Softly, She Floats

Katlyn Snowden mystery Book 2, Volume 0

Natalie Stefan

Published by Payella Pty. Ltd., 2023.

SOFTLY, SHE FLOATS
A KATLYN SNOWDEN NOVEL
Book 2

Natalie Stefan © 2023

Published by: Payella Pty. Ltd.

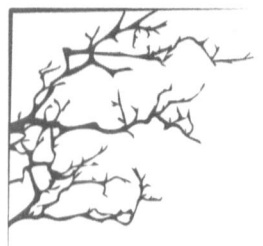

Dedications

This book is dedicated to my family for
supporting my writing efforts.
Squirreled away in some cave, a writer creates. After the story is created, the
editing starts. Many eyes troll through the manuscript to make something that
is a garbled mess into a story.
A big thank you to:
Victoria Chie for helping me craft this story into something better than it was
and allowing me to pick her brains when I couldn't find a solution.
To Shirley for her eagle eye editing my manuscript.
Marc Kelly for suggestions on policing in the UK. Any errors in policing are
mine alone and not a reflection on Marc's suggestions.
The Fab Coasties chat group for their suggestions and support.
And a thank you to my beta readers who gave me feedback on whatever
needed to be changed to make this a memorable story.

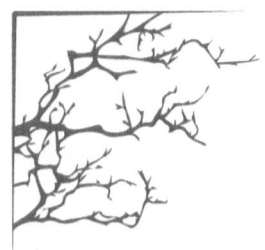

Chapter 1

Casterton-on-Sea, UK

Unemployed and in a foul mood, Katlyn Snowden stumbled out of bed after a restless night. She shrugged off her pajamas and yawned her way to the wardrobe. Her day held little purpose other than researching the suspect responsible for the warehouse fire that claimed her partner's life a few months ago.

A brisk walk was the only thing she looked forward to each morning. With a cup of coffee and some buttered toast, she donned her all-weather jacket from the mudroom and stepped outside. Sipping the hot beverage, she crossed the two-acre lot towards the back gate. An autumn wind mercilessly battered the lone oak tree in the yard.

She struggled to open the gate, nearly concealed by overgrown vines. Reminding herself to trim them later, Katlyn let herself out. She maneuvered through blackberry brambles and low bushes in the shared space along the cliff edge, the crashing waves below filling the air. Stone steps cut into the rock led down to the beach. Careful not to slip, she descended slowly, gripping the handrail. By the time she reached the bottom, her leg grafts ached.

The angry sea with white-capped waves and the dark sky loomed ominously. But, she was determined to get some exercise. With her hands in her pockets to ward off the cold, she strolled along the pebbly shoreline, dodging clumps of seaweed. The sudden sound of seagulls squawking as they fought over a morsel of food gave her a start.

Her walks along the shore gave her time to think. The termination notice she handed in at the station two weeks ago was the most satisfying thing she'd done all year. Chief Inspector Henry White, of Casterton-on-Sea police station, was furious and tore up her notice in front of her. She'd made a duplicate, which she handed to the desk clerk after collecting her belongings on the way out.

Scaling rocks covered with limpets and cockle shells, she ventured towards the next beach, smaller than the one she'd just left. Today, an urge to explore tugged at her. The odor of the seaweed was stronger here, and she wrinkled her nose.

In the shallow water among the weeks, a large blue suitcase floated. Her stomach tightened. She noticed black hair protruding from it. "Must be a wig."

She kept walking and tried to enjoy her time in the fresh air, but something pulled her back to the suitcase. Lost in thoughts of her uncertain future, she was drawn to the way the hair was floating in the water. Something was wrong.

Katlyn hesitated for a moment, then her police training took over. Walking into the water, she pushed aside the seaweed and struggled to drag the heavy case over the pebbles to the shore.

Squatting, she worked the rusted clips on the suitcase. Finally, she opened it and recoiled in shock and horror. "Bleeding hell!"

The smell of a decomposing body slapped her. She had seen plenty of bodies at the mortuary when the pathologist was performing an autopsy, but this body was in the worst state she'd ever seen. The woman's legs tucked up to her chin.

The putrid smell was overpowering and turned her stomach. She retched. Straightening, she wiped her mouth with a tissue.

Surveying the grim scene, she stared at the hand protruding from the suitcase. Overwhelmed and her mind racing with unanswered questions, she stumbled backwards. Her foot slipped on a patch of slippery seaweed and the sound of waves crashing against the jagged rocks filled her ears. Losing her balance, she fell, hitting her head on the unforgiving rocks.

Pain shot through her skull, her vision blurred, and her world spun. Panic gripped her as she realized she was alone, with no one to help her. Attempting to stand, her legs weak and unsteady, gave way and she slipped and fell again. "Oh, shit!"

As she lay there, the crashing waves grew louder, echoing the chaos in her mind. The morning sun grew higher on the horizon, but fear and confusion consumed her as layers of blackness consumed her consciousness.

GROANING, KATLYN SLOWLY came to. Her head pounded, and she touched the lump at the back of her skull. The tide was coming in and she was lying in a puddle of seawater. Shivering, her clothes and sneakers wet with sea water, she muttered. "What the bleeding hell?"

The suitcase rested in the shallow waters nearby. A bloodless, wrinkled hand poked out of the partially open suitcase as if it was reaching for her. A jolt of fear surged through her. Questions raced through her mind - whose hand was it? How did this body end up here?

Cold sweat broke out on her skin. She was rooted to the spot, unable to tear her eyes away from the eerie sight before her.

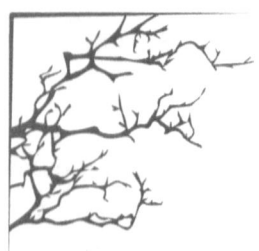

Chapter 2

Colin's car pulled up, bringing a flicker of relief to Katlyn. He must have been in the area when she called in the 10-55, dead body. Jumping out of his vehicle, he bounded down the steps to the beach.

He greeted her with a smile. "Hello, Kat. How are you?"

"Brilliant, now that I'm unemployed." She regretted her decision to leave the crime scene to change into dry clothes. She kept her gloved hands tucked in her pockets.

Colin shook his head. "You're on leave. That's what White told everyone. Quite a few members told him what a great job you'd done on that last case."

"I submitted my resignation. I even left a printed copy on his desk."

"Did you know the mayor came in to congratulate you, but White informed him you were on leave." His frowned. "I saw White tear up your resignation letter."

"He's making a career of tearing up my letters. I'm not going back."

"The team is lost without you," he said.

"Flattery won't help." However, the comment lifted her spirits.

He raised an eyebrow before he scanned the beach. "I don't see a body on the beach. Where is it?"

"There's no direct access to that beach. It's hidden around the next bend. We'll have to climb over the rocks to reach it."

"Let's see what you've found."

"We should wait for the forensics team. Otherwise, they won't find us and with the tide coming in, access will be cut off in a few hours. The team will have to move quickly."

The seagulls rode the air currents, their cries spreading the news of the body.

He eyed her. "Keeping out of trouble?"

"I've been packing up a few of my dad's clothes." But she hadn't taken them down to the charity shop yet. That would be the hardest part, the letting go.

"Good for you. It must be tough." Colin shivered. "I should have worn a beanie."

"Here. Take mine." She didn't expect him to accept, but he did. The chilly air made the lump on the back of her head throb. "Do you have any headache pills on you?"

"What's wrong?" Colin said.

"I fell and I think I may have blacked out for a bit. I've got a lump on my head and it's bothering me."

"Let me see." He touched the back of her head. "Does it hurt?"

"A little. At least, it's not bleeding."

"I'll check if one of the team has some supplies when they arrive."

Three police vehicles arrived, almost at the same time. White emerged from the first one, and waved. Katlyn didn't return the greeting. He almost stumbled down the stairs, but regained his footing just in time.

Katlyn's jaw tightened. Why had he bothered to come? She'd expected the forensics team, but not him.

The SOCO (Scene of Crime Officers) team alighted from the police van loaded down with the usual equipment. They donned their person protective equipment (PPE) to minimize contamination of the crime scene. Two uniforms began cordoning off the area.

"You're in for a treat." Colin remarked, nodding toward White, who was approaching.

White had a face the color of raw beef and his shirts strained across his ample stomach.

She sighed. "I should try to relax. But I can't."

"You can do this," Colin encouraged. "I'll be right here with you."

"Good morning, Kat, Colin. Where's the 10-55?" Chief White inquired.

"Around those rocks there's a small beach, Tide Cove." She pointed toward the area. "We better get everyone out there. In a few hours, the high tide will cut off all access and the suitcase with the body might be dragged back into the deeper water."

"What were you doing here, Kat?" White said.

She controlled the urge to snap back at him. "I go for walks along these beaches," Kat said. "I live just up there." She gestured towards her home.

"Hmm! You're keeping my team busy. We've gone months without a 10-55, but since you've arrived, we've had four dead bodies and now this is the fifth two weeks apart."

"That's good of you to notice," Kat said.

He glared at her.

She ignored him and greeted the two forensic team technicians who had joined them.

Victor Sabrige, the pathologist, emerged from the second vehicle. He walked towards them with a wide smile. His short, dark-brown hair, which was usually tidy, was a mess, suggested he'd been in a hurry to get here and had forgotten to comb it. He nodded to her. "Good morning, detectives," he exclaimed. "Where's the floater?"

"Very funny, not." She told him where to find the body.

"I'm cooped up all day with bodies. I know, I could have been a doctor in a regular practice, but the dead don't talk back, and you don't have to cure them of their ailments," Victor joked, trying to lighten the mood.

Colin glanced at her and chuckled. "He never fails to entertain."

Katlyn shook her head, but she couldn't help smiling. "Okay let's go."

She led them across the pebbles while seagulls squawked overhead as the forensic team followed closely over the rocks to the next small beach. "This beach is called Tide Cove."

The darker side of her hoped White would fall in, but she didn't truly wish him any harm.

White huffed and puffed as he negotiated the rocks. "How much farther?"

"Not too far," she reassured him.

As they reached the secluded cove, the suitcase came into view, partially covered by seaweed. "I dragged it from the water."

White scowled. "I would think you know better than to tamper with evidence."

"I didn't know there was a body inside until I opened it. And with the tide on the way in, the water would have dragged the suitcase out to sea if I hadn't saved it."

White harrumphed, looking disgusted with her.

The cameraman took photos from every angle while the others stood back and waited.

White turned to Katlyn. "Monday, you get working on this. You need to lead the team."

Guess he thought, because she had two weeks away, it was enough time to forgive him and his abrasive manner. She shook her head. "Find someone else."

He grunted. "There is no one else. But, you'll do better this time."

"That does it," she said. "You ungrateful, despicable man."

"Name calling won't get you anywhere," White said. "You...."

"Colin, get him away from me!" Kat stood her ground and folded her arms. She itched to slap some humility into him.

Colin stepped between them. "Chief, she did a great job wrapping up the Braithwaite case."

"Well...." White didn't finish.

Amazingly, the Chief was lost for words. She'd have to thank Colin later for his support.

The forensic team circled the suitcase, their gloved hands poised. With precise movements, they removed the seaweed from the suitcase and opened it to reveal the lifeless body within.

The photographer moved in and went to work.

Victor glared at White before returning to the task at hand. He put down a rubber mat beside the suitcase and kneeled.

White disappeared around the rocky outcrop. When he reappeared, Katlyn saw him huffing and puffing up the stairs that led to the common area above.

She pointed to a nearby rock partly coated with seaweed and some clams and mussels. "I threw up, slipped, and fell backwards, hitting my head on that rock. I was out for a little while," Kat said to Victor. "Sorry. I contaminated the scene."

"Are you alright?" Victor stood and approached her.

She went to nod, but stopped as it increased the pain. "My head hurts."

"Let me see." Victor stepped closer and examined her eyes. "No dilation of the pupils. Are you feeling dizzy?"

"Not so far."

"Experiencing double vision?"

"No."

"Can you turn around? I want to see where you hit your head."

She complied.

Victor gently parted her hair. "A scab has formed. A little swelling, but that will go down in a few days."

"Ouch," she said. "That hurts." His touch, even though she was hurt, made her stomach flutter.

He reached into his pocket and handed her a blister pack. "Take one of these. It's paracetamol. Sorry, I don't have any water."

"It's not a problem. Thanks." She dry swallowed the capsule.

Victor shook his head. "I don't know how you swallow those dry."

She shrugged.

"You should see your doctor so he can check that you're okay," Victor said.

"Thanks, I will later."

Katlyn's breath hitched as she looked at the lifeless young woman with a bloated face, wearing black lycra leggings and a long-sleeved t-shirt. Her knees up to her chin and her black hair fanned out across her body. Katlyn had seen many crime scenes, but the sight of a dead body never ceased to send a chill down her spine.

The smell was overpowering. She stepped away, saddened that someone had cut a young life short in this vile way.

"Hmm. Interesting," Victor said.

"What do you mean?" she said.

"The killer didn't bother to weigh down the suitcase. I would say they didn't know the body would float after a few days. A weighed down body may float eventually if the weights aren't too heavy, but not this soon."

He gently turned the victim's head from side to side.

Again, Katlyn forced herself to look at this female who was once a living, breathing person. "What do you see?"

"Some trauma on the side of the head. The question is, was this the cause of death? I won't know until I get her on the table."

Katlyn knew the pathologist was always busy, and she preferred not to push him, but this was important. "When can you do the autopsy?" Kat asked.

Victor looked up from his kneeling position. "I'll ring you."

As the forensic team collected evidence, Katlyn's discomfort from the egg on her head asserted itself. She couldn't ignore it any longer.

"Colin, I'm sorry, but I need to see a doctor."

"Let me drive you?"

Katlyn nodded.

"Someone did this to her. We must find this piece of trash and bring them to justice. Are you in? I can't do this without you." Colin said.

She didn't answer.

He gazed at her with pleading eyes. "Come on, Kat, can't we work together on this one?"

How could she say no? This young woman didn't deserve to die in this way, no matter how good or bad she may have been. "Okay." She had to stop herself from swearing at White. "But he has to apologize for his behavior before I'll show him any respect!"

The Katlyn turned to Colin. "We'll need to establish the victim's identity and trace any possible leads. We'll go through the usual routine, starting with the suitcase."

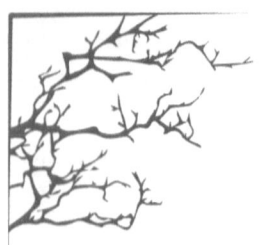

Chapter 3

Billy, his nickname from his school days, parked his car down the road from Katlyn's home. Disabling the security cameras was crucial for his plan. He hired someone skilled in that area to take care of it. Now the CCTV was running on a loop. This ensured Katlyn remained blissfully unaware of his presence.

Silently, Billy crept around the back of the house. He used the key he'd gotten from a locksmith to enter through the back door. He moved through each room with methodical precision, determined to find the gun he sought. His motivations ran deep, rooted in a past that involved Katlyn. A fire and a scar on his face served as a constant reminder of her actions.

As he meticulously searched every drawer and explored every nook and cranny, frustration grew within him. Only weeks ago, when he'd been observing Katlyn, he'd seen her using the Glock 17 at the practice range, and he knew it had to be somewhere in the house. Yet it remained elusive, taunting him at every turn.

As he searched, he encountered Katlyn's cat, which was perched on her bed. It hissed and spat at him, retreating under the bed. He made a mental note to deal with that bleeding animal later.

He searched every drawer, every corner of the house again, even areas he'd already checked before. Still, he found nothing. Frustrated, he punched the brick wall. As he felt the pain shoot through his hand, he knew it was a stupid move.

Determined not to give up, Billy ventured into the shed, an area he had yet to explore. With a piece of wire, he bypassed the antique lock and gained access. The shed was cluttered with old chairs and various items, triggering a sneezing fit because of the accumulated dust. He persevered, sifting through the bedding inside an antique pram, hoping to uncover the hidden gun.

He'd set fire to the abandoned warehouse, intending to kill Katlyn and her partner while they were inside. However, she had escaped, while the fire claimed the life of her partner. The bullet from Katlyn's Glock had left a scar on Billy's once attractive face, requiring reconstructive surgery to fix his appearance. The process wasn't yet complete. He'd have to endure more pain and more surgery to make his face look "normal" again.

Each day was a battle for Billy. Every day he faced his scarred reflection in the mirror, and was reminded of Katlyn's handiwork. For that, she would pay. He was planning a big surprise for Katlyn. Revenge was sweeter for the waiting. Soon enough, he would have his revenge."

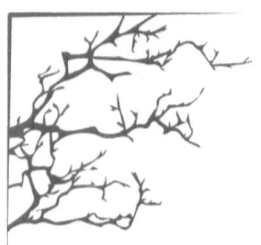

Chapter 4

As the heavy door swung open, Katlyn stepped into the sterile autopsy room. Victor, dressed in his protective gown, snapped on his gloves. His mortuary technician, Teresa Holgate, unzipped the plastic pouch that concealed the young woman's body.

"Good afternoon, Kat." Victor's voice carrying a mix of professionalism and warmth.

"Afternoon to both of you," Kat replied.

"How are you feeling?" He inquired, concern evident in his blue-gray eyes.

"The paracetamol did the trick. Had the doctor check me over. I'm healthy except for this lump on the back of my head."

"That'll subside in a few days," Victor reassured her. "Turn around and part your hair. Let me look."

Katlyn complied, trusting Victor's expertise.

"Don't worry." His concern brought a comforting warmth to her.

"Thanks."

Victor returned to the table. "This is going to get messy."

She mentally prepared herself, standing at a suitable distance from the body. The pungent odor emanating from the corpse filled the air.

"I didn't expect to see you here today," he said.

"I'm fine."

"I should have clarified my statement and said I didn't expect to see you again in your professional capacity," Victor's soft tone acknowledging her return to active duty after resigning over two weeks ago.

"Nor did I." Her eyes meeting his briefly.

"I heard on the grapevine about the growing tension with White."

He witnessed her altercation with White at the crime scene as well. "I don't want to dwell on that. I'm working on this case because this woman didn't deserve to die so soon. Not for any other reason."

"You must be a wonderful, caring person," he said with sincerity.

"I don't know about that." Katlyn blushed, genuinely surprised by the compliment. Victor's kind words, coming from someone who had been a little brusque during their last encounter, were not something she expected.

"Have you seen a body that's been in the water for a while?" Victor asked.

"Only this one." She avoided looking at the unfortunate woman lying before them.

"Well, you're in for an experience. I won't mind if you have to leave," Victor said, in his attempt to ease any discomfort she might feel before clipping on the microphone and testing the sound. The crackle in his voice prompting Teresa to adjust the settings.

Victor announced the date, time, name, and the location where the body was found. "Visual observation reveals some vascular marbling, discoloration of skin and soft tissue and general bloating. Fingertips exhibit typical wrinkling due to water immersion. Victim is wearing blue nail polish. I note abrasions on her hands and feet, but we may attribute these to various factors. These abrasions could have occurred antemortem or could result from perimortem or postmortem cutaneous trauma."

Victor performed a y-incision and began removing the major organs. "No water found in the lungs indicating the victim died prior to immersion," Victor stated.

Pausing for a moment, Victor glanced at Katlyn. "She's pregnant, approximately eleven weeks along." His voice carrying a mix of professional detachment and underlying empathy.

"That raises more questions than it answers." Katlyn's mind racing with possibilities and implications.

"It certainly does," Victor said.

Teresa carefully placed the organs into bags, recording their weight and preparing them for further analysis.

"There's so much the water hides from us. But we'll see what the toxicology lab finds." He remarked, his gaze shifting back to the victim's head. Gently, he examined it, moving it from side to side. "Trauma to the side of the head. Ah, her neck is broken."

"Is this the cause of death?" Kat asked, seeking clarity amidst the grim details.

Victor nodded. "It may be the cause, as the fracture has severed the cord above C3. This is because the phrenic nerve, which controls the diaphragm and breathing, emerges from spinal nerves C3-C5. Severing the cord above C3 would lead to complete denervation of the diaphragm, leading to asphyxiation. It's not instantaneous, but anyone with this break will suffocate within a few minutes. However, I can't confirm it as the definitive cause of death until we receive the toxicology reports."

"How old was she?"

"I'd estimate her age to be between sixteen and eighteen. She's been dead for possibly forty-eight hours, but that's my best estimate since she's been immersed in 10C° seawater," Victor explained.

"Poor girl. So young to be pregnant and so young to die, especially in this manner." Katlyn lamented. Glancing at her watch, she realized the passage of time. "Gosh, it's after six. I'm supposed to be meeting the team at the local pub." She grimaced. "To celebrate, or not, my return to active duty, or something like that. I must be daft for coming back."

"Not you. You're the brightest star in the dungeon. They're lucky to have you," Victor said. "You came back because of your commitment."

"I can't turn my back on this young girl. I need to find the person who did this to her. I don't know how you do this every day."

Victor shrugged, a hint of weariness in his gesture. "It's what we do."

Teresa laughed. "My partner doesn't let me talk about my day. Your dinner conversation tonight, huh?"

Katlyn laughed, feeling lighter for a moment.

"I hope you can enjoy your catch up with the team," Victor said. "But afterward, I cook a mean spaghetti carbonara. Care to join me?"

The invitation took Katlyn by surprise. Unsure of Victor's intentions, she said, "Thank you, but I'm not dating."

"It's not a date. Just a meal. I'm about to ask Teresa and her partner to join us as well." Victor turned to his assistant. "Would you join us and make it a foursome?"

Teresa nodded. "I've nothing planned, and Kasper doesn't cook."

"Excellent," Victor said with a smile. "It's much more enjoyable to share a meal with company. I typically make too much and end up throwing the leftovers away. After you leave the pub, Katlyn, come to my place."

"Okay." Katlyn left with a mix of curiosity and intrigue filling her thoughts.

She threw her protective gear into the nearby bin and made her way to her car.

The deceased female was pregnant and her neck broken. It appears someone didn't want her to continue with the pregnancy, and perhaps the woman didn't want an abortion.

She hoped the lab found something significant in the toxicology reports and provide some insight into the suspect. Determined to find justice for the young girl and her unborn child, she took a deep breath and started the car, driving off into the evening. Eager to unravel the secrets that lay ahead.

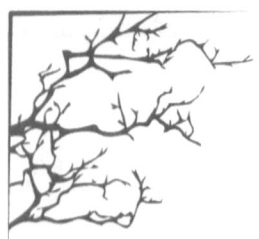

Chapter 5

Katlyn drove toward the local pub, her mind still in turmoil from the autopsy. Normally, autopsies didn't affect her so much, but this one was different. The teen had evoked such a strong sense of sympathy within her. Perhaps, because she had a teenage daughter of a similar age. The mere thought of someone doing this to Briony had tugged at her heartstrings.

As she drove, her phone rang, and she answered via the button on her steering wheel.

"Hi, mum. Where are you?" Briony Snowden said.

"What's wrong, love?"

"I rang you at home, but you weren't there."

"Sorry about that. I was attending some work matters. It's best to ring my mobile phone."

"Jeez, mum. Don't tell me you're back working for that horrible man again?" Briony said, referring to Chief White.

Mental note, she would not complain about White to her daughter again. She also wouldn't share the gruesome news about the autopsy with Briony. "The lads begged me to come back." Well, Colin did.

"Sure, the guys did." Briony sounded skeptical. "Sorry, mum. Your face was all over the news reports last week and they said you did a great job of finding the murderer."

She stopped at the petrol station. "Thanks, love. I'm working on a new case now."

"Did Mr. White apologize to you for the way he treated you before?"

"Sorry, love, I have to go." She didn't want to upset her daughter further by telling her exactly what happened with White. "I'm about to get some petrol. Can I ring you later?"

"I was considering moving back with you for a bit, but now that you're working again, I'll stay with Dad."

She felt a pang of sadness at her daughter's words. "You know you're welcome anytime, day or night, love." Her ex promised to support their daughter through university next year and that she didn't need to contribute. This made her even more determined to help financially. But she needed a paying job to do that.

"Why don't we meet at that café again for a bite? Sunday suit you?" Kat said.

"I think so. But don't call me and cancel because of work," Briony said, making it obvious she hadn't forgotten about the last time they made plans and Katlyn had canceled.

"I'm sorry about last time," Katlyn said.

A tall lanky lad wearing black-rimmed glasses that looked too small for his face served her when she paid for her petrol and mineral water. After taking another paracetamol for the headache caused by the bump on the back of her head, she drove to the pub.

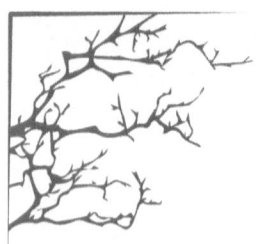

Chapter 6

S he stepped inside the busy pub, maneuvering through groups of people enjoying a beer, and joined her colleagues, who were gathered at a table.

A cheer rose when she announced she would not be leaving.

"You're the best team leader, Kat," Amanda said. "And ... another female on my side to help balance the testosterone is sorely needed."

Katlyn nursed her drink. "Thanks. We females have to stick together." Katlyn spoke up. "But, I need to make a confession. I've been neglecting the most important person in my life—my daughter. I want to spend more time with her, no matter how busy work gets."

"Here! Here!" Amanda said. "Family comes first."

Katlyn did a lot of smiling and made some bland comments. Briony's remark that she was lowering her principles by continuing to work for White played on her mind. She had bills to pay and not working wasn't an option.

She laughed at some anecdotes shared by the Colin, Amanda and the other team members about their past experiences. Katlyn felt a sense of belonging and gratitude for her colleagues, knowing that they were not only her workmates but also her friends.

"I don't know how you can watch that decomposing body being carved up," Derrick said.

Silence fell over the group as they turned their attention to Katlyn, waiting for her response.

"It's part of the job," she replied, taking a sip of her drink. "I admit, I haven't seen a body in such a state before."

Derrick motioned for another round. "I'll have another pint."

Most of the team were still nursing their first lager.

A murmur went through the group. "No, thanks."

Interrupting the moment, Derrick's phone rang. He glanced at the screen, then answered. "I haven't forgotten. I'm just having a few drinks with the lads at the local." He paused, listening intently. "Don't be like that. A man needs a bit of social life." He waved goodbye and left the pub.

Katlyn checked the time, and was surprised it was after seven. Seizing the opportunity with Derrick's departure, she decided it was a suitable time to leave as well. "I'm heading out too. Thanks, everyone. It was great."

Colin raised an eyebrow. "What's the hurry? Going on a hot date?"

"Joining some friends for dinner," Kat said. "See you tomorrow, bright and early." She bid her goodbyes, grabbed her handbag, and made her way back to her Corolla.

Fifteen minutes later, she pulled up on the circular drive of Victor's mock Tudor-style house on an acre of land.

Katlyn stepped out of her car and walked up the brick path to the front door. As she tapped the ornate bronze knocker against the strike plate, doubts crept in. Should she have accepted Victor's invitation? Footsteps echoed down the hallway, and Victor opened the door. His blue eyes twinkled as he welcomed her. "Welcome to my humble abode. The others are in the reception room."

She stared at the interior to distract herself from his gaze. "You have a lovely home."

"It's comfortable." Victor hung up her Mack on the coat rack. "How are you feeling?"

"My headache has finally subsided."

"Glad to hear that." He seemed genuinely concerned. "Come through."

They walked down the hallway adorned with black and white tiled hallway and a carpet runner down the middle. A few paintings of country scenes dressed the walls. Victor led Katlyn into the reception room, his hand lightly grazed the small of her back. She felt a shiver run down her spine and a flush rise to her cheeks.

"The aroma coming from the kitchen is divine."

"I hope it lives up to your expectations."

"I'm sure it will."

They walked into the large reception room with an eclectic blend of antique and contemporary furniture. It looked lovely.

Inside the reception room, Teresa and Kasper had been talking as they sat on the lounge. They fell silent as Katlyn and Victor entered and Teresa introduced her partner, Kasper Goch.

"Hello again, Teresa, and pleased to meet you, Kasper." Katlyn took a seat in an armchair.

"I'm the local cabinetmaker and carpenter." Kasper had black hair tied back in a short ponytail.

"If you need something made, or some carpentry work done, then I can recommend him," Victor said.

"Stop with the praise," Kasper said. "It's a bit embarrassing."

"The accent? Eastern Europe?"

He nodded. "It's hard to shake off. I'm originally from Poland, but I've been living in the UK for fifteen years now."

"Do you handle major projects, or do you take on smaller ones as well?" Kat asked. "I'm interested in getting a new vanity for my bathroom. The current one has seen better days."

"I handle projects of all sizes, as long as I have the workers available. Currently, I work with a part-time laborer. Give me a couple of days to finish my current project, and then I can fit you in. Here's my card." He reached over and handed it to her.

"Thanks."

"As I mentioned, give me a ring and I'll come over and you can show me what needs to be done."

"Kasper has been a lifesaver for me," Victor said. "He's remodeled my staircase when I initially purchased this place, as it was in terrible disrepair. And the list goes on. I kept him in work for months."

Victor went to the drinks trolley. "What's your poison?"

"I've just come from the pub, so I'll pass, especially since I've got this bump."

"Ah. My cooking skills will be put to the taste test. I'd better check on our meal."

She chatted with Teresa and Kasper while Victor saw to their dinner.

Victor returned. "Dinner is served. Please join me."

They followed Victor into a well-appointed kitchen with an open-plan dining area. The table was set with cutlery, plates, glasses and a centerpiece of roses in a crystal vase.

"Please take a seat anywhere," Victor said.

He brought over a serving bowl with the spaghetti carbonara and placed it on the table. "Give me your plates and I'll serve."

Katlyn took a mouthful. "This is absolutely delicious."

"It's the best I've tasted," Teresa agreed. Victor beamed. "Thank you."

As the night wore on, and they laughed and talked over their meal. Katlyn found herself increasingly drawn to Victor.

For dessert, Victor brought out a store-bought chocolate cake. They all enjoyed a slice, with Kasper helping himself to a second. Teresa commented on Kasper's sweet tooth.

After they'd polished off their dessert, Kasper said, "I've an early start tomorrow on a new project. Thank you for the invitation and a lovely meal." They both stood, and Victor saw them out.

When he returned, Kat said. "Let me wash up."

"There's not much to do. I've got a dishwasher. Want a tea or coffee?"

She was about to shake her head, but thought better of it. Her headache was gone, but she didn't want to push her luck. "I'd better go home, too."

"Come sit on the sofa and I'll tell you what I found."

She was intrigued. She felt at ease in his company and followed him into the reception room.

"The Jane Doe had nothing in her stomach." Victor sat opposite Katlyn and leaned forward. His voice, low and intense as he spoke about the gruesome details they had uncovered. "That means that she hadn't eaten for about twenty-four hours before her death."

Caught up in the moment and the intensity of his gaze, she leaned in.

"You mean she was being held captive somewhere?"

He nodded. Unless the lab results show something unexpected, the report will say Jane Doe's death was probably caused by a broken neck."

"I have several theories running through my head," Kat said. "First scenario: the suspect found out she was pregnant and killed her. Second scenario: the suspect demanded she have an abortion, but she refused, so he killed her. Third scenario: it was an accidental death resulting from the suspect physically assaulting her, causing her to fall."

"That's your area of expertise, not mine," Victor admitted. "However, I prefer to believe it may be something else entirely. What if she was kidnapped, and someone was keeping her as his house slave?"

"When he found out she was pregnant, he got rid of her." Kat added.

"That's exactly what happened in a case I worked on last year." Victor said.

"Unfortunately, these things have a habit of reoccurring."

Katlyn suppressed a yawn. "Thanks for dinner. Everything was delicious, but I should call it a night. It's late and we have work tomorrow."

He gazed into her eyes. "You don't have to."

She swallowed. The message he conveyed was clear, but she tried to make light of it. "I have to feed my cat, Lucy. She'll be annoyed that I haven't come home yet."

"I used to have a Havana Brown, named Pebbles. I adored her." He shook his head and grimacing. "Sadly, I had to put her down. Pebbles was 15 and could hardly walk."

"That's so sad."

"Yep. Yep. I thought about getting another cat, but I can't bring myself to replace her."

"Thanks for dinner, Victor. And, for checking on me this morning, and giving me some paracetamol."

"Happy to help." He leaned over, touched her arm as he kissed her cheek.

His touch sent a jolt through her, and she had to stop herself from turning to meet his kiss.

"If you change your mind, you know where to find me," he whispered.

"One-night stands aren't my thing," she replied softly. His touch sent a quiver low in her belly. "I'm not ready for anything more permanent, either." Katlyn's heart raced as she tried to make sense of her body's response. She walked to her car in a daze, her mind spun with questions and doubts. Getting involved with Victor seemed like a bad idea. She just wasn't ready for any romantic entanglements.

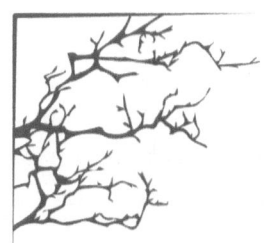

Chapter 7

The detectives gathered in the squad room and waited for Katlyn's update. The two weeks she had been away seemed a distant memory. Katlyn pinned a photo of Jane Doe on the board, alongside photos of the location where she was found, her silver chain, bird earrings, a heart friendship ring, clothing, and a waterlogged and faded dry-cleaning ticket discovered in her jacket pocket. She turned to her team, ready to share the new information.

"Three things we know for certain," she began. "She wasn't physically restrained, her stomach was empty, and she was pregnant."

Amanda interjected. "Do you think she was being held captive somewhere?"

"It's unclear at this point," Kat replied. "It could suggest she was drugged and didn't want to eat. Or she may have been sick and vomiting with morning sickness due to her pregnancy. These are all speculations for now. We're still waiting for the blood analysis to come back from the lab. In terms of physical description, she had black hair, aged between sixteen and eighteen, pregnant and five-six in height. And we know she was into running based on her clothing: lycra leggings, a t-shirt, bomber jacket and sneakers."

Brady and Silvester (Syl) were absorbing the details, while Derrick was absorbed in his phone.

"Near the beach, close to the cliff, our team found tire tracks on the grass," she continued, drawing them in. "Forensics is still trying to match the tire tracks to a specific brand and vehicle." She glanced at her notes. "We also need to initiate a search on the database for missing girls around that age."

"I can help with that. I can check missing persons databases," Amanda offered.

"I was about to ask you to check in the nearby counties as well."

Amanda nodded in agreement.

"Derrick, can you try the local dry cleaners?" Kat asked.

His head jerked up. "What?"

"I'll send you a copy of the dry-cleaning ticket. Check the local dry cleaners to see if there is any dry-cleaning not picked-up, who dropped it off and anything else you can about the item," she said, tapping the ticket. "Due to immersion in the seawater, only two numbers are visible. Whatever it was, it cost £10.00. Make inquiries in the nearby villages, too."

He scowled. "That sounds like a lot of legwork."

It wasn't just his words, but the condescending tone that bothered Kat. She had heard rumors that Derrick was vying for her position, and it seemed he didn't relish getting his hands dirty. Coming from a privileged background, he likely hadn't experienced hardship or manual labor in his life.

Katlyn sighed, aware of Derrick's laziness. "I understand it's not the most exciting task, but it's an essential part of the investigation. We need to cover all possible leads."

She carried on. "I'm appearing on TV to show photos of the jewelry and clothing found with Jane Doe," she said. "We need volunteers to man the phones. Who's willing to help?"

Most of the team eagerly raised their hands.

"Thank you all for your commitment. I'll keep you informed about the interview schedule." She couldn't help but notice Derrick hadn't raised his hand. "Our goal is to uncover the truth behind Jane Does' death. Let's get to work."

Katlyn noticed White leaning against the wall outside his office, clearly waiting to speak with her. She sighed and squared her shoulders, mentally preparing for their conversation. He walked in to the office, leaving the door open.

She knocked and went in. He looked up from the computer. "You finished out there?"

"Yes, Chief. You summoned me?"

White's double chin wobbled as he gave her a nod. "Yes, yes. The spare office is next door. You can use that."

"Thank you, but no thanks. I prefer to work with the team." Katlyn declined the offer, suspecting that White's sudden generosity was influenced by higher authorities rather than genuine goodwill. He was unlikely to be thoughtful towards her; he would sooner choke on his breakfast cereal. "The desk I currently use in the squad room suits me perfectly."

"Be sure you only give the TV interviewer the bare facts. No mention of Jane Doe's pregnancy, the suitcase, or the location where she was found. No leaks or I'll hold you personally responsible. Do you understand?" White's tone remained abrasive.

"I've been a detective for five years now. I believe I can manage that," her frustration evident. "Is that all?"

"Just try to behave and avoid any involvement with the staff," White warned.

"What the hell do you mean?"

"Do I have to spell it out? You had dinner with Victor, and I don't know what else."

"What are you insinuating? Sure, I had dinner with him, and Teresa and her partner, and afterwards I went home. What the hell's wrong with that? Who told you?"

"None of your business," he snapped.

Opening the door, she retorted, "Besides, Victor isn't part of the station staff here."

Someone was clearly trying to undermine her credibility. She'd have to watch for that proverbial knife in the back. She had experienced enough of that at her previous station, Tellford, where people unfairly blamed her for her ex-partner's death. "I'm done here. I've work to do."

She slammed the door on her way out and counted to twenty. But it did little to calm her anger. Fuming, she made her way back to her desk.

The squad room fell into a hushed silence, and her colleagues watched her with anticipation. They must have heard parts of the conversation, perhaps not the exact words, hopefully just raised voices. Collapsing in her chair, she felt the weight of the obstacles she faced. The desire to resign welled up inside her, a momentary impulse to escape the challenges and frustrations. But then she remembered Jane Doe, the girl found in the suitcase, and her commitment to justice. With a renewed determination, she shook off the thought of quitting. Who else would fight for justice for Jane Doe? It was her responsibility, and she wouldn't let anything or anyone deter her from uncovering the truth.

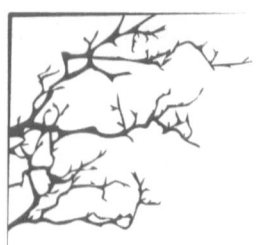

Chapter 8

A manda rushed over. "Kat, forensics searched Jane Doe's clothes and found a concealed pocket in her jacket. Inside, they discovered a plastic bag containing nine hundred pounds"

Katlyn stopped typing and looked up. "How would a teenager get this amount of money?" Kat said. "Maybe, she stole it?" Amanda suggested.

Katlyn nodded thoughtfully. "That's a significant amount." An unsettling sensation moved up her spine. "We know the teen was pregnant."

"Perhaps she planned to get away and stole the money. But the father of the baby found out and killed her," Amanda speculated.

Katlyn grimaced. "Anything's possible. It's too early to draw any conclusions. But if he knew she was pregnant...." Katlyn rose and made her way towards the big board. "Derrick. Any success with that dry cleaner's ticket?"

He slouched in his chair and shrugged. "Nah. The woman said... most items are collected. She couldn't identify anything from the ticket since the paper had faded."

"What kind of dry cleaning would the cost ten pounds?"

"How would I know?" Derrick said.

"I specifically asked you to find out. Didn't you inquire about it with the woman?" Katlyn sighed. "You should've asked which items weren't picked up?"

He straightened and put his hands on his hips. "Look. I went and asked the woman."

"Go back and ask more questions."

He crossed his arms. "I did already."

"I expect you to include details about your conversation with this woman in your report. I'll expect it on my desk by this afternoon," Kat said.

"What! Who do you think you are?" Derrick challenged.

"I'm D.S. Snowden and you're D.C. Johnson. And I'm heading this case. Therefore, you will abide by my decision."

"I'll see about that." Derrick huffed, before storming towards White's office.

Just breathe, she told herself.

Colin stood. His face, a mask of anger. "He's out of order."

Katlyn slammed down her pen on the edge of the big board and returned to her desk. "You're damned right about that."

White emerged from his office. "Kat. In my office now."

Rolling her eyes at Colin, she strolled in to meet the impending firing line.

Derrick sat in the only chair free of clutter, looking like Lucy when she'd caught a mouse. Well, she was no mouse, and she wouldn't take any shit. She stood waiting with her hands at her sides.

White, elbows on the desk, glared at her with open hostility.

She was subordinate to White, but not to Derrick. They aimed to put her at a disadvantage, but she wouldn't play their games. She picked up the papers on the only other chair beside Derrick, dumped them on the floor, and sat. She waited, knowing the silence would irk White more than it did her.

"What do you think you're doing by treating your colleagues like lackeys? I plan to report you to the Superintendent," White threatened.

"Go ahead," she said, undeterred. She'd only met Chief Superintendent Higgins once, right before starting her position here. "I'll be questioned and, in my report, I'll document Derrick's refusal to comply with my instructions."

"I did not!" Derrick burst out.

White gave a slight shake of his head to Derrick, which she would have missed if she hadn't been watching their exchange.

Derrick's lips tightened.

"I'll give you a warning this time. Don't let this happen again, or I will report you. You will treat your team with respect."

She jumped from her seat. "I give 110% and expect the same from my team." She flung the door open, and strode out.

Breathe, just breathe, she reminded herself.

Amanda caught her eye and made a drinking gesture with her hand.

Katlyn nodded. She noted the okay signal from her colleague. "See you at the local later?" She mouthed to Amanda.

Amanda smiled and gave an affirmative nod.

Katlyn dialed the lab's number and provided them with the case number. "What can you tell me about the suitcase? Was there anything unusual about it?"

"The suitcase your Jane Doe was found in didn't have wheels. The outer case was vinyl, which suggests it may be vintage, possibly from the sixties," the woman said.

"What about the jewelry?" Kat asked.

"Nothing expensive. It was all cheap costume jewelry."

"Thanks," Kat said.

Jane Doe wasn't from a privileged background. How did she get such a large sum of money for one so young? Was it possible she was doing tricks, and that's why she was pregnant?

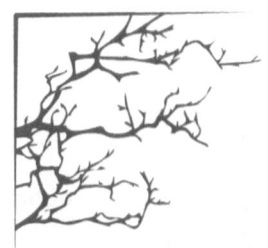

Chapter 9

Katlyn rummaged through her wardrobe, trying to find an outfit suitable for her upcoming TV interview. She discarded several dresses and a couple of suits before finally settling on a black dress and matching jacket. After putting on some tights, she noticed a hole in one leg. She considered changing them but decided it wasn't noticeable enough since it was high up to warrant a full wardrobe change. Completing the look, she added a pale blue scarf.

Why did she bother to look nice? The higher ups only wanted her to convey a message and nothing more.

Hastening to her car, she received a call from Kasper. He wanted to visit the next morning to measure up her kitchen. Agreeing to the meeting, she hung up and drove towards the interview studio on the other side of Casterton-on-Sea.

Negotiating down a narrow lane, she arrived at a small converted barn that served as the studio. The interviewer, Jody Coffrie, was inside waiting for her.

Katlyn entered the studio. Jody, seated in one of three tub chairs arranged in a semi-circle, waved her over. "Good morning, Detective Sergeant Kat Snowden."

Katlyn took a seat beside Jody. Her chair wobbled slightly as she leaned forward. "Three questions on the list I won't be answering. The exact location of the body is not for public release, nor will I be commenting on how she died."

Jody, displaying her long-painted fingernails, brushed her long blonde hair to the side. "You don't have to be so formal."

"Please don't ask any surprise questions as I won't be answering them either. I have photos of her clothing and her jewelry to provide viewers with something they can identify. I'll also be giving a general description of the Jane Doe."

"I'm trying to make the interviews I do fun. Boring, and the viewers switch to something else."

"This poor girl is dead. That's not a matter for entertainment, it's a very serious business."

Jody beckoned to the makeup girl, Blossom, standing in the shadows, and asked her to fix Katlyn's face for the camera.

Blossom nodded, grabbed her bag of cosmetics, and placed a bib around Katlyn's neck to prevent any makeup from marking her clothes. Then she leaned over Katlyn and began her work, moving quickly before Katlyn could object. "Not too much make-up, please." Katlyn almost got a mouthful of face powder, as the woman whirled around with her brushes and blushers. While Blossom worked on her, a male hurried in with glasses of water. He set down one on each side table: beside Jody and another beside Katlyn.

Once Blossom was done, she stood back and admired her work. "You were too pale. Now you're pretty. Like a model." Blossom held up a mirror.

Katlyn shook her head. She wasn't one for primping and preening.

Jody picked up the microphone. "The light's flashing orange. Thirty seconds to go. We're a low-budget county station, so we're lucky to have Blossom. The last place I worked had nothing as nice as this studio." Jody nodded, adjusted her earpiece, and the light turned green.

"Good morning, viewers. We're here in the heart of Casterton-on-Sea to bring you the latest news." She told the viewers about a local robbery, some drunken youths causing problems at the pub, and some London news. "We're so excited to have a special guest today. Please welcome Detective Sergeant Kat Snowden. She'll give us an update on the investigation of the unidentified woman found on a remote beach yesterday."

The light went red, and Jody drank some water. "Ready?"

Katlyn nodded. But she'd rather walk on hot coals than be interviewed on TV.

The light flicked green again.

"Good morning, Detective Sergeant Kat Snowden."

"Is it unusual for a female to be leading a case like this?" Jody asked.

First stupid question. "No. I've handled many similar cases during my career."

"How old was the young woman you found?"

"The pathologist estimates her age to be between sixteen and eighteen years old."

"That's incredibly tragic. Did she drown?"

"I cannot comment on that."

"Do you suspect foul play?"

"I cannot comment on that." If Jody was miffed that her questions went unanswered, she didn't let on.

"I believe you have some pictures to show the viewers to help identify the female."

Katlyn held up the photos, hoping her hands didn't betray her nerves by shaking. "If anyone recognizes any of the clothing or jewelry, please call the Casterton police station."

Jody took over. "The number is displayed on your screen. Please call now if you have any information."

Katlyn reached over to pick up the glass of water. As she grabbed it, her tub chair tipped over. She let out a yell as her legs flew up.

Flailing, in a futile attempt to regain her balance, the glass sailed towards Jody. It struck the reporter on the top of her head, causing water to cascade down her face and hair. All of this on live local TV.

Shit. Katlyn blushed. "Sorry."

Jody blinked the water from her eyes, shot Katlyn daggers, smiled at the camera, and continued with her commentary as if nothing had happened.

A male assistant rushed over from the wings as Katlyn slid from the chair, her dress riding up even higher before she stood.

Katlyn noticed the advertisement break light come on.

"Sorry, love. I told management the chair had to be fixed or go, but they didn't do a thing about it." He dabbed her face with some paper toweling, which absorbed the liquid and removed some of her make-up. Her face probably resembled some skin disease. Hopefully, the camera hadn't caught too much of her mishap.

The young male returned carrying a different chair. "Sorry, it's the best I could find."

Jody seemed calm and composed as she talked about a truck accident at a railway crossing while all this was going on.

The male gestured towards Katlyn with an okay sign, and Katlyn nodded. But she wasn't okay. She was utterly mortified.

Jody ended the conversation about a politician's expensive trips paid for by taxpayers and returned to Katlyn. "Do you have any suspects?"

We're interviewing all the residents in the vicinity to gather information about any unusual activities," Kat responded.

Jody bombarded Katlyn with more questions, and Katlyn struggled to contain her anger. The interviewer delved into personal matters that Katlyn had no intention of addressing. "I'm asking the public if they have any information about the unidentified woman found on the beach. If you recognize the clothing or the jewelry, please call-"

Jody took over. "Please call the number displayed on your screen. Thank you."

Despite being broken up by Katlyn's mishap, the ten-minute interview felt like an hour by the time the green light finally went off.

Jody flicked her long hair away from her cheek. "Thank you. You enjoy stealing the spotlight, don't you?"

Katlyn's mouth opened and closed in surprise at the sudden attack.

Jody abruptly marched over to Blossom, who had re-emerged. "You made her look better than me. Never do that again if you want to keep your job. No one looks better than me." She strode from the room without a backward glance.

Blossom rolled her eyes and gave Katlyn a knowing look.

"Thanks for doing my makeup. Sorry I messed it up. I hope never to come back again."

Blossom packed up her makeup and said in a low voice, "She's a show pony. Just ignore her."

Katlyn appreciated the reassurance and made a mental note to remember Blossom's advice.

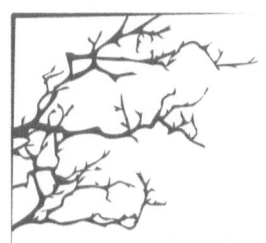

Chapter 10

White stormed through the squad room, his face twisted in a scowl. At least he hadn't stopped to berate her about her tumble from the tub chair earlier today. "What's got him so worked up?" Kat said to Colin as they stood by the coffee machine, nursing their cups.

Colin shrugged as he filled his cup and looked at her sympathetically before responding. "You're the talk of the town. That doesn't sit well with White."

Kat's cheeks grew hot as she realized her embarrassing fall had been caught on camera. "Did you see me fall?"

He nodded. "Quite a show. White said you've dragged the station's reputation down to the gutter. Said you did it on purpose to gain attention. Everyone heard him ranting."

"Great. Now I'm the laughing stock of the station."

"No, you are not. Don't let him get to you," Colin reassured her.

"It was an accident," she said, her voice tinged with a hint of annoyance.

Colin whispered. "He likes to be the center of attention and you've stolen his limelight."

"I didn't ask for any of this," Kat muttered, her frustration evident.

"You're upset."

"He's a self-centered shit. Just one kind word about my mishap would have been nice."

"He doesn't know how." Colin said, recognizing White's shortcomings.

"If he doesn't want me here, he can fire me." Katlyn's frustration boiling over.

"That's not going to happen. The mayor called in to see White," Colin said. "I overheard him saying you've brought policing into the twenty-first century, and raised the profile of the department."

She kept her voice low. "Eek. Does the mayor want to get in the cot with me or something?" She raised an eyebrow, considering the political dynamics at play.

Colin gave sappy smile, but had the decency to change the subject. "You received a call that was patched through to me right after your interview. The guy said he'd only speak with you and said he'd ring back. He hung up before I could ask for his details."

"Thanks." As she went back to her desk, her phone rang. Katlyn hesitated, debating whether to ignore the call, but her intuition told her it could be important. With a deep breath, she forced herself to answer. "Casterton-on-Sea Police Station, D.S. Kat Snowden speaking."

"Hi, sexy. Want to hang out with me tonight?" the male said.

That didn't deserve an answer. She hung up and called reception. "Please screen all my calls. Some idiot has propositioned me."

"I'm sorry," the female desk assistant said. "It must be because we all saw your mishap. It took up the whole screen before they blacked it out."

Katlyn reddened. The entire interview was cringe-worthy.

The moment she hung up, her phone rang again. Katlyn hesitated, debating whether to ignore the call, but her intuition told her it could be important. With a deep breath, she forced herself to answer. "Casterton Police Station, DS Kat Snowden speaking."

"I saw a man killing that poor girl on the beach," a male said.

Katlyn's heart raced, her attention fully captured. She sat up straighter, her voice firm. "How did he do it?"

"He hit her with a rock. She fell to the ground, and he dragged her body into the water," the male explained.

"Any reason you didn't come forward immediately after you saw this?" He was obviously fabricating the story as she found Jane Doe in a suitcase.

"I thought she might be okay," the caller responded, his voice filling with concern.

The downside of TV interviews was it attracted oddballs who made up stories for their five seconds of fame. But Katlyn couldn't dismiss this call outright. "Are you absolutely sure you witnessed a murder?" she probed, her voice reflecting a mix of skepticism and concern.

"Yes, yes. It was horrible. He was tall, and he had dark hair."

"Thank you for reporting this. Just leave your details with me and we'll call you."

Sylvester came over. "I've gone through the entire UK missing persons list. No matches, I'm afraid. Either Jane Doe hasn't been missed, or she was homeless."

"I was at the autopsy. Her neatly kept nails had a coat of blue nail polish, and her clothes weren't those of a person living on the streets. No needle tracks to indicate she was on drugs. Jane Doe had a place to call home."

He nodded. "Caught you on the news segment."

"Don't. I want to forget that."

"That's not likely. You caused something of a sensation here. The public loved you. Said you were authentic."

"Shit. You mean flashing my tights? That's all I need." Now her ex would call her and telling her she was a slut. It wouldn't matter that he was the one carrying on with his personal assistant.

The results they'd been waiting on arrived from the lab. The female had recently had a breast enlargement. Why would a teenager have this done? And where would she get the money for such an operation? The baby in her belly was a male and Jane Doe was eleven weeks pregnant at the time of death.

JANE DOE WAS NEAR HER daughter's age. That squeezed at her heartstrings. Someone must be missing her. Why hadn't they reported her missing?

She pushed those thoughts aside as she and Colin arrived at the first cosmetic surgery clinic on their list. It was a small, dingy place that smelled of disinfectant and chemicals. They spoke to the receptionist, but she could not provide any useful information.

"Colin, do you think there's any chance Jane Doe could be connected to a human trafficking ring?"

Colin's eyebrows shot up. "That's a possibility. But why do you think that?"

"Well, the breast enlargement surgery means she had some money or someone had paid for her to have this done."

"It's a wonder her parents hadn't noticed." Colin said.

"Maybe, their style of parenting was laid back. No. That's unfair. Anything's possible," Kat said.

"She didn't have any identification on her, which suggests someone was trying to keep her hidden," Colin added.

"We need to follow every lead, no matter how small."

Why hadn't anyone reported Jane Doe missing? Was she from out of town or had her family given up on her?

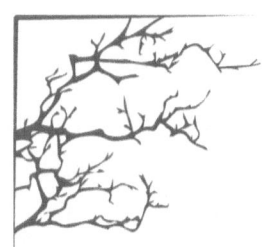

Chapter 11

Katlyn ended yet another unproductive call and glanced over at Colin. They had been working tirelessly, but the breakthrough they desperately needed remained elusive. Colin appeared concerned as he jotted down notes from his own phone conversation.

Her phone rang again, and she recognized Victor's voice on the other end. "Hello, Victor."

"Would you like to join me for a meal at Jamie's? They serve a fantastic beef wellington."

Katlyn's mouth watered at the thought of a beef dish. "Thank you, but..."

"No 'buts,' please. I can pick you up or meet you there."

She couldn't think of an excuse to refuse him. "I'll meet you. Thanks."

While she was on the phone with Victor, she noticed Colin listening intently on another call. He appeared concerned as he jotted down notes. She was about to inquire about it when her phone rang again. It was Dean, her ex-partner.

"Kat, you have shown the world what a slut you really are in that interview. How can you think of having Briony with you when you're behaving in such a way?"

"Need I remind you that you were the one having an affair?"

"That was a one-night stand. It was nothing," Dean said.

I'm aware that your one-nighter was more than that. Don't go calling me a slut. I have evidence you were playing around for over a year. You can't keep your zipper done up." She slammed down the phone, anger pulsing through her veins.

Breathe. Just breathe. The squad room had fallen silent, but they all pretended they were doing something. Let them listen. She didn't care. She'd done nothing wrong. Maybe she should have told Briony. But her daughter was too young to be dragged into her father's sordid affairs.

She walked over to Colin and waited until he finished his call. "Any luck?"

"Maybe. I just talked with a guy who said the jewelry belonged to his girlfriend. He hasn't seen her all week, and she's not answering her calls. I've got an address for the girlfriend." He finished his coffee.

"Girlfriend's and the guy's name?"

"Tina Game, and the boyfriend is Albert Park."

"Let's get our skates on and check out the address." He glanced at his watch. "We've got half an hour to get there and meet this Albert. My car?"

"Sure," she said, then waited for Amanda to finish her call. "Conduct a search for Tina Game at this address."

Amanda nodded while she wrote down the information.

"We're heading there now." She followed Colin downstairs. "Was this Tina Game living at the address when she was alive?"

"Mr. Park said so."

As she opened the door of his Jeep, black boxing gloves fell out. "Boxing gloves?"

"Just throw them in the back. I meant to leave them in my locker at the club."

She slipped into the passenger side. "You box?"

"I'm an amateur. Just took it up to get fit. I go when I can." Colin drove through the town.

"I'm impressed. Are you sure the guy who recognized the jewelry is waiting for us at the address?"

"Said so. It's way out of town. Probably a farmhouse." Colin turned into a single lane road with hedgerows on both sides.

"I'm not fond of driving on these narrow roads."

"I grew up on a farm."

"A country boy," Kat commented.

"My parents sold up when I left home and moved into town. They used to keep a few cows for the milk and some laying hens to sell eggs at the farmer's markets."

"I don't even like milk," Katlyn said. "Our neighbor had a cow and mum used to make me drink the stuff. Even today, just the thought of warm cow's milk makes me shudder."

"You and me both."

Colin turned down another lane with dry-stone walls on either side.

They drove in silence for several minutes, the tension building with each mile they covered. The absence of house numbers along this stretch of the laneway made her think they were lost, until they neared a farmhouse set amongst overgrown with bushes and weeds. The front gates were at a crazy angle, with the house number still attached. Colin glanced at Katlyn. "It's the right place, but I expected someone to meet us here."

"I don't like the look of this." It seemed the place was abandoned. Katlyn shivered, feeling a chill down her spine. Colin parked the Jeep further down the lane beside a large oak tree. The atmosphere was heavy with an eerie stillness, broken by the occasional rustling of leaves in the wind.

"It doesn't look lived in," Kat said. Something wasn't right. "I thought you said the guy was meeting us here?"

Colin glanced at his watch. "I said half an hour, and it's only been twenty-five minutes. Maybe, he's late. You can wait here while I check it out."

She pulled a small folding pocketknife from her handbag and slipped it into her pocket. "I can't let you go in alone."

Colin gave her a long look. "You come well prepared."

"I hoping I don't need this, but you never know." She slipped it into her pocket.

Colin grabbed two tasers from the back seat and gave her one.

They both got out and walked down the uneven, moss-covered stone path. They cautiously approached the farmhouse, its windows boarded up, and the paint peeling off the weathered walls. Katlyn couldn't shake the feeling that they were being watched.

Katlyn slipped, and Colin caught her. "I find it hard to believe that Tina Park lived here."

"I agree."

Katlyn got a creepy feeling climbing up her spine. "If we see any sign of trouble, we'll call for backup."

Katlyn stood on the worn stone porch. Colin knocked on the front door. The stillness seemed to envelop them.

"This place is giving me the jitters," she whispered.

Colin knocked again and tried the door. It wasn't locked, so Colin pushed it open with a loud creak. They stood in a dimly lit hallway. He glanced at her. "Let me go in alone."

"And miss out on all the fun. I can't let you go inside alone." She put her finger to her lips as a sign they should refrain from speaking.

Colin nodded, his eyes scanning the darkened rooms. "Let's split up and search." "Stay within eyesight, though," she said. He readied his taser and edged inside. She followed him into the cold, unwelcoming house.

Dust-covered fixtures greeted them, and the air was heavy with the scent of decay.

Their every step echoed on the wooden floor as they advanced. A double doorway opened to a large reception room. All the furniture was covered with dust cloths. The heavy drapes were closed, and the room shrouded in semi-darkness.

Katlyn shook her head and indicated for them to keep moving.

Scattered over the vintage counter tops in the kitchen, were dead insects and droppings from creatures who might still inhabit this place.

They explored the house. Each step echoing through the desolate rooms. Katlyn's heart pounded in her chest, her senses on high alert.

Her breath caught when a creak had the short hairs on the back of her neck standing on end. Katlyn's heart raced as she stood in the dimly lit hallway.

She went further along the hallway and saw the basement door was open. A sliver of light beckoned from below. "I'm going down," she said.

Colin grabbed her arm gently, concern etched in his eyes. "It could be dangerous. Let me go first."

She pulled her arm free, giving him a determined look. "I have to know."

"Please, I'll call you if there's a problem."

She watched him descend in the flickering light until he disappeared around the bend.

A pervasive silence assaulted her. "Colin?"

She hesitated a moment before following him.

Katlyn went down the creaky wooden stairs when the light suddenly failed. Each step intensified the tension in the air. Her thudding heart drowning out her rational thoughts. "Colin, where are you?"

As she descended, she could barely see her own hand. A dank, moldy smell rose from below. She continued with her phone light to guide her. Suddenly, she heard a loud noise, and her heart jumped in her throat.

"Colin, is that you?" But there was no answer. Her palms were sweating with dread as she continued. She couldn't shake the feeling that something was wrong.

Reaching the bottom, the beam from her phone illuminated a grimy forgotten space. Dust particles danced in the light, and the stale air hung heavy. Old storage boxes and discarded furniture were revealed in the dance of light as cobwebs hung like ghostly veils.

A muffled sound reached her ears from the far end of the basement. Her heart raced as she cautiously moved forward. "Colin? Where are you?" Barely a whisper of something unidentified drifted to her.

The room narrowed, forcing her to squeeze through a gap between two dilapidated shelves. Suddenly, a sharp blow struck the back of her head. Her vision blurred, and she struggled to stay conscious.

Thuds and scraping noises echoed and then subsided. "Colin?" she called out, her anxiety mounting.

A door slammed somewhere above. "Colin?" Katlyn's worry deepened. Footsteps faded away, leaving her lying on the cold ground, defenseless. Then she passed out.

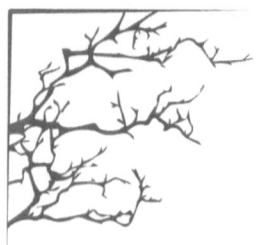

Chapter 12

Katlyn woke with a splitting headache, greeted by darkness. Lying on a cold, damp floor, her hands were bound behind her back. She blinked, attempting to clear her vision, but the gloom persisted. Closing her eyes momentarily, she opened them again, noticing a faint glow filtering through a gap somewhere.

The dank, fetid smell filled her every breath. It made her stomach churn. Was this a dream? No. Her hands were tightly tied.

Confusion clouded her mind. She struggled to discern her whereabouts. "Is anyone there?" she whispered. The silence was deafening.

Someone had struck her on the head and left her here. Her mind raced with questions. Why had they done this to her? And what did they plan to do next? Suddenly, a groan reached her. She tensed. "Who's there?"

No answer.

Another groan followed, and Katlyn's heart pounded with dread. She called out again into the void, seeking any hint of a presence.

Struggling relentlessly, she fought to free her hands from the tight ropes. Her exertion causing sweat to bead on her forehead. Gasping, she continued even when her wrists burned from the friction.

Soon, her skin became slippery, and she managed to wiggle them out of the bindings. But she was exhausted with the effort.

"Help me," she pleaded, hoping that someone was listening.

Another groan followed, but the source remained elusive. "Who's there?" she called out again. No answer.

Determined to stay focused, Katlyn felt around in the darkness, searching for her phone. Instead, her hands encountered rocks and dirt, and a small creature scuttled across her legs. Suppressing a scream, she shivered in disgust. It must have been a mouse. She despised those filthy creatures. "Help!" she called out again, fear coursing through her veins.

Was she going to die here? A sob rose in her throat. She wasn't ready to die.

Stop this, she told herself. At least she was still alive and wearing clothes. That was something to hold on to.

Gradually, she mustered the strength to sit upright and resumed her search for the phone. This time, her fingers brushed against something wooden. Reaching into her pocket for her pocketknife, she realized it was missing.

Trying to piece together her memories from the time she blacked out proved futile. She couldn't recall what had transpired. "Is anyone there?" she called out once more, hoping for a response.

A faint groan. It sounded like a male. Was he groaning because he couldn't speak?

Rubbing her eyes attempting to improve her vision, she said, "Can you make another noise?"

The person obliged, prompting Katlyn to rise slowly and stumble towards the sound, her hands outstretched in front of her. Where was she? Her thoughts were scattered, and nothing seemed to make sense. "Colin? Is that you?"

Several steps later, her foot hit an object, causing a male to grunt in response.

Uncertain if it was her partner in the darkness, she questioned, "Colin, is that you?"

The male another groan.

"Thank God it's you," she whispered, relieved, as she kneeled and touched the figure before her. "Can you get up? Make one sound if you can, and two if you can't."

Two groans.

Feeling around in the darkness, Katlyn located the rope binding Colin's ankles. She tugged at the twine, persisting despite the burning sensation in her fingers. Finally, the rope fell away.

"Are you hurt?" She asked.

Another groan.

Brushing her hands over his body, she discovered his arms were secured behind his back. Fumbling with the knots, she attempted to free him. The throbbing in her head intensified, but she pushed through it, determined to release him from his restraints.

She sat back for a moment to regain her strength and gave it another shot. Finally, his wrists were freed.

"I'm going to remove the tape from your mouth. I'll be as gentle as I can." She ran her hands over his face. Grabbing the edge of the tape, she peeled it away slowly.

"Thanks," Colin whispered, his voice hoarse.

"I've lost my phone. Do you have yours?"

"They took it."

"We have to find a way out. Where's the stairs?" Katlyn spoke with an urgency, aware their captors may return at any moment.

"I'm not sure of anything," Colin said.

Katlyn and Colin cautiously navigated the dark room, their hands probing for any obstacles in their path. The air was thick and musty, making each breath a challenge. Every step was a struggle, but they persisted, driven by the desperate need to escape.

As they moved, Katlyn stumbled and collided with what seemed like an armchair.

Colin swiftly pulled her back up. "Be careful."

"I'm trying." Resuming their journey, she continued until she encountered a solid wall. Her hands touched something that felt like wood rather than the cold brick. Tracing her hands along, she eventually closed her fingers around a door handle.

"Hush. Let me listen," she whispered, pressing her ear against the door. No sound did she hear.

She tried the handle, but it wouldn't budge.

"Let me." Colin pulled and pushed, to no avail. "Stand aside. I'm going to find something to use "

She heard him rummaging around. "Try not to make too much noise. If someone's upstairs, they might hear us."

"Bugger that." Colin returned with a length of wood and swung it at the door. The blow echoed loudly in the silence. "If anyone's here, we'll soon find out." He tried again, and the door cracked.

"Listen."

"I think they've scampered," Colin said. He struck the door again, and more wood splintered.

Once more, he delivered a forceful blow, causing the door to give way. Dim light spilled into the room. They stumbled into a narrow hallway, which led to a flight of stairs. Hurrying up the steps, they emerged into the sudden brightness, disoriented after being engulfed in complete darkness.

She breathed a sigh of relief, but it was short-lived.

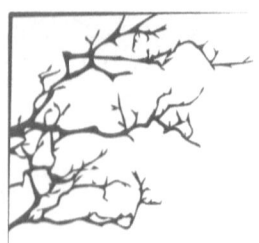

Chapter 13

A chilling sight awaited them as they stepped into the doorway.
A figure clad in a balaclava stood before them. The assailant swung a cricket bat at Colin.

He ducked just in time to evade the blow. Seizing the opportunity, he swung the makeshift weapon he still held, connecting with a resounding thud. The attacker stumbled backward and collapsed, motionless, on the floor.

Katlyn returned to the basement and grabbed the length of rope used to restrain them.

Colin secured the man's wrists behind his back. Two phones lay on the countertop next to the back door. "Look! I think they're our phones," Katlyn said, grabbing both.

Her heart raced as they made their way through the kitchen. Could more of the thug's pals be lying in wait outside? She tightened her grip on Colin's arm. "It might be a trap."

"I can't see anyone. We'll just have to take our chances," Colin replied firmly, flinging open the door to assess the situation.

They burst into the open air, raced across the overgrown yard, and into the tall bushes and brambles beyond.

Concealed in the bushes, Colin attempted to dial the emergency services. "I haven't got a signal. You?"

"Mine's the same," Katlyn confirmed.

"Bleeding useless when you need it. Let's make a run for my Jeep."

She nodded.

Colin gripped the lump of wood.

Colin gripped the makeshift weapon as they cautiously crept along a path of uneven cement pavers at the side of the house. Suddenly, a loud noise froze them in their tracks. Had it originated from the front yard?

"They're waiting for us," Katlyn whispered, dread gripping her. "Let's try this way."

"I'm with you," he said fearfully.

They darted through the undergrowth behind the farmhouse. Thorns tore at their clothes, but they ignored the stinging pain and pressed on. Startled thrushes took flight, creating a commotion that they tried to silence their movements.

Katlyn saw a gate and pushed through it.

They'd tramped a long way through the dense vegetation, and eventually reaching the road. Katlyn and Colin continued down the road, with farm cottages scattered in the vicinity but none in proximity. Their pace quickened as they caught sight of Colin's Jeep in the distance. However, as they approached, their hopes were dashed when they saw that someone had shattered the windows and ransacked the interior of Colin's Jeep.

Colin cursed under his breath. "They've wrecked my Jeep."

Katlyn put a hand on his arm. "That's fixable. At least we're alive."

"Yeah, but now we're stranded."

"I'll call for backup if I can." She checked her phone and breathed a sigh of relief. "I've got a signal." She called the station and just before the signal disappeared again, she relayed their location and situation.

Startled by an approaching vehicle, she hurriedly took cover behind some bushes. The van slowed down, sending a surge of anxiety through Katlyn. Had they been seen? She crouched lower, hiding deeper within the foliage.

The van increased speed and disappeared around the bend. She got to her feet. "Phew. That was close. My heart was in my mouth."

"Mine too," Colin admitted.

"Did you see who was inside?"

"I glimpsed two guys," Colin said. "Unfortunately, nothing that could help identify them."

"I didn't do any better. Couldn't even see the number plate," she said.

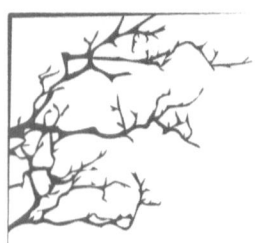

Chapter 14

"We were lucky we made it out." Katlyn remarked as Colin parked outside the police station after leaving the forensic team at the farmhouse. "It could have turned out very differently, otherwise."

"But, we made it."

The man Colin had knocked out had vanished.

"Are you sure you don't need to get checked over at the hospital?" Colin inquired.

"Just a few scratches and bruises," she replied dismissively as she rubbed the welts on her wrists caused by freeing herself from the bindings.

"What about that bruise on your forehead?"

"I'm fine, really. I have a check-up appointment with the doctor later. And what about you?"

"A few scratches. Otherwise, I'm good."

"Alright then, let's get on with it. The guys are combing through that house. I'm hoping they'll find some fingerprints," Katlyn said.

Colin nodded, and they both stepped out of the Jeep. As Katlyn reached for her phone, a message from Victor popped up.

Victor: 'What happened to you? I waited for ages.'

Katlyn cursed inwardly. She had completely forgotten about their dinner plans after all that had happened.

Katlyn: 'Sorry. We were following a lead and got locked in a farmhouse. I'll explain later.'

Victor: 'You're forgiven. Ring me tonight. Dead bodies are keeping me busy all day.'

Katlyn: 'Thanks. I'm busy too. Speak tonight.'

As they entered the station, the uniformed officers turned their heads and greeted them.

"Welcome back!" they cheered.

"Thank you. I might look worse for wear, but I'm okay and so is Colin," Kat said.

"Glad to hear it," Desk Sergeant Hardy said as he scratched the eczema patch on his neck.

When Katlyn crested the stairs, she saw White, hands on his hips outside his office, waiting for them. News traveled fast. Her heart sank, anticipating what was to come. She dropped her bag on her desk and was about to sit down when her boss marched over.

"What do you think you were doing going into that abandoned place without backup? This could have ended badly."

Criticizing her in front of her team was wrong on so many counts. "I'm well aware of that, but I resent the way you're speaking to me."

He glared at her. "I'll speak however I want."

Colin joined Katlyn, folding his arms and positioning himself right next to White. "Chief."

White sneered. "What?"

"We went because we had a call from Jane Doe's supposed boyfriend," Colin said.

"I informed Amanda, but there was no reason to suspect an ambush," Katlyn added. "We couldn't get a signal on our phones to call for backup when we arrived."

"We went to have a conversation with a man named Anthony Park," Colin interjected.

"Use your brains next time," White seethed before storming off toward his office.

"Bastard," Colin muttered softly.

Determined to make her point, Katlyn raised her voice. "I'm off home to shower, and then I'll go for my check-up at the doctor's."

White halted in his tracks, then slammed his office door shut.

She dismissed the thought of filing a report about White's behavior to his superior. He would check with White, and the usual shit would happen. Nothing at all.

Amanda hurrying over. "I tried ringing both of you several times and was about to round up Brady go with me to the address when your call came in."

"Thanks." Katlyn picked up her handbag. "Colin, go home and clean up, too."

"You still think forensics will lift some prints?"

She nodded "But, they might have worn gloves."

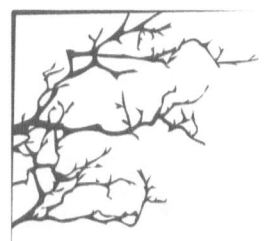

Chapter 15

Katlyn opened the front door. "Good morning, Kasper. Glad you could come."

Kasper, in navy work overalls, had a carpenter's pencil in his chest pocket. With his certain cheeky demeanor, he had a certain charm that some women found appealing, reminiscent of David Beckham.

"I always make time for Victor's friends. He's been a good client and friend." He bent over to take off his work boots.

"No need for that. Just wipe your feet. I'll show you what I need done," Katlyn said, leading him down the hallway.

"Three of the bedroom doors are sticking. I never close them fully because I struggle to open them again."

Kasper opened and partially closed the second bedroom door, examining how it met the door frame.

Standing over six feet tall, he easily reached up to run his hand over the top of the door. "The frame has twisted a little with age, which is to be expected in old houses. I'll plane it. But that'll leave a raw surface, which will need to be undercoated and painted." He stared at the two large black garbage bags in the middle of the second bedroom, but didn't comment on them.

The bags held some of her father's clothes. She still couldn't bring herself to donate them to charity. "I want to paint all the rooms, anyway. The color chart is on the kitchen countertop. I circled the colors I want for the doors and skirting boards. Also, this window falls when I try to open it. The other bedroom has the same issue."

"Let me see." He skirted the bed and tried opening and closing the window. "The rope sash is broken. Old age. These are easy enough to replace. What else do you need done?"

"I need to replace the vanity cabinet in the bathroom." Her dad had propped it up with a wooden post. "I'm not fussed as long as it has a basin, a mixer for hot and cold water, and some drawers. I'm working on a case that's taking all my time. So, I'll leave it up to you to pick something suitable if it's not too costly. A kitchen renovation is on my to-do list."

He nodded. "Let me see your kitchen first, then I'll measure up the bathroom cabinet space."

"That's okay." She led him to the kitchen.

Kasper leaned over and opened and closed the kitchen cabinet doors. "Do you want to give these a face lift or new cabinetry?"

"I'm thinking something new and basic, if it's not too costly. But the vanity cabinet and the doors are the priority," Katlyn explained.

Nodding, he suggested, "I'm actually installing a new kitchen for a client in a few days. The current kitchen is only seven years old, comes with a cooker, dishwasher, and range hood. Are you interested? Just pay me for the labor and get an electrician to install the new appliances."

That would save a significant amount of money. Katlyn was grateful that she had gone to Victor's for dinner and met Kasper. She'd spoken to Victor last night and promised to have dinner with him next week. "Can you take a few pictures of the kitchen and send them to me?"

He nodded. "Of course," Kasper agreed. "I'll be going there tomorrow to measure the space and see what needs to be done."

"Thank you. Please keep me updated on the cost as you progress," Katlyn requested.

"Sure."

She nodded and glanced at her watch. "I'm off to work now. If I'm not here, my neighbor, Gail Babcock, can let you in. She's always home. I'll give you her phone number just in case she needs to go out." Her father had given Gail a spare key when he had bought the place. She'd asked her neighbor to keep it in case she lost hers and for times like this.

Kasper keyed in the Gail's number into his phone. "Thanks."

As Katlyn made her way to her car, her mobile phone started ringing. She didn't recognize the number. "Hello, Kat speaking."

"Kat Snowden?"

"Yes. Who am I speaking with?"

"I can't tell you."

"Look, don't waste my time. Why are you calling? How did you get my number?"

"I saw you on TV. You were genuine. I like that," the male voice said. "I liked your acrobatics."

She sighed. She'd never live this down. "If you have any information about the case, I suggest you ring the station and let them know. Goodbye."

"I know who the Jane Doe is."

Now he had her attention. Damn, she wished she could put a trace on the call. "What's her name?"

When he remained silent, Katlyn assumed he had hung up. She asked again, "So, who is Jane Doe?"

"No, no. Her name isn't Jane Doe; it's Emily Green. It was all a mistake," the caller revealed.

"How do you know that? Who are you?" She was speaking to dead air. He'd hung up before she could get his name. She noted the phone number and called Syl. "Can you trace a number for me?"

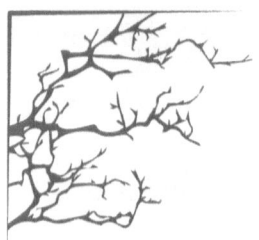

Chapter 16

As Katlyn stepped from her vehicle, her phone beeped a message from Victor. "Hey, just checking in. How's the case going?"

She smiled, grateful for the distraction. "Making progress, I hope. Got a call from an anonymous tipster claiming to know Jane Doe's name."

"Really? That's great news!"

"Syl's running a trace on the number now."

As she walked into the station, Colin was waiting for her at her desk.

"Morning, Katlyn. Any updates on the case?"

Katlyn nodded. "An anonymous caller informed me Jane Doe's name is Emily Green."

"Good. White is going to want an update on our progress soon."

Katlyn sighed, feeling the weight of the case on her shoulders. She turned to Derrick. "I need you to go over the forensic reports on that farmhouse in Bransgrove Road and see if there's anything we've missed."

Derrick glared at her. "Fine."

"Syl, did you trace who rang me this morning?"

"A dead end. It's a burner phone."

She sighed again. "Anyone tell me something I can use."

"I've made some enquiries and found ten Greens living within a twenty-mile radius from where Jane Doe was found," Colin said.

"Let's split the list." She tore the sheet in half. "You take this lot. Let's ask them if they have a teenage daughter and if they know where their daughter is?"

"I'm on it," he said.

Katlyn dialed the number for the first Green on her list, hoping to make progress in her search. The phone rang for a moment before a hesitant voice answered. "Hello?"

"Hi, is this Mr. Green?" Katlyn asked, her voice filled with anticipation.

There was a brief pause on the other end before Mr. Green replied. "Yes. What is this about?"

"She introduced herself. Do you have a teenage daughter?"

A heavy silence hung in the air before Mr. Green spoke again. "You're sick, do you know that? Why don't you leave us alone?"

"I'm sorry. What happened to your daughter?"

"Are you serious? I... I lost my child to suicide six months ago."

Katlyn's heart sank as she realized the impact her call had on Mr. Green. She responded gently, "I'm truly sorry for your loss, Mr. Green. Please accept my apologies for disturbing you."

She hung up, pondering what other surprises awaited her. Logging into the database, she searched for any individuals named Green reported missing or involved in any incidents. She discovered the record of the girl who had tragically taken her own life. At least she now knew that none of the other Green families had experienced a recent death.

The next number on the list almost growled when he answered. "You've dragged me from watching Everton playing Leeds."

Oh, a passionate soccer fan. Katlyn introduced herself. "Am I speaking with Mr. Green?"

"Yes. This better be good."

"Do you have a teenage daughter?"

"No. Is that all you want? I don't have time for this nonsense. Goodbye," Mr. Green replied dismissively.

Katlyn moved on to the next number with no luck. By the time she dialed the last name, she hoped that the family would be home and that they would inform her that their daughter was missing. She hung up from that unsuccessful call and stood. Another coffee would boost her spirits.

She crossed the room to the coffee machine while two of the team were still fielding calls from her interview at the local station. The calls had almost petered out now.

Crossing the room, she made her way to the coffee machine while two team members continued fielding calls from her recent interview on the local station. The influx of calls had dwindled now.

Sometimes reaching out to the public for help in identifying a Jane Doe yielded results, and sometimes it didn't. However, the call she received on her mobile phone could be the breakthrough they needed. She quickly fired off an email to White, informing him they might have a lead on their Jane Doe.

She made a coffee for Colin and carried it over to his desk. He looked up from his computer as she placed the cup down.

"How did you fare?" she asked.

"Thanks." He took a sip. "Out of my five Green families, one was elderly, the next had two toddlers, and the others didn't have teenage daughters. How about you?"

"We need to visit the addresses of the Greens who weren't answering their phones. Perhaps speak to their neighbors."

He gulped the hot liquid. "Not bad."

She laughed. "That's about the extent of my cooking."

He stood. "Let's go."

She grabbed her handbag, informed Amanda of their destination, and together they headed down the stairs to the car park.

Colin waited in the unmarked police car. She fastened her seatbelt. "Let's hope this isn't a fruitless hunt."

"Yeah."

"How are your plans for your renovations going?"

"I've found someone to fix my doors and a few other jobs. He's Teresa's partner."

"The woman who assists Victor," Colin said. "I can't imagine working with dead bodies."

"I guess you must get used to it," she said. "You settled where you are now?"

"I'm looking at moving into something bigger shortly."

"From your two bedder. Do you need help with the move?"

"Nope. I can move the sofa you loaned me and a few clothes."

"The sofa is yours to keep."

"Gee, thanks. I'm your charity case now."

"Not at all."

"Sorry. I'm... never mind."

He still seemed reluctant to discuss what was bothering him.

She wondered if he was still grieving for his wife despite his better judgment. Even if she had left him for someone else, it would still leave a void.

She knew from her own experience with Dean, her ex, that it was difficult to adjust and trust someone after infidelity.

They traveled past the local shops—cafes, hairdressers, a Coop food store, a pharmacy, a couple of dress shops and some tourist traps. A jetty ran down to the pebbly beach where seagulls squabbled over the chips children threw and fishing boats were moored.

A man walking down the street waved at Colin, and he waved back. "A guy I went to school with. I grew up about ten miles away in Gyvennerville. When I entered the police force, I swore I'd never come back."

"So why did you?"

"The divorce."

"Bugger."

"It wasn't working out, especially with three people in the marriage. I had enough of her excuses and her spending my hard-earned money. I closed all the credit cards down. Now she'll have to rely on her lover boy to support her expensive shopping habits. My ex kept the house as she had a baby on the way. Not mine. And I couldn't afford to live in the suburbs of London. So here I am. How about you? How did you end up here?"

"I inherited my dad's house. I didn't take a thing when I moved out because my daughter is still living with her dad."

"You didn't ask her to live with you?"

"I did, but she's going to school near her dad, and I didn't want the house to be sold and uproot her."

"That's admirable, but it's a sacrifice for you."

"I might consider my share when my daughter moves out, but while she's still studying, I couldn't do that to her. Plus, my dad's place is well set up."

Colin stopped to get petrol at the local station.

Katlyn climbed out. "Let me get this."

"So, I'm a charity case."

"Don't be silly. You can pay but this goes on my expense account for the station. No sense in you paying."

"How did you manage that? I'm not so privileged, and I've been there longer."

Katlyn shrugged. "Just did. I thought it came with the job, and White didn't object." She went inside to pay.

The youth looked at her strangely. "Just the petrol, hon?"

Katlyn glared at him. His name tag identified him as Martin. The lad must have seen the TV interview, and his imagination was running wild. "I'll thank you to keep your dirty thoughts to yourself."

Martin blushed as he handed her the receipt.

She climbed into the car.

"Are you okay?" Colin said when she returned.

"That lad called me 'hon'. He must have recognized me from the TV interview."

Colin chuckled. "Your mishap was revealing."

She folded her arms. "Oh, shut up."

Colin slowed down as they approached the address in the rundown area on the outskirts of Casterton. "Is this it?"

The front yard was unkempt and cluttered with junk. Katlyn nodded. They both got out. "Let's see if they have a missing teenage daughter," Colin said.

They walked up the gravel path, negotiating around car parts, to the unsound wooden front steps. Each step Katlyn took creaked.

Colin knocked. The front door badly needed a coat of paint.

An overweight, unshaven male opened the door. "What?"

Katlyn stepped forward and showed her warrant card. "DS Kat Snowden."

"Ain't done nothing wrong. What do you want?"

"Do you have a teenage daughter?"

"What's she done now?"

Maybe they were finally getting somewhere. "Is she at home?"

He turned from them and shouted, "Jane! What have you done now? Get out here."

An overweight teenage girl appeared. "I done nothing. Why are they here?"

"Sorry we bothered you. Thank you for your time," Kat said.

The male slammed the door as they left.

The next place they visited, no one was home.

Katlyn knocked on the door of the last place. "I'm hoping someone recognizes the photo of the jewelry Emily Green, if that's her name, wore."

No one answered the door. "Let's split up."

They began knocking on doors. The door was opened promptly by the nearest neighbor. Katlyn showed her warrant card and introduced herself. "Can I ask your name?"

"Mrs. Badger. What's this about?"

"Is Mr. or Mrs. Green home?

"Oh, they left to visit her sister in Scotland a week ago."

"Do they have a daughter?"

"Yes. But she's staying with friends most of the time. Comes back to do her laundry and grab some meals."

"Can you describe her?"

"I don't think that's anybody's business. Why do you want to know?"

"We looking for the parents of a girl found on the beach."

"You surely don't think it's Emily?" The woman looked alarmed.

"We don't know. But, we need to locate the parents and get a description of their daughter."

"She's a nice girl."

"Please...."

The woman nodded. "Emily has long black hair, has been into fitness lately, and she has diabetes, which has caused her parents a few problems. I haven't seen her here for a week or more. She used to wave to me when she was home."

"If I show you a picture of her jewelry, could you tell me if it was hers?" Katlyn retrieved the photo."

Mrs. Badger hesitated. "Looks like her jewelry, but I couldn't be certain. I do hope it's not her."

"Would you have the Green's mobile phone number?"

"I'll get it for you."

Colin glanced at her and gave a single nod, but said nothing.

Her heart raced. They had potentially found Jane Doe's family, and the teenager's name was Emily Green.

The woman returned with a slip of paper. She put her hand over her mouth in distress.

"Thank you for your help. Please don't call Mr. or Mrs. Green. Let me contact them."

Now came the dreaded task of informing the parents their daughter was dead. That was the toughest part of her job.

Once in the car, she dialed the number Mrs. Badger gave her.

A woman answered. "Who is this?"

She introduced herself. "Good morning, Mrs. Green?"

"Yes."

"Do you have a daughter named Emily Green?"

"Yes. What's she done now?" Came the response, with the husband cursing in the background about his daughter.

"I need you to return as soon as possible," Katlyn said.

"It's not convenient. Whatever she's done, Emmy can manage on her own for the week."

"I'd prefer to tell you in person. Please return as soon as possible to Casterton."

The woman harrumphed. "You'd better tell me now or I'm not coming."

Telling parents this devastating news to parents and relatives over the phone was heartless. "We need you to come home."

"I'm not cutting my holiday short to return because Emily has gotten herself into some trouble. Sort it out yourself."

"Do you have your family with you now?"

"My husband... is with me," the woman responded, her voice quivering slightly.

The woman finally grasped the severity of the situation. "Please sit down," Kat said.

"Don't drag this out, just tell me."

"I'm sorry to tell you we've found a girl's body on a local beach. We believe it's your daughter."

"It can't be." Her voice trembled.

A male voice spoke on the phone. "My wife's had a shock."

"Get her a hot cup of tea with plenty of sugar."

"I'll do better," Mr. Green said. "I'm pouring her a whiskey. What's this about?"

"We've found a body at Tide Cove. We believe it's your daughter, and we need you and your wife to return to Casterton and identify her."

"Oh God. It can't be our Emmy. It can't. You're making a mistake. What happened to this girl you say is our daughter?"

Mr. Green still held onto hope that it wasn't Emily. Katlyn's heart went out to them. "It's what we're trying to discover. Please call me when you get back, and I'll arrange a viewing."

She pushed her hair away from her face. This was the worst part of the job. It never got any easier. She dialed Brady at the station. "Can you contact the local dentists and see if they have an Emily Green in their records?"

"If they do, I'll get them to send through the dental records for identification," Brady said.

"That's tough. Telling the parents," Colin said.

"I need a stiff drink. Care to join me? My dad had quite a collection of spirits."

"Can't say no to that."

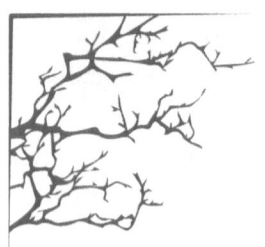

Chapter 17

Mr. Green held his wife's hand. Mrs. Green's eyes were red from crying. "Are you sure it's our Emmy?" he asked, his voice filled with desperation.

Katlyn's heart was heavy, trying to understand the pain they were going through. She couldn't imagine how torn she would be if something happened to Briony. "We need you to identify her body, but we are fairly certain," she replied gently.

Mrs. Green stared at the ground, lost in her thoughts. Following a moment of silence, she looked up with resolve. "I want to see my baby," she said, her voice trembling with sorrow as tears streamed down her face.

Katlyn nodded, her own eyes moist with sympathy. "Of course. Follow me. The viewing window is just through the door."

She'd made plans with Victor last night to have the parents identify the remains this morning. Surprisingly, Victor had been chatty and even complimented her on the way she was leading the case, leaving her momentarily speechless.

Mr. and Mrs. Green entered the room nervously, their faces etched with anxiety and dread as they prepared to confront the horror of their daughter's body. Victor met them in the hallway, introducing himself and leading them to the curtained viewing window.

"Now, it may not be your daughter. Take as long as you need to be certain," Victor said softly, his voice filled with compassion.

"Honey, maybe you should wait outside. This is going to be too hard on you," Mr. Green suggested, concerned for his wife.

"I want to see my baby. I want to say goodbye." Mrs. Green wiped away her tears.

Mr. Green stood closer to his wife and gripped her hand tighter.

Teresa pulled aside the curtain, revealing the covered body on the table. Then she drew the sheet to reveal the face of the teenager. Mrs. Green let out a piercing scream. "My Emmy, Emmy, Emmy!" Overwhelmed by her grief, she collapsed, her legs giving way beneath her. Colin rushed forward to catch her, eased her to the floor gently, while Katlyn called for assistance.

Katlyn spoke softly to the girl's father. "I'm sorry for your loss. If your wife needs more support, I can put you in touch with a counselor," she said.

"We'll manage. We don't need help, thank you," Mr. Green replied, his face lined with grief as he fought to keep his emotions in check, his voice carrying a mix of sadness and determination.

Colin helped Mrs. Green into a nearby chair, offering her a glass of water. Katlyn approached Mr. Green once again, her voice filled with compassion. "I'm sorry, but I must ask. Could I get a recent photo of your daughter to circulate?"

"What the hell for?" Mr. Green asked, perplexed, his brows furrowing in confusion.

"It may assist us in our investigation, and we'll also need to interview both of you. The longer we delay, the colder the trail gets," Katlyn explained, hoping to convey the necessity of their cooperation.

Mr. Green sighed heavily. "Very well. Come by tomorrow evening."

"A constable will collect the photo. We'll need to see your daughter's room as well to search for any clues as to who may have done this."

Mr. Green nodded.

"Thank you. We appreciate your cooperation during this difficult time," Katlyn said sincerely. "And once again, I'm sorry for your loss."

The Greens slowly made their way outside, their grief palpable as they climbed into their battered Volkswagen and drove away.

Katlyn and Colin stood outside the mortuary, both burdened by the weight of the parents' anguish. It was a heavy reminder of the impact this had on the lives of those involved.

Victor joined them, acknowledging the difficulty they were facing. "It's hard on the parents."

Katlyn nodded. "We'll have to monitor the Greens. Given the proximity to the victim, they may provide valuable leads to the suspect."

"Of course," Victor said.

"We can't disregard the possibility that the killer might be someone they know," she explained, her voice tinged with concern. "They might unknowingly provide us with crucial information."

Victor nodded thoughtfully. "Well, let me know if there's anything I can do to help."

She appreciated his genuine concern, but the weight of the case was something she needed to shoulder herself. "Thank you, but we'll manage."

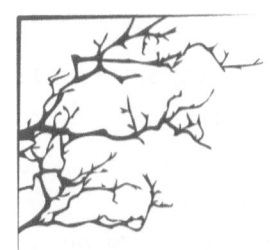

Chapter 18

Katlyn phoned DS Jules Buckford, her old friend and former colleague, who worked at Tellford police station, which was about 20 miles southwest of London. Jules was one of the few remaining friends Katlyn had from her time there. "Did you find any new information about the warehouse fire?" she asked, her voice carrying a mix of angst and sorrow. It was the incident that claimed her ex-partner's life.

"Forensics discovered that bags of crisps were used as the accelerant to start the fire. It's an unusual choice, but here's what we know," Jules explained. "Crisps, because of their high fat content and the packaging, can burn effectively. The breakthrough came when one of the forensic arson experts revisited the warehouse. He found a fragment of a crisp packet near the remains of a three-gallon bottle of methylated spirits that was used for cleaning machinery."

"Crisps! it's been two and a half months since the fire. Why didn't they find out before?" Brian Palmer, her ex-colleague, died in that fire and to this day, she regretted not being able to save him. Jules knew this. "I can't thank you enough for looking into this for me."

"You owe me a pint for this," Jules teased.

"Happy to oblige, but you still owe me a round for when I found the knife used in the murder you were investigating."

"Fair point," Jules conceded. "Let's have a lager next time you're in the area. Hopefully, that'll be soon."

"It's a deal," Katlyn agreed.

"I've just emailed you a list of individuals who rented the warehouse over the past ten years. Most of them are involved in drug dealing," Jules informed her. "However, I couldn't trace the actual ownership of the warehouse. They have a complex network of shell companies that lead to dead ends. But I'll keep digging."

"Thanks again for your help," Katlyn said.

"You've been through the mill and I don't understand why some of the team are still blaming you for Brian's death. Take care of yourself," Jules advised sincerely.

Katlyn choked up with emotion and blinked away a tear. "I will."

Colin approached at her with a raised eyebrow. She pretended not to notice.

"That photo of Emily Green on the TV... well I've just had a conversation with a man who claims to have seen her with a guy down on the beach a few times." Colin shared the information about the informant. "I took down his details and said we'd meet him at a café."

"That's promising," Katlyn responded cautiously. "No more meetings at secluded places, right?"

"Absolutely," Colin grimaced. "He works at the local hospital."

"That's a relief. Shall we go now?" Katlyn asked. "Brady and Derrick should be at the Green's searching Emily's room."

"Good. Let's hope they come across something of value to the case," Colin responded.

Katlyn glanced at Syl as entered the room wearing a frown. "Did you find anything useful on Emily Green's social media pages?"

Syl shook his head. "Her posts appear to be quite ordinary. No boyfriend pictures either, but there might be something we're missing. I'll keep digging."

"Just keep looking. Something might turn up." Katlyn picked up her handbag and met Colin at the stairs.

Colin and Katlyn made their way to the car park. Colin had his keys at the ready. Katlyn glanced at him. "Have you had your windows fixed?"

"I did." Colin said. "Lucky the glass company had the replacements in stock."

As they drove, he brought up a more personal matter. "Is Victor... this is a bit awkward. I saw the way he looked at you. Do you want me to tell him to back off?"

Katlyn let out a weary sigh. Colin was crossing a line by mentioning this. "Thanks, but I can manage my own life. After what happened with my ex, I'm just not ready. One-night stands included." She didn't want to get hurt again.

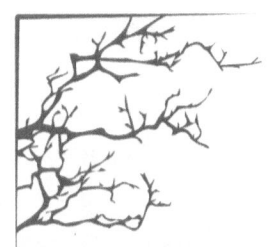

Chapter 19

Colin and Katlyn sat in a booth at the café across the road from the general hospital, patiently waiting for their contact to arrive.

"He should be out in a few minutes," Colin said, keeping an eye out for their informant.

Katlyn's phone rang.

"Hello, it's Kasper. I've measured the other kitchen, and with a few minor adjustments, it will fit perfectly. I've sent you some photos."

She scrolled through the images. "It's a great kitchen. Yes, thank you. When can you install it?"

I'll need to store it in your garage while I dismantle your old one. There's just one catch, though. It will have to stay in your garage until I finish another job."

"Thanks for the heads-up. I'll inform Gail that you'll need access to my garage."

"I'll let you know the day prior," Kasper said.

"Yes. Keep in touch." Katlyn hung up.

Just then, a tall, thin man in his mid-fifties, wearing hospital scrubs, caught Katlyn's attention. He seemed nervous from the way he kept glancing about while speaking on the phone. Katlyn subtly gestured to Colin. "I believe that's our man crossing the road."

Colin glanced at the man through the café window. "Let's hope he's not wasting our time."

As the man ended his call, he glanced at Katlyn and Colin. He appeared undecided whether to enter the café. Finally, he pushed open the door and limped inside, wearing an orthopedic elevated boot on his left foot.

Colin stood up and addressed the man. "Bernard Young?"

Startled, Bernard responded, "Yes, that's me."

Colin made the introductions after they both showed him their warrant cards.

"Please, take a seat," Katlyn invited, gesturing towards the empty chair. "We were hoping to talk to you about something you witnessed on the beach a few days ago."

As the waitress approached to take their orders, Bernard settled into the seat opposite them, continually scanning the room with a nervous gaze. Did he fear being seen talking to them?

Katlyn started a conversation to help put Bernard at ease. "So, Bernard, what do you do at the hospital?"

"When doctors need something delivered or done, they call me. It could be anything from fetching a walking frame to accompanying a patient to the x-ray department," Bernard explained.

"Sounds like you have a busy job," Katlyn said.

He nodded.

"Bernard, do you frequently take walks on the beach?" Colin inquired.

"I love walking. It's quite relaxing," Bernard replied.

"You mentioned seeing the girl on the beach," Katlyn said. "We're investigating the murder of Emily Green, and we were hoping you tell us about the man you saw her with."

Bernard nodded, his eyes darting around nervously. "Yes, I remember her. She was so beautiful. She was with a man, possibly in his thirties, wearing a blue shirt and jeans."

"Did you get a look at his face?" Colin asked.

Bernard shook his head. "No, he had his back to me."

"Which beach was this?" Colin probed further.

"Turtle Beach. It's my regular spot. The boyfriend was tall, had dark hair, and wasn't particularly good-looking. I'd say I'm better looking than him," Bernard said.

Katlyn and Colin shared a knowing glance. Bernard was clearly fabricating his story. First, he said he didn't get a look at the face and now this. "You believe Emily was found at Turtle Beach?" Kat said. "We haven't released the exact location where Emily was found to the public."

"Yes, that's right," Bernard replied confidently. "I saw her lying on the beach. I thought she was asleep, or I would have immediately called the police. Over the past few months, I've seen her there a few times."

Bernard omitted any mention of the suitcase which contained Emily's body or the accurate location. She pushed further. "Let's be honest. Have you actually seen Emily at all?"

A red flush crept up his neck. "What do you mean? I'm trying to help you. I have seen her but.... She was...."

Katlyn cut in to warn him. "Bernard, you are aware that providing false information can lead to serious consequences."

He stood. "Stop, stop! I was trying to help you. You people don't appreciate my help. I've exceptional vision and hearing. I know what I saw and heard. You stupid people can go to hell." He ran out of the café.

The waitress arrived at their table, carrying a tray of coffees. "Is that man coming back?"

Colin shook his head. "No, he's gone. But don't worry, we'll enjoy his coffee."

Just as they settled back into their seats, Katlyn's phone rang. "Hello, Brady."

"We've just left the Green's home," Brady informed her. "We found a few items in Emily's room that might be of interest. The parents didn't know if Emily had a boyfriend. They seemed to be wrapped up in their own lives, and didn't have a clue what Emily was doing."

"Thanks," Kat said.

Colin pondered the situation. "Now I'm thinking that perhaps Bernard overheard something, but not at the beach. He concocted the beach story to make us believe him."

"Maybe we should question him again," Katlyn said.

Colin nodded. "And find out what he truly knows."

Katlyn sighed. "I still think he wanted his five minutes of fame, but it won't hurt to dig deeper and see if he knows something." She'd get Brady on to it.

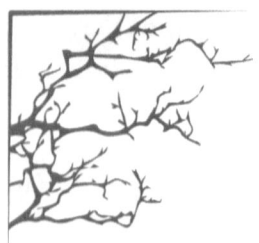

Chapter 20

Colin parked outside a row of tenement houses. "Her name is Lola Belcher. She rang and said she had something to tell us."

"And she couldn't tell you over the phone?" Katlyn zipped up her navy puffer jacket. "Hmm. I hope this isn't another wild goose chase."

They squeezed past an old black Saab with dents and scrapes on the sides, parked near the front door. Katlyn pressed the doorbell.

The curtain on the side window lifted, revealing the face of a young girl. Katlyn heard the girl call out to someone inside. "There's people at the door." The girl disappeared.

She heard a muffled response from inside. Judging by the tone, it didn't sound positive.

The door opened to a sullen teenager with blue streaks in her hair, wearing leggings and a t-shirt adorned with the logo of the latest band. "Yes?"

They both showed their warrant cards. Katlyn introduced herself and Colin to the teen. "Are you Lola Belcher?"

She seemed taken aback for a moment. "Yes?"

"We'd like to speak with you about your friend, Emily."

"I didn't really know her that well." What or who had changed this teenager's mind about speaking with them? Katlyn paused at the entrance. "Is your mother or father at home?"

"Mum's out the back."

"We prefer to interview you with your mother's or father's consent, as you are underage."

"My dad left us years ago. I can get my mum."

"Yes, please."

Lola led them into a cluttered living room. "Wait here."

The teen disappeared through a doorway and returned shortly later with her mother in tow.

The woman appeared weary from hard work and carried a basket of laundry on her hip. She placed it down and extended her hand. "I'm Carol Belcher."

Katlyn introduced both Colin and herself.

"Lola told me you're here to interview her about Emily."

"That's correct. We hope Lola may assist us in our investigation."

"It's so sad what happened to Emily. I hope you catch the fellow responsible."

Katlyn wondered why Carol assumed a male ended Emily's life. "We're doing everything we can to apprehend her killer. May we speak with Lola?"

"Of course. Can I offer you a tea or coffee?"

"No thanks," they both said in unison.

"Take a seat. I'll be in the kitchen if you need me." Carol left.

The teen slumped into an armchair while Colin took out a notepad and pen.

Katlyn leaned forward from the lumpy sofa. "Did Emily ever confide in you if she were seeing someone?"

She shook her head.

"You were her friend," Kat said.

Lola nodded.

"What if something happened to you? Wouldn't you want your friends to help the police?"

"I don't want to get anyone into trouble," Lola said.

Lola was having second thoughts about sharing any information. "Just tell us what you know."

Lola shrugged. "This was a mistake. I'm sorry."

Katlyn knew she had to appeal to Lola's emotions. "Lola, Emily Green is lying in the mortuary. A killer cut her life short."

Lola winced, showing the appeal had struck a chord. "Don't you want the person responsible brought to justice?"

The teen said. "I guess so. I used to hang out with her a lot last year. But this year, she didn't hang out with me so much anymore. I think she was seeing someone." Lola nervously tugged at strands of her black hair.

Colin lent forward and said. "Was she seeing a boy?"

"I don't know. I just know lately she was moody." She played with her hair again.

"Do you think she had a row with the boyfriend?" Colin suggested.

"Maybe. Boys can go hot or cold on you for no reason." Katlyn reflected on her own teenage years when her first crush hadn't even noticed her. "Did she have any close friends?"

"She sometimes hung out with some of the other girls. And sometimes she would just disappear right after school."

"When did you last see Emily?"

"A week ago. It must have been on Thursday in biology class. She seemed worried and sad at the same time. I asked her if something was wrong, but she didn't want to share. Anyway, after class, she left."

"Did you see her later that day?"

Lola shook her head.

"Is there anything else you can tell us about Emily?" Colin asked.

"Not really."

"Did she keep a diary?"

"I don't know. If anyone would know, it probably would be Poppy. But, don't tell her I told you."

"Who's Poppy?"

"Oh, Poppy Connolly. Emily is good friends with her."

Katlyn rose. "We appreciate your help. If you think of anything else, please don't hesitate to call." She handed her card to Lola.

They said their goodbyes and went to the car.

As Colin drove away, Kat said, "Next, we need to go to the school and interview Poppy Connolly the rest of Emily's friends."

"And her teachers," Colin said.

"It's too late today. I'll call the school in the morning." Katlyn's phone rang. "Hi, Brady. Did you have a chat with Bernard?"

"Our five minutes of fame Bernard. Honestly, I think he's a waste of time. He gave me the same information as he did for you."

"Okay," Kat said. "It was worth checking all the same." She said goodbye and hung up.

"Want to get a bite to eat at the pub?" Colin asked.

Katlyn yawned. "I'm tired. How about some takeaway? We could try that new Thai restaurant?"

Colin agreed.

She brought up the menu on her phone and went over it with him. They picked up their order on the way to her place.

Katlyn opened the front door to her cottage, and Lucy sashayed around her mewing. "So sorry. I forgot to put out some dry food for you. I won't be a moment, Colin." She hurried into the kitchen and prepared the cat's meal.

"Where can I put these?" Colin followed her to the kitchen with two bags. One with two servings of rice, and the other with cashew nut chicken and lime chili pork.

He set them on the table. "What's that smell? Have you been doing some painting?"

"Kasper has been fixing my bedroom doors. I couldn't close them properly, so he planed them and repainted them." She opened the cupboard door. "Would you like some wine?"

"Sure." She handed him the bottle to open while she got the glasses and some servers. "I have a feeling that Lola was hiding something." Katlyn opened the containers of food.

"I feel the same way. We should interview her again." He helped himself to a serving of rice and some pork. "We will after we talk to the teachers and her friends. I'll get Amanda to check the social media pages and see what she can find? Was Emily was chatting with any particular boy?" After they ate their meal, Colin said. "I'm glad the chief made us partners."

"Don't speak too soon. I might still turn out to be a bitch. Let's take our wine into the lounge room." She glanced at her father's ornaments on the mantlepiece, waiting to be packed up.

He stared at the oil paintings adorning the walls before he sat down. "You into art?"

"It's my dad's. He left this place to me. He used to enjoy going to markets and if he spotted something that caught his eye, he'd buy it if it was cheap enough. Some of it is junk and some probably worth a penny."

"Don't get rid of anything without an appraisal. Just look at the old frame. This oil painting might be valuable."

She eyed the country scene. "It's a bit dark. But it's growing on me." She poured some more wine into her glass. "I might sell it and retire if it is."

"Half your luck if it is." Colin finished his glass of wine.

"Can I top up yours?" Kat asked.

"I guess I'm driving back to mine. So, I'd better not." He stood. "Thanks for the company."

Katlyn got what he meant and his gaze conveyed he wanted something more. She wouldn't get involved with him just because she was lonely sometimes. "See you tomorrow, Colin."

After showering and changing into her pajamas, Katlyn put her phone on the nightstand and lay in bed, staring at the ceiling.

She couldn't shake off the feeling that she was missing something crucial to the case. She closed her eyes and tried to push away the thoughts, but they continued to swirl in her mind.

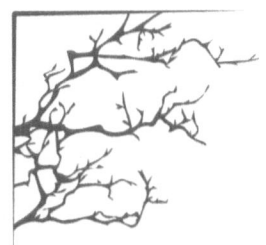

Chapter 21

"Good morning. How may I help you?" The red-haired office assistant at the Casterton Community Secondary School smiled.

Katlyn showed her warrant card, as did Colin. "D.S. Kat Snowden and my partner, D.C. Colin McKenzie. I have an appointment with the headmaster, Mr. Williams."

The woman straightened her beige cardigan. "Oh, it's concerning that schoolgirl the police found. I'll buzz him for you." The office assistant spoke it to the intercom. "Those detectives are here to see you, Samuel."

The school, like many in rural areas, had outdated furniture and wood-paneled walls adorned with cheap prints. At least, the office assistant had added a personal touch with a vase of lilies on her desk. The school reminded Katlyn of her old inner-city London school that had overcrowded classrooms and insufficient funding.

They were shown to Mr. William's inner office and exchanged greetings with the headmaster, who sat behind a large oak desk. The only sign of modernity was a computer console perched on the corner. A photo of him with his wife occupied the other corner.

The headmaster stood and buttoned his sports jacket. "Welcome. Please take a seat."

Katlyn settled into an old wooden chair while Colin remained standing. "Thank you for seeing us on such short notice," she said. She had called earlier and insisted that the headmaster make time for them.

He pushed his glasses up his nose. "I had to rearrange my schedule to fit you in."

Katlyn bit back a retort. Emily Green was more important than any meeting. "We appreciate your co-operation."

He pursed his lips. "We are very proud to be classified as a specialist school in math and computing. Our school has a very high overall performance rating, with top marks in some areas."

Why was he boasting about the school's merits when he knew the serious nature of their visit? "We're investigating the murder of Emily Green," Katlyn stated.

"Mr. and Mrs. Green identified their daughter just yesterday," Colin said.

"How awful for them. Our students were as upset to hear this as I am. Some of her classmates were in tears."

"How was Emily doing at school?" Katlyn asked.

"Her form teacher would have more information than I do." He pressed an intercom button. "Bring me the file on Emily Green, please."

Moments later, the office door opened, and the redhead entered, holding a folder. "Thank you, Analise," the headmaster said. He flipped through the file and then passed it to Katlyn. "Emily was a talented student. She ranked in the top ten percent of her year group for both math and computing. She also had a keen interest in science. Her behavior was exemplary, and as far as I'm aware, she had no disciplinary issues."

Katlyn nodded and flipped through the file. "Did Emily have any close friends at school?"

"Emily's Form Coordinator would have more information on that."

"In that case, we'll need to interview the form coordinator and Emily's classmates. Could you arrange a room where we can conduct these interviews, please?"

"Is all of this really necessary? The news of her death has traumatized Miss Green's friends."

"We assure you it's necessary," Colin interjected.

"This is causing disruption to the school's operations. You have no idea how upset her classmates were when I announced Emily Green's death during our assembly today. Some parents are considering counseling for their children."

"Those parents are fortunate they still can protect and care for their children. Emily's parents are not so lucky anymore." Colin said.

Katlyn shot Colin a warning glare, urging him to be more cautious with his words.

Mr. Williams scowled in response. "How dare you say such a thing!" He angrily reached for the phone on his desk. "I'll organize a room for your interviews."

Mr. Williams said, "Mrs. Pickering will be here shortly. She'll take you to the room I've organized for the interviews."

As they stepped out of the headmaster's office, Analise, the office assistant, stopped typing and stared at them. Katlyn mustered a smile, although she could sense the woman's resentment in her hard gaze.

Colin shrugged and typed a text message.

Her phone pinged.

Colin: 'Not very helpful, was he?'

Katlyn: 'Next time, don't speak your mind.'

Colin: 'I know, but he acted as if Emily wasn't important and this was an inconvenience.'

Katlyn: 'Let it go.'

A tall, reed-thin woman approached them. She wore black trousers, a faint-pink striped blouse, and flats. Her unconventional touch was evident in her bright orange nail polish and cherry-red hair. She flashed a smile as she stopped before them. "Good morning. I'm Nicole Pickering."

Colin and Katlyn stood and introduced themselves.

"It's a terrible thing. The students are grief stricken, so please be gentle with them," Mrs. Pickering expressed a genuine sadness in her eyes.

"We must ask questions to determine if any of her friends know anything that could help with our investigation," Katlyn reassured her.

"Please come this way." She hurried down the hallway, her ponytail swinging.

Katlyn had to quicken her pace to keep up.

Nicole Pickering led them upstairs to a room containing half a dozen desks, chairs stacked against the wall, and two whiteboards. "Just make yourselves comfortable, and I'll bring Emily's schoolmates."

"We'd like to start with you, please?" Katlyn said.

Nicole Pickering's demeanor sank, and she slumped into a chair. "Me?"

"We need to form a picture of Emily's life."

"Emily was one of my students. I was her math teacher."

"Have Emily's grades been consistent?"

"Actually, her grades dropped over the last few months."

"Do you have any idea why?"

"I noticed she seemed preoccupied in class and didn't take part as much as she used to. I tried to talk to her about it, but she wouldn't say anything."

"Did she have any close friends in the class?" Colin asked.

"Yes, she was quite close to a girl named Poppy. They often sat together during class."

"Can you give us Poppy's full name and contact details?" Kat asked, retrieving her notebook. Lola mentioned a girl with that name.

"Sure, it's Poppy Connolly." She gave them the Poppy's details.

"Any boy problems that you're aware of?"

"If you're asking if she had a boyfriend at school, then I'd have to say I hadn't noticed. If anything, she seemed to avoid the boys in her year. It's not uncommon. Many girls her age consider teenage boys of their own age immature."

"Did Emily have any conflict or trouble with classmates?" Kat asked.

"She was a sweet girl. If there were any arguments, the teachers usually report them to me, and I address the issue by speaking to the students involved. But I didn't come across any such incidents with Emily," Nicole replied.

"Did she have any other close friends?"

"Lola Belcher is another close friend," Nicole said.

"Okay, let's start with these girls." They'd spoken to Lola previously.

"I assume you noticed the flowers at the front gate," Nicole said. "The students and their parents have been leaving them as a memorial for Emily. Every time I see them, I can't help being upset about what's happened." A tear rolled down her cheek, which she brushed away.

"Seems Emily had quite a few good friends. The flowers are a touching tribute."

Nicole nodded and started for the door. Then she turned back. "I nearly forgot. Emily was absent on Friday."

"So, Thursday was the last time she attended school?" Katlyn clarified.

"Yes. Typically, we contact the parents in these situations. This time, we didn't receive a response from her parents."

"What do you mean you didn't get a response from her parents?" Kat asked.

"Parents may be unavailable to answer the phone due to work commitments. Normally, I receive a callback from them eventually," Nicole explained before heading out. "I'll get Emily's friends for you."

When she left Colin said, "Nicole seems genuinely upset about this."

"Someone wanted Emily dead."

Mrs. Pickering arrived with three nervous teenage girls. After introducing themselves, Katlyn and Colin asked for their help in investigating Emily's murder. The girls appeared even more frightened upon hearing the word "murder." Katlyn quickly reassured them they weren't suspects and only wanted to ask a few questions. She asked two of the girls to wait outside while she spoke with the third girl.

A young petite blonde teen sat beside the grade coordinator.

"Mrs. Pickering's right. We don't bite. Take a seat and let's get started," Kat said.

The young woman sat beside the grade coordinator.

"Let's start with your name, please?" Kat said.

"Let's start with your name, please," Katlyn began.

"Sophia Winslow. Emily was my best friend," the blonde girl replied.

"When did you last see Emily?" Katlyn inquired.

"A week ago. We caught the bus from school together. But she got off before me. It's awful what happened to Emmy." She wiped tears away.

Nicole gave her a tissue.

"Did she seem upset or worried about anything?" Colin asked.

The blonde shook her head. "No, she seemed fine. We talked about the school dance next month."

Kat asked? "Do you know if Emily was seeing anyone, or had a boyfriend?"

Sophia scrunched the tissue tightly in her hand. "I think she was. She stopped sharing things like that with me months ago."

"Anything, no matter how small may help us find out what happened to Emily," Colin said.

"We used to walk together to the bus stop, but sometimes she wouldn't catch the bus and would go off somewhere. When I asked her if she was seeing someone, she gave me a dirty look and walked off." Sophia fidgeted, nervously smoothing down her uniform.

Katlyn noticed her fingernails were chewed down to the quick.

"It was like she was scared to share her secrets with us," Sophia said.

"Do you think it was an older man she was seeing?" Kat said.

Sophia looked away. "Older? I don't really know."

Sophia was lying. "Please think hard. We need to know everything we can about Emily. It may help us track down her killer."

Sophia blushed. "I swear I don't know. Can I go now, Mrs. Pickering?"

"Think hard for Emily's sake, Sophia," Nicole urged.

"We need to find her killer," Kat said.

Sophia stared at the floor. "She was seeing someone, but I don't know who or anything else. Please, I want to go Mrs. Pickering."

"One last question," Kat said. When did you last see Emily?"

"I don't remember," Sophia shrugged. "Maybe, days ago."

"Thank you for helping." Katlyn addressed Nicole. "Please send in the next student."

The interviews carried on for another two hours, but they yielded little useful information. As Katlyn and Colin were preparing to leave, Sophia came running. "I forgot to tell you that Emmy has a phone. She was always texting someone. The teacher took it away from her during sport because she wouldn't stop."

Katlyn asked, "Did the teacher return the phone at the end of the lesson?

Sophia nodded.

"Do you know where Emily's phone is?"

"I don't know," Sophia admitted.

Another search of Emily's room was necessary as Brady and Derrick didn't find Emily's phone. Katlyn asked one more question. "You mentioned a boyfriend when we spoke earlier."

Her eyes widened. "I remember something else, too. She called someone when a group of us were walking to the library. She referred to the person as H.B., I think. I don't know if that's any help. It might be a joke or something."

"Everything you can tell us helps us get a better picture of Emily. Thanks very much," Kat said. Finally, they were making progress. They'd established that Emily may have a boyfriend with the initials H.B.

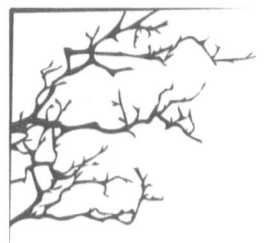

Chapter 22

Katlyn sat at the old wooden desk in the second bedroom and stared at her laptop open before her. The room, serving as a bedroom for now, held the potential to become her study—a sanctuary where she could delve into the depths of her investigations. With a furrowed brow, she reviewed the files Jules, her friend and colleague from Tellford Police Station, had sent her.

These files contained information about the fire that had burned Katlyn's legs and claimed the life of Brian Palmer, her former partner. The accelerant was packets of crisps scattered around the factory floor. The owner of the premises was a company listed in the Cayman Islands, and the previous tenant also had an offshore address.

As Katlyn immersed herself in the details, an unsettling feeling washed over her. She paused, her hand resting on the table, searching for the source of her unease. Something about these offshore companies nagged at the back of her mind, but she couldn't quite put her finger on it. Was it a gut feeling, an instinct honed through years of detective work? Or was there a trigger, an external piece of information that eluded her grasp?

Setting aside her laptop, Katlyn reached for a glass of wine, hoping to calm her racing thoughts. But as the liquid touched her lips, the unsettling feeling only intensified. It wasn't the first time she'd experienced this unease since delving into the unsolved case. Also, the lack of explanation left her questioning her own instincts. What was she missing? Were there hidden connections waiting to be uncovered?

Taking a deep breath, Katlyn set aside her thoughts and focus on her dinner. She heated a ready-made meal of curried chicken and rice, savoring each bite as she contemplated the enigma before her. The crime show playing on the television provided a temporary distraction, albeit an unrealistic one. Detective work was far more complex and nuanced than what they portrayed on TV. She finished the rest of her wine, hoping it would lull her into a peaceful sleep.

After undressing, Katlyn stepped into the shower, letting the hot water cascade over her tense muscles. The ache in her shoulders and neck, a result of long hours spent hunched over the computer, subsided. But as she rinsed off the soap, a familiar voice echoed through the kitchen, cutting through the running water.

"Katlyn?"

She turned off the shower, her heart skipping a beat. It couldn't be. Her father had passed away six months ago. Trembling, she hastily wrapped a towel around herself and hurried out of the bathroom, a mixture of hope and confusion consuming her.

"Dad? Is that you?" Her voice quivered as she called out, yearning for a connection she knew was impossible.

A loud crash resonated from the kitchen, snapping her back to reality. Her pulse quickened, and she grabbed another towel, cautiously tiptoeing barefoot toward the source of the noise. The sight that greeted her was far from what she had expected. The cookie jar lay on its side on the counter, its lid shattered.

Lucy must have knocked it over. Her initial confusion giving way to a sense of relief. That mischievous feline had a knack for causing trouble, and she had already lost a few of her father's beloved ornaments to Lucy's antics. The remaining valuable ones likely belonged to her father's partner, as he had never shown much interest in such trinkets.

Paintings had been more his style, though none of the several he owned held significant value, at least as far as Katlyn knew. The ornate frames probably held more worth than the imitation oils.

Sighing, Katlyn gathered the broken pieces of the cookie jar and tossed them into the bin. But as she turned to leave the kitchen, her gaze drifted toward the open window, a curtain flapping ominously in the breeze. Her heart skipped a beat, and a surge of anxiety coursed through her veins. Hadn't she locked the window? She was certain she had.

The tightness in her stomach grew. With trepidation, she approached the window, her body tensing. Bathed in the moonlight, she caught sight of a chilling silhouette lurking in her yard.

Her breath caught in her throat. Someone was outside her home, watching. She swiftly closed the window and drew the curtains tightly shut, attempting to create a barrier between herself and the unknown intruder. Panic surged within her, urging her to take precautionary measures.

With a sense of urgency, Katlyn embarked on a thorough sweep of every bedroom, checking each window meticulously. The tightness in her stomach persisted, fueling her determination to secure her surroundings. Returning to the kitchen, she retrieved her Glock 17 from its concealed spot beneath the kick panel. She knew it was a necessary precaution, a means to defend herself if the need arose.

Leaving a bedside light on to keep the darkness at bay, she quickly changed into her pajamas and climbed into bed, gripping the weapon tightly under her pillow. Every sound, every creak in the house, seemed amplified in the silence of the night. Sleep wouldn't come easily, but Katlyn resolved to stay vigilant and protect herself. The safety of her well-being hung in a delicate balance, and she refused to let her guard down.

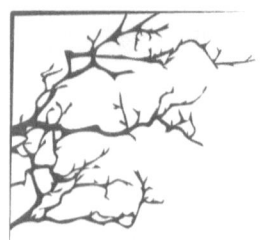

Chapter 23

Billy's eyes widened with lust, watching an almost naked Katlyn as she moved about the kitchen. She certainly had delectable breasts—not big, but delectable all the same. His desire was twisted with malice, fueled by the belief she was responsible for his downfall. He observed her slender figure, appreciating the allure it held, but his gaze also landed on the small tattoo on her shoulder and the scars that marked her legs. These reminders of her involvement in his loss stoked a simmering anger within him. He was determined to make her face the consequences of her actions.

When Katlyn approached the window, he shrank back into the shadows. She closed the window, and he waited until she'd gone.

Billy gazed at the camera feed on his phone, but she was gone from view. He made a mental note to adjust the camera angle to better track her movements.

Soon enough, she reappeared, now dressed in pajamas, holding the Glock 17. A surge of rage coursed through Billy, but he knew it wasn't yet time to act. He patiently awaited the perfect moment to strike.

A sinister grin twisted his lips as he reveled in the impending fear that would consume Katlyn's eyes. She had disrupted his world, and now it was her turn to suffer. He savored the anticipation, deriving twisted pleasure from the moments that would lead to her demise.

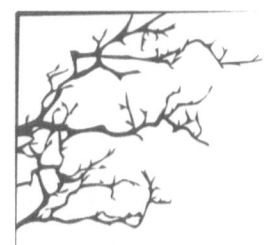

Chapter 24

Katlyn, battling exhaustion, approached the whiteboard, suppressing a yawn. Despite having a restless night because of prowler lurking about in the street, she knew she had to focus on organizing the details of the ongoing case. She wasn't sure what she saw, so she hesitated to tell anyone, afraid they'd think she was imagining things.

Summoning her team for a briefing, Katlyn noted Colin's absence because of his scheduled day off. Derrick, as usual, appeared engrossed in his phone. "Derrick, would you mind paying attention?" Her tone filled with mild exasperation.

Derrick frowned, momentarily torn away from his digital distractions.

"Good morning, everyone," Katlyn began, tapping the image of the unfortunate victim, Emily Green, displayed on the whiteboard. "Let's review what we have so far. Miss Green wore lycra leggings, a t-shirt, and sneakers." She pinned up visual representations of the clothing items. "We found a dry-cleaning ticket in her pocket and some jewelry. This rules out a simple robbery motive. Her stomach was empty."

Katlyn paused for a moment, her mind racing to make sense of an inconsistency. As she thought about Emily's secretive behavior, a realization struck her. "Wait a minute," she said, her voice tinged with curiosity. "If Emily had become so secretive lately, not sharing anything with Sophia, how did Sophia know about Emily having a mobile phone? We haven't found the phone yet. It doesn't add up." Katlyn furrowed her brow, pondering this. She made a mental note to investigate further and chat with Sophia again.

Brady raised his hand, prompting a smile from Katlyn. "No need to raise your hand, Brady. We're not in class," she said. Brady dropped his hand, returning the smile. "Please, go ahead."

"It's possible that she was being held captive, maybe by the baby's father," Brady suggested, his voice filled with earnestness. "She refused to have an abortion, so he resorted to kidnapping her. And when he didn't know what to do, he ended up killing her."

Derrick snickered, earning a disapproving look from Katlyn. "Do you have something to add?" she asked.

Derrick shook his head dismissively, indicating he had nothing substantial to contribute.

Amanda chimed in. "Hmm. What if the guy killed her because he's already married?" she said.

Katlyn nodded appreciatively. "Both good thoughts, Brady and Amanda. Emily was an excellent student, but her grades had been slipping lately. We know she was pregnant, but we're still uncertain whether it was with a boyfriend or from a one-night stand."

Pointing to the card with Sophia Winslow's name on it, Katlyn continued. "According to Emily's friend Sophia, she had become secretive in recent times, not sharing anything with her. Sophia mentioned Emily had a mobile phone, but it hasn't been located." She added a note on the board, 'phone missing'. "Sophia revealed Emily had been seeing a boy, referring to him as HB, though Sophia never met him. Poppy Connolly and Lola Belcher, friends of the victim. Lola Belcher didn't provide any significant new information. We've yet to interview Poppy."

"Next, we have Bernard Young, who claimed he saw Emily with a male at the beach where her body was discovered. He didn't know the body was concealed in a suitcase. Nor did he correctly identify the location of the body. We haven't released this detail to the press. I'll remind everyone that White will come down heavily on anyone who leaks this information to the public."

A murmur went through the group as Chief Inspector White joined them, positioning himself at the back of the room, arms folded over his ample belly. White's angry expression was nothing new. His ruddy face always carried a scowl, and his plump lips were tightly pressed together. As he plodded, due to his hip problem, towards the big board, the squad could sense the tension in the room.

"The nine hundred pounds found on Miss Green raises another question," White interjected, his voice gruff. "Was she planning to run away, or was something else going on?"

Amanda stood up from her chair. "That amount of money doesn't stretch far in today's world."

"Agreed. "And let's not forget both Colin and I were trapped in that abandoned farmhouse," Kat said. "It appears the suspect wanted to send us a warning, a clear message to back off. Colin and I believe if we hadn't escaped, the suspect might have returned to kill us. The suspect is dangerous and willing to take any measures to stop us. We need to redouble our efforts to apprehend them."

White turned to face the squad. "The press is giving us more flack for not solving this case yet. I need every one of you to double down and get on with it."

"But, Chief, we're working as hard as we can," Brady said.

Ignoring the comment, White directed his attention to Katlyn. "In my office, now."

Puzzled by his sudden summons, Katlyn prepared to respond, but White was heading back to his office. She followed him, knocking on the door before entering.

White didn't look up from his computer. "Close the door."

Katlyn complied and waited, curiosity piqued.

"Just a minute," he mumbled, finally lifting his gaze. "You're holding a press conference after lunch in the town hall."

Glancing at her watch, Katlyn realized it was just past nine o'clock. "You can't spring that on me. I'm not..."

White's frown interrupted her protest. "This is part of the job. Get yourself organized. I'll see you there."

Katlyn stormed out of the office, slamming the door behind her. Her stomach tightened into a knot of nerves. She had no idea how to handle the press. Grabbing her handbag, she nodded to Amanda, who was nearby.

Amanda put down the phone and mouthed, "What's happening?"

"Outside," she whispered, leading Amanda to the car park.

"I have a surprise press conference shortly," she said.

Amanda cursed. "I ought to deck that bleeding so and so. Don't worry. I'll stand by you."

"Thanks."

"First, get yourself spiffed up," Amanda advised.

"I'm not a show pony. What I'm wearing will have to do. I'm more concerned about being ready." Katlyn felt a tinge of embarrassment from the previous clothing mishap.

Amanda shook her head. "No, wear something nice. Make sure it's trousers this time."

Katlyn managed a small smile. "Thanks again. Can you organize a fresh image of Emily Green while I'm gone? And send it to the reporters who are attending the press conference."

"Will do."

Before they parted, Amanda continued to encourage her. "Remember, you're in control. Don't let them intimidate you."

Katlyn nodded, grateful for Amanda's support. She knew she had to gather herself and face the press with confidence. It was time to show the world that their team was making progress in solving Emily Green's murder. Determined, she squared her shoulders, ready to face the challenge head-on.

Katlyn hopped into her car and called Colin to inform him about the press conference.

As she drove home, she mentally rehearsed the points she needed to address during the conference.

Katlyn arrived home and swiftly changed into a pair of black trousers and a blue blouse. She quickly brushed her hair and applied a touch of makeup. Nervously, she assessed her reflection in the mirror, knowing the press conference would be a challenge.

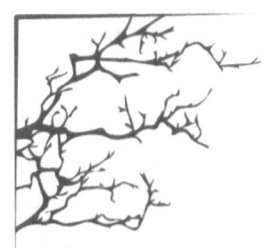

Chapter 25

U pon returning to the station, Katlyn found Amanda had already sent out the updated image of Emily Green to the reporters. She left the station with Colin in tow. "Don't let them intimidate you. Go slay them, Kat," Colin said. "I wish I had your confidence." Taking a deep breath of salty air, Katlyn strode along the footpath toward the town hall.

She reminded herself to thrust her shoulders back and not let the nerves show. As she entered the packed room filled with local reporters. Their casual attire stood in contrast to the few who'd traveled from London to get the latest scoop. As she walked toward the podium, they all began clamoring for a statement. *Don't let them know how unnerved you are by this, she told herself.*

White spoke into the microphone. "Can we have some quiet?" He retreated to the side. Voices subdued as Katlyn stepped to the microphone. "Good morning. I am Detective Sergeant Katlyn Snowden. I'm here to provide an update on the Emily Green case."

The room fell silent. "Emily Green's life was cut short by persons or person unknown. Currently, we are investigating a few strong leads."

One reporter raised their hand. "Can you give us any indication of who the suspect may be?"

"We are not prepared to release that information at this time," Katlyn replied firmly.

The same reporter asked another question. "There's a rumor about a suitcase Miss Green had with her." Someone had leaked this information. Though it wasn't entirely correct, it was too close to the mark. Stern words with the team about leaks today. "No comment." Photographers' cameras were flashing in her eyes.

Another reporter spoke up. "Can we confirm the suitcase was Emily Green's?"

"No comment."

The same reporter spoke again. "There have been rumors circulating that you've been threatened. Can you confirm this?"

Katlyn paused for a moment. "No comment."

Reporters badgered her with more questions. But Katlyn avoided giving any details that could harm the ongoing investigation. After several minutes, she concluded the conference, thanking the reporters for their time. All the while, White stood to the side, his arms folded across his ample belly.

Colin handed out photos to the reporters of Emily's jewelry and clothing she'd been wearing.

As she exited of the town hall, Amanda approached her. "Well done, Katlyn. You handled that brilliantly."

Katlyn breathed a sigh of relief. "Thanks, Amanda. I was really nervous, but I think it went okay."

Amanda grinned. "Of course, it did. You have a natural talent for this."

Katlyn chuckled. "I don't know about that, but I'm glad it's over."

As they walked back to the station, Katlyn couldn't help but feel grateful for Amanda's support. She knew she couldn't have done it without her.

"You'll be quoted in all the evening newspapers." Amanda fluffed up her pink hair.

Katlyn sighed. "We still haven't apprehended the suspect."

"At least they have an image of Emily Green and her jewelry to circulate," Amanda added.

"Let's hope someone who hasn't come forward will recognize the picture and ring us," Kat said.

As they walked into the station, Brady hurried over.

"Just received an anonymous call," Brady said. "The man said he has some information for you."

She sighed. "He couldn't tell you over the phone?"

He shook his head. "He's at work, but wants to meet you later."

After being locked in an abandoned cottage and the time wasted on Bernard, Katlyn hesitated to get her hopes up. "Later... what time?"

"He gets off his shift at two o'clock, so I suggested two-thirty. I have the address."

"And he didn't provide his name?" Katlyn inquired.

Again, Brady shook his head. "As soon as I got the time and address, he hung up."

"How did he sound?"

"Serious. I didn't get the feeling that it was a prank call."

She glanced at the address. "This is quite far from town."

"I know. Since Colin is off today, dealing with his divorce, I can accompany you," Brady offered.

"Thanks, but I need you to continue going through those interviews, just in case you find anything," Katlyn replied, a sense of unease creeping into her thoughts. "On second thoughts, perhaps you should come along."

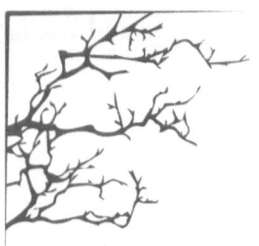

Chapter 26

Katlyn gripped the steering wheel as she drove down the narrow lane. Brady sat silently beside her, probably anticipating, as she was, this lead provided by the anonymous tipster was of use to the case and not an ambush. Ancient hedgerows lined the road, standing tall and weathered. Occasional farmhouses and fallow green fields, contrasting with her unease at the impending meeting.

As they continued down the lane, Katlyn's senses were on high alert. Suddenly, the distinctive sound of an engine roared behind them. She glanced at her rearview mirror and saw a dark van rapidly approaching, tailgating their car with alarming proximity. The van seemed to loom closer.

"The nerve of some drivers," Brady grumbled.

"Can you see their number plate? I can't," Katlyn said.

Brady turned his head. "He's too close. Bleeding nuisance drivers. They shouldn't let these people drive."

"I hope he doesn't try to pass us. I can't get out of the way, the layby's too far back." Katlyn's stomach clenched.

As the van continued to tailgate, Katlyn felt a mix of anger, fear, and determination. She urged Brady to communicate with the van driver, hoping they would back off.

Brady rolled down the window and signaled for the driver to back off, but the van persisted in its relentless pursuit.

The tension in the car grew as the dirt track crested the hill and they descended into the valley, with the van closing in. Katlyn's anxiety mounted with each passing moment.

The first time it bumped the car, Brady said, "Maybe, his breaks are gone. Be careful."

"I'm trying." She swerved to avoid a cow grazing by the side of the road, narrowly missing a collision. "Shit!"

The van mirrored her every move, almost crashing into their car with each passing second. Her grip on the steering wheel tightened, her knuckles turning white.

She accelerated, trying to get clear of the van.

Brady reached for his phone, intending to capture evidence of the dangerous pursuit. But a sudden jolt shook the car, causing the device to slip from his grasp and disappear into the footwell. "Oh, bugger."

The van rammed into her Toyota, sending it careening sideways.

"What the hell?" Fear etched across his face. He tried to reach for his phone, but couldn't get it.

Katlyn's instincts kicked in, her mind laser-focused on one aim: to escape their relentless pursuer. As she regained control, she punched in Amanda's number. "Code DD40. Someone's trying to run us off the road."

Brady shouted into the speaker. "We need backup now."

She pressed harder on the accelerator, determined to escape the van. Adrenaline coursed through her veins as she defied the speed limit.

The van increased speed and squeezed beside her with metal grinding on metal. The wheel wrenched from her hands as she spun out of control.

Amidst the chaos, Katlyn's phone rang, momentarily distracting her. She fought to regain focus. An oak tree was suddenly in front of them. Katlyn swerved, but the van crashed into her vehicle once more, sending them hurtling toward a massive oak.

Their car collided with the tree, the impact shattering the world around them. Everything went dark as the wreckage enveloped them, trapping them within its unforgiving embrace.

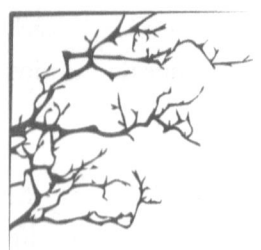

Chapter 27

Katlyn sat on the edge of the hospital bed, dressed in her street clothes, eager to leave. "I'm fine, really," she assured the young doctor who stood before her, holding her patient notes. "Just a headache and some sore ribs."

The doctor raised an eyebrow, concern etched on his face. "You lost consciousness, and we need to run some scans to rule out any underlying issues. It's important to be cautious."

Katlyn sighed, feeling restless. "I can't stay here. I have work to do. Three hours in hospital is more than enough for me. I've endured weeks at the East End hospital's Burn Unit, and if I have a choice, I'd rather not stay any longer than necessary."

The doctor gave her a stern look. "I strongly advise you to stay overnight. We need to monitor you and ensure there's no sign of concussion."

Reluctantly, Katlyn conceded. "Fine, I'll stay for the scans. But how is Brady Denko? Is he okay?"

"He was fortunate to escape with a few scratches. He left an hour ago."

Katlyn felt a sense of relief wash over her.

AFTER WAITING HOURS, the scans were finally done and the nurse wheeled Katlyn back to the ward, where she gathered her belongings from the locker. Glancing at her phone, she noticed several missed calls from Colin. She dialed his number, and he answered, his voice filled with concern. "Hello, I've heard about the accident. Are you okay?"

"I've got a headache and some sore ribs."

"What does the doctor say?" Colin asked.

She looked up as the doctor entered the room. "He wants me to stay to ensure I don't have a concussion, but I feel fine." Katlyn sighed.

The doctor's face bore a look of disapproval. "I can't release you until I'm satisfied that you're not at risk of a concussion. I strongly recommend staying overnight."

Katlyn felt torn, frustrated by the fuss and longing for her own comfort. "I can't stand being cooped up in this place."

Colin said. "Maybe you should listen to him. It's better to be safe."

Katlyn groaned inwardly. Both of them were ganging up on her. "I can't stay here. Please, Colin."

The doctor sighed, giving in to her insistence. "Is someone picking you up?"

"Yes, my partner," she replied. "I'll ring you back, Colin." She hung up.

The doctor gave her his card. "Promise me you'll go home and get some rest. I'm relieved you have someone who'll be with you."

Katlyn contemplated her response. Was remaining silent was akin to lying. "Thank you," she said, accepting the card.

"Call me if you feel woozy, want to vomit, or otherwise, off. I'm also giving you a script for pain killers to take if your headache gets worse. I want you to see your local doctor tomorrow." He turned to go, but swung back. "Give me his details and I'll fire off an email to him with the results."

"Thanks."

"Is someone picking you up?" The doctor asked again.

"My partner is on his way."

"Good. I don't want you traveling alone or driving for twenty-four hours," the doctor warned.

"I promise. Thanks for taking care of me." Katlyn expressed her gratitude sincerely. Driving was not an option as her car was being repaired.

The doctor nodded and left.

Colin strode into the room, but his steps faltered when he saw Katlyn. The surprise on his face was clear, and she couldn't blame him. With bruises scattered across her body and cuts on her face, she must have looked quite a sight.

"Are you sure you're not hurting anywhere?" he asked with concern.

"I'm made of tough stuff, you know," she replied, dismissing any pain she felt. She grabbed her handbag and phone, ready to leave.

As she climbed into Colin's Jeep, the sun peeked through the clouds, brightening the day. "It's come out especially for me."

Colin chuckled. "You think so?"

"I overheard you tell the doctor I'm your partner," Colin said.

"It's the truth, well, not the way he thinks."

Colin laughed. "No doubt about you."

He buckled up his seatbelt. "I don't know if you've had lunch, so I've picked up some sandwiches for us."

"Thanks." Katlyn answered her ringing phone.

"Where are you?" White asked.

"Colin's taking me home."

"Good. I'm considering taking you off the case pending medical advice," he said.

"What? I have a headache and some sore ribs. I've had enough scans to last me a lifetime. Nothing else is wrong with me." Katlyn's heart sank. She knew it was the right decision, but she didn't want to be sidelined. "I understand, Chief," she said, trying to keep the disappointment out of her voice.

"I'll get Colin to keep you updated on any developments, but for now, focus on your recovery," he said before hanging up.

"White just rang. I'm off the case for the time being," she informed Colin.

"You need to rest," Colin said.

"How did your meeting with the solicitor go?"

"Well, just as I expected. My ex gets to keep the house," Colin replied with a tinge of bitterness in his voice.

"That's tough," Katlyn sighed. "Can you stop at the pharmacy? I need to get a prescription filled."

"Let me get that for you," Colin said, pulling up at the pharmacy. While he went inside, she waited in the car and noticed Brady approaching her.

He leaned down to speak through the window. I came to see you, but you had left for a scan."

"I've got some bruised ribs and a headache." Katlyn observed the grazes on Brady's face. "How about you?"

He touched his cheek. "Just a few scratches. We're both lucky that your car hit the exposed roots of the oak tree and not the trunk. It could have been much worse for both of us. Your news has spread around the station like wildfire," he remarked.

"I'm giving them something to gossip about," Katlyn said. "Glad you were with me."

"Anytime." Brady smiled and left.

Colin returned to the car with her medication.

As he got in, she asked, "Did you schedule interviews with Emily's grade teachers?"

"I arranged them for late this afternoon."

"I want to come along."

"I'll check on you later to see how you are," Colin said. "Then we'll decide."

She nodded.

She thanked Colin as they arrived at her doorstep. Getting out of the car, she winced and clutched her side, feeling a sharp pain in her ribs. She let out a soft groan and leaned against the wall.

Colin noticed Katlyn's discomfort and approached her with concern. "Are you sure you don't want me to help you?" he asked.

"No, it's fine. I'll manage," she said, trying to sound strong.

He gave her a skeptical look but didn't push it. "Okay, well, take care of yourself. Call me if you need anything."

"I will. Thanks again, Colin," she said, walking into her house. Her recovery should be her priority, but the investigation was constantly on her mind.

Resting on the couch, she contemplated the events of the day. The close call with the van, the crash into the oak tree had all been terrifying. She questioned who would wish to harm her and for what reason.

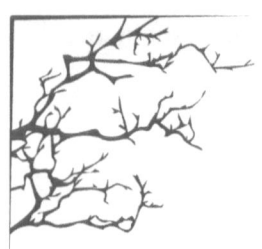

Chapter 28

Billy surveyed his surroundings, ensuring that no prying eyes were watching his every move. Nosy neighbors tended to peek through their front windows. The wind howled, gusts blowing in from the North Sea, tearing leaves from the trees and creating an eerie atmosphere. But Billy was undeterred from his mission.

He crept along the laneway, between Katlyn and her neighbor's homes. Upon entering the common ground, he navigated the prickly blackberry brambles to reach the back of her property. How could she afford to live near the sea on a detective's salary? That she may be involved in illicit activities intrigued him. Determined to dig deeper, he aimed to gather evidence that would tarnish her reputation and ruin her career. It would be payback for her role in shutting down his illegal import businesses, causing him substantial financial loss.

Having previously installed hidden cameras in Katlyn's kitchen and at the exit doors, Billy knew she wasn't home. The video feed on his phone confirmed this. Besides, this was the time of day she was at work. However, when he reached the gate, he discovered the vines had partly grown over it again, and it wouldn't open enough to allow him in. Frustration welled up inside him as he realized there was no time to wrestle with it. In a split-second decision, he leaped over the fence and made his way to the back door.

Inside the dated kitchen, she'd left a single breakfast dish in the sink. Was, no one else living here? The cat prowled the hallway, its fur bristling as it caught sight of Billy. He attempted to kick the feline, but it deftly evaded his strike, darting into Katlyn's bedroom. Reacting quickly, Billy slammed the door shut, effectively trapping the terrified animal inside. A sense of satisfaction washed over him as he moved on to search the next bedroom.

As he entered the room, he noticed large garbage bags filled with old men's clothes on the floor. The sight of the bags sparked curiosity in Billy's mind, wondering if someone else was moving in or out of the house. He hadn't observed any males entering the house, except for that detective, who hadn't stayed overnight. If Billy succeeded in his plans, Katlyn would never share a bed with anyone again.

Satisfied with his reconnaissance, Billy made his way to the shed, a bag of tools in hand. From a compartment, he retrieved a video camera and a microphone. Then he carefully set them up in a discreet corner of the shed's ceiling frame.

Just as he finished, the sound of a vehicle pulling into the driveway startled him. Hurriedly gathering his belongings, he swiftly made his way to the back of the property. He leapt over the fence again and vanished into the common ground, leaving no trace of his intrusion behind.

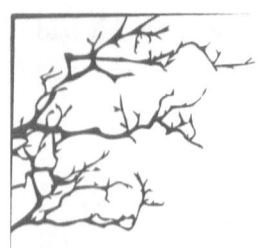

Chapter 29

Colin sat at Katlyn's kitchen table. "Maybe, you need to rest. "Brady can come with me," he said. He must have noticed the discomfort reflected on her face.

Katlyn shook her head determinedly. "I can't afford to rest. We need to solve this case as soon as possible. If I'm not there, White will pair you up with Derrick."

"He's as useful as a bull in a china store," Colin said.

Katlyn chuckled at the accurate description. "Just so you don't worry, I made an appointment at the doctor's for later. Let's focus on the case for now."

"You know what White said," Colin said.

"He won't know if we reschedule some of our interviews for today," Kat said.

Colin rolled his eyes. "Alright, but promise me you'll take it easy afterward. I'll drop you off at the doctor's surgery."

"Deal," Katlyn agreed, grateful for Colin's support.

Just then, Victor called. "I heard what happened. Are you hurt? Do you need any help?"

"Thanks for asking, but I'm fine," Katlyn reassured him.

"I can come over this evening and make dinner for you?"

"I've got Colin here." That didn't come out the way she intended. "Thanks for the offer, but we're going to conduct some interviews, and I'm not sure when we'll be done."

"You should take it easy and rest."

"I'm having a quiet night tonight and going to bed early."

"Maybe next time," Victor said, concern evident in his voice.

"Sounds good." Despite her initial reservations, Victor was getting under her skin and she wasn't sure how she felt about this.

Colin glanced at her with a curious look but refrained from asking any further questions.

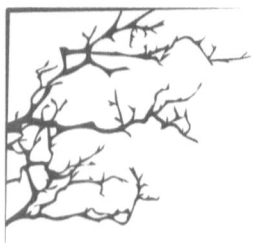

Chapter 30

Colin and Katlyn climbed from the Jeep and entered the Casterton Community Secondary School. They walked along the path between three-story brick buildings that bore visible signs of age. The mortar was crumbling, serving as an indication of the school's lack of maintenance.

Analise, the office assistant, looked up from her computer as they entered. "You're back. You're wanting to speak with the headmaster again?"

Colin stepped forward. "I believe Mr. Williams has organized a room for us where we can interview Emily Green's grade teachers and Poppy Connolly."

"Oh, right you are," Analise replied. "Please go down the hallway and turn left. The room is vacant now. I'll contact the teachers you'll need to speak with."

"Thank you," Kat said. The ache in her ribs was getting worse, but she didn't want to return to the car for a painkiller as they were on a tight schedule. "Can I ask if you have any paracetamol and a glass of water?"

Analise nodded. "I'll bring that along for you shortly."

As Katlyn walked down the hallway, the scent of sweaty teenagers and raging hormones triggered a wave of memories of her own high school days. Feeling a poorly, she took a seat in one of the metal chairs.

"You're not looking so great. Maybe we should leave it for another day," Colin suggested.

Katlyn shook her head firmly. "No, we can't afford any delays. Let's get through the interviews first. I'll be okay."

Just as Colin was about to respond, Analise entered the room, carrying a glass of water and a packet of pills. "The first teacher will be here soon. Let me know if you need anything else."

"Thank you," Katlyn replied gratefully, taking the pills and a sip of water to ease the growing discomfort.

"Let me conduct the interview and you observe?" Colin suggested.

Katlyn nodded, realizing it was the best course of action. "That's a good idea. You lead, and I'll take notes."

They interviewed all of Emily's grade teachers. Every teacher they spoke with mentioned Emily had seemed more preoccupied recently, and her grades had slipped.

Once the last teacher had left, Colin closed his notepad. "We should ask Analise to call in Poppy Connolly."

As they waited for Poppy, Katlyn couldn't help but wonder why Emily had become so preoccupied in the last few months. Was it related to the boyfriend mentioned by Sophia, or the pregnancy?

"Let's hope Poppy can shed more light on the situation," Katlyn remarked, her focus shifting back to the task at hand.

Someone knocked.

A few minutes later, Poppy entered the room, her face a mix of nervousness and determination.

"Please take a seat," Katlyn said. "Would you like an adult present for the interview?"

"No, thank you," Poppy said.

"Poppy, thank you for joining us," Colin began, adopting a calm and reassuring tone.

"We appreciate your willingness to come forward and assist us with our investigation," Katlyn said. "We're trying to understand more about Emily's recent behavior and any factors that might have contributed to her death."

"We understand you've been friends with Emily for quite some time," Colin said.

Poppy nodded, her fingers fidgeting with the edge of her sleeve. "Yeah, we've been friends since primary school."

"Can you tell us about your relationship with Emily Green?"

Poppy shifted uncomfortably. "We weren't that close, but we were in the same year. I think we had a class or two together."

"Can you tell us if there was anything different about her behavior of late?" Katlyn asked.

Poppy shrugged. "I don't know."

"Did you ever hear her mention anyone she was afraid of or something that was troubling her?" Colin asked.

Poppy shook her head. " There was a boy she was seeing. I don't know his name, but Emily mentioned he was older. I saw Emily holding hands with him. That's when I asked and she told me he didn't like her spending time with other people and to keep it a secret. But, I suppose that doesn't matter now."

Katlyn indicated for Colin to take notes. "I need to caution you about telling us stories. You can get into serious trouble if you do."

The girl looked about furtively again and crossed her arms. "Please believe me. I'm telling the truth. My dad's been in jail for ten years, and I can't remember what he looks like anymore. My mam doesn't like the cops, but I want the bastard that killed Emily locked up."

"Did she mention anything specific about his behavior or any incidents that alarmed her?"

Poppy's voice trembled slightly as she recalled the memories. "She said he got angry easily, and he was possessive."

Hmm. Katlyn noted down these details, her mind racing with possibilities. "Thank you for sharing that information, Poppy. Is there anything else you can tell us?"

Poppy hesitated, her eyes welling up with tears. "I... I think she might have been pregnant. She told me she missed her period, and she was terrified."

Katlyn's heart sank at the revelation. "So, you were quite close with her."

Poppy nodded. "I guess."

"Did she mention any plans or what she intended to do about the pregnancy?"

Poppy shook her head, tears streaming down her face. "No, she didn't say. She was so overwhelmed and confused."

Katlyn handed Poppy a tissue, offering her a comforting smile. "You're doing great, Poppy. We appreciate your honesty and willingness to share this information with us. It could be crucial with what was happening in Emily's life and state of mind."

"Can you give us a description of the older man?" Colin said.

"I'm not sure about his age because it was getting dark when I saw them. About in his twenties or thirties. He had black hair and was tall. He was wearing some sort of tradesman clothes."

"Can you tell us where you saw Emily with this man?" Colin said.

"They were in the unlit part at the back of the park. He was arguing with her."

"How do you know they were arguing if they were a distance away?"

"She was shouting at him. I couldn't hear what they said. And he was waving his arms at her. Then he pushed her. She nearly fell."

"When was this?" Kat said.

"Nearly two weeks ago."

"Why were you there?" Kat said.

"I was on my way to meet a friend."

Katlyn jotted this down. "What time was this?"

Poppy shrugged. "About half five."

"Who were you going to see?" Colin said.

"I just told you. A friend."

She was hedging. "Can you give us a name? We need to verify your story. No one is going to get into trouble, Poppy," Kat said. "Emily's in the mortuary, and we need to find her killer."

Poppy wiped away a tear. "Sorry. It's Sophia Winslow I was going to see."

They had interviewed Sophia yesterday. She didn't say anything about Poppy seeing a man. "Does Sophia know what you've just told us?"

"I didn't tell anyone."

Teenagers liked to gossip. "Why is that?"

Poppy shrugged. "I just didn't."

"Thank you. You've been very helpful." Katlyn looked at Poppy, her voice filled with empathy. "We'll do everything we can to find out what happened to Emily. If there's anything else you remember or if you think of anything that might be important, please don't hesitate to contact us."

A knock had Poppy turning toward the door.

A gray-haired woman in sensible shoes, a navy skirt, and a cardigan walked in, frowning. "Are you interviewing Poppy without an adult present? She's only sixteen."

Colin and Katlyn exchanged surprised glances, taken aback by the sudden intrusion.

"Poppy came to us of her own free will. She was asked if she wanted an adult present and she declined. There was no coercion, if that was your concern." Kat said.

Poppy hurried out of the room.

"This is simply not right. Just because you're with the police does not give you carte blanche to do as you please." The woman put her hands on her hips. "Identify yourselves, please."

Katlyn stood up, maintaining a calm demeanor. She introduced both Colin and herself to the woman. "We are investigating the murder of Emily Green, and Poppy came forward voluntarily. We asked her if she wanted an adult present, and she declined. There was no coercion or violation of protocols."

"And your name is?" Colin asked.

The woman's frown deepened, but she seemed to consider Katlyn's words. "I'm Barbara Snodgrass, Emily's grade English teacher. Right then, I will report this to the headmaster. He'll certainly lodge a complaint with your superiors."

Colin gave Katlyn a guarded look, implying they'd be in hot water over this with White.

"That is simply not good enough. Humph!" Barbara stormed out.

As they made their way back to the car, Katlyn sighed in frustration and said, "There's still too many unanswered questions." But, she wasn't about to give up.

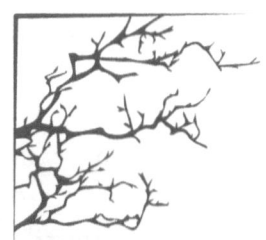

Chapter 31

Katlyn sat in the staff common room at Casterton Community Secondary School. "I hope Sophia will know who boyfriend was?"

"In her previous interview she didn't have any knowledge of a boyfriend. I'm not sure if she will. Emily was very secretive," Colin said.

The room smelled of indoor heating, and when the sports teacher entered, it smelled of sweaty armpits too. He held a lunchbox, but when he saw Katlyn and Colin, he retreated.

"We'd better get Nicole Pickering."

Colin nodded. "We don't want any more trouble with that Barbara woman." He left to get the grade coordinator.

Sophia stood in the doorway. "Hello." Her voice was filled with uncertainty.

"Good afternoon." Katlyn pushed her hair from her face. "Please take a seat. My partner will be along shortly with Mrs. Pickering."

"Okay," Sophia said.

"We need to go over your statement again. There are a few areas that remain unclear," Katlyn explained, hoping to coax the truth out of the young girl.

Chewing on her fingernails, Sophia tucked her feet underneath her. "Am I going to get into trouble?" She asked, her voice barely above a whisper.

"You won't be in any trouble. Just be honest with us, please." Sophia was hiding something, and only the right questions would tell if it was something significant.

Colin returned with Mrs. Pickering in tow. The grade coordinator entered the room, a puzzled expression on her face. "Good afternoon. They informed me you need to revisit Sophia's statement?"

Katlyn stood. "Please take a seat. We need to go through all the evidence with a fine-tooth comb to ensure we haven't missed anything that could be important. And we thought it best to have an adult present while we conduct the interview."

"I see," Nicole Pickering said as she took a chair next to Sophia. "Are you okay with this, Sophia?"

The girl nodded. "I guess."

"Now, Sophia, I need you to think carefully before answering each question," Mrs. Pickering advised, her tone gentle.

"You told us previously you saw Emily with an older man. Is this correct?"

The teenager blinked, hesitating momentarily before responding. "There was someone. But I only saw Emily with a man once. I couldn't say if he was her boyfriend or not."

Mrs. Pickering leaned over and touched the girl's shoulder. "It's okay. You won't get into trouble."

"There was someone. But I only saw Emily with a guy once, and they were far away in the park. I couldn't say if he was her boyfriend or not."

This confirmed her suspicions that an older male was in Emily's life. "How long ago was this?"

"About two weeks ago."

"Can you describe the man?" Colin said.

Sophia sighed, visibly contemplating her response. Was she on the verge of fabricating a lie? "I understand that the memory might not be fresh, but we need any details you can provide," Katlyn urged gently.

Sophia shrugged. "He was tall and wore a cap."

"Would you be able to identify the male?" Colin asked.

Curiosity piqued, Katlyn probed further. "No, he was facing away from me."

"What were they doing?"

"He was holding her hand and leading her to the back of the park. But, I don't think she wanted to go because she stepped away from him. Emily didn't seem happy. That part of the park is a bit overgrown, and no one goes there."

Nicole Pickering leaned forward. "Sophia, are you sure there's nothing else you can remember? Even something small can be important," Kat said.

Sophia fidgeted with her hair. "I don't know. Emily was secretive about texts she received during our walks. I always thought it was a bit weird."

"I'm sorry. I can't remember anything else. Can I go now?"

Katlyn jotted down notes, her mind buzzing with new possibilities. "Thank you for sharing that, Sophia. One last question before we conclude. Did Emily ever mention having a diary?"

Sophia tensed, her eyes darting around the room. "I... I don't know," she stammered.

"Are you sure?" Katlyn pressed. Did teenagers still have diaries? They probably did if they were so inclined.

Mrs. Pickering pursed her lips. "Excuse me, Sophia told you she didn't know."

Katlyn glanced at the woman. "I just need her to be certain. It could be critical to the case."

"Did you see Emily with a diary, or did she talk about writing in a diary?" Katlyn asked.

"I never saw her with one. It's a personal thing," she frowned. "And I don't remember her talking about any diary."

"Thank you, Sophia. You've been very helpful," Kat said.

Mrs. Pickering rose. "You can go back to class now, Sophia." She turned to Katlyn and Colin. "I can't be sitting here all day. I have work needing doing."

"Thank you for your help. I'll let you know if we need you again."

The coordinator hurried away.

Colin tapped his foot. "That woman doesn't like us, does she?"

"Doesn't make our job any easier." Katlyn sighed. "Ask Amanda to check the park CCTV for the last month to see if Emily was there with a male. And get some door-to-door inquiries going with residents living near the park. Someone must have seen Emily with that man."

"On to it." He dialed and spoke into the phone.

When he was done, Colin turned to her, eyebrow raised. "I thought you were leaving the questions to me?"

"Yep. Sorry. The pain killers kicked in and I was feeling better."

"That's good. Are your ribs still sore?"

"A little, but I'm definitely on the mend." She rose.

"Glad to hear it," Colin said as he opened the staff room door. Students were bustling around them, chatting with friends, some hurrying and others dawdling.

Katlyn lowered her voice. Although the students were making enough of noise that they wouldn't hear their conversation, anyway. "Sophia confirmed what Poppy said about an older boyfriend," Kat said.

She climbed into the car. "Why do I have a gut feeling that Emily had a diary when none of her friends know about it?"

Colin started the car. "We can't go back to the Green's home on a gut feeling."

Katlyn nodded. "I know. There's something bothering me at the beach where I found Emily that I need to check."

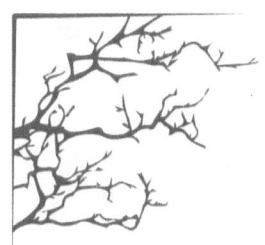

Chapter 32

K atlyn carefully stepped down from the boulders onto the pebbly beach. Squawking seagulls and the sound of waves lapping were pleasant, but for the memory of that gruesome discovery in the suitcase.

Colin joined her, taking in a deep breath of the salty air. "I love the smell of the ocean."

Katlyn nodded. "There's nothing quite like it. But we have work to do. You take this side," she gestured toward the far end of the beach, "and I'll search the other. Let's meet in the middle."

"Sounds good." Colin bent over, looking for anything out of the ordinary that could be evidence.

As Katlyn made her way to the far end of the beach, she felt a twinge of pain from the bruised ribs. The car accident reminded her to be cautious, but she pressed on. The next hour passed slowly as she carefully maneuvered over the moss-covered boulders between the rock wall and the beach.

Finding nothing of interest, she retraced her steps, feeling they had missed something during the previous search. Kicking a few small stones aside, she discovered only dried-up seaweed. Stepping away, she accidentally slipped on some moss, trapping her foot between two boulders. "Bugger!"

Colin hurried over to her. "What happened? I knew you should take it easy."

She struggled, but couldn't free herself.

"Just a minute." Colin bent down to move the boulder and with some effort, shifted it slightly.

Katlyn pulled her foot out. "Thanks." She made to move on when she something caught her attention. "Look at this." The nagging feeling that they had overlooked something proved correct.

Among the rocks lay a pair of men's designer sunglasses. Katlyn snapped on some disposable gloves, picked the glasses up, and placed them in an evidence bag. "These aren't cheap imitations."

"They could belong to the killer?" Colin said.

"I hope they do," she said.

"Do you think they were dropped from the cliff face?"

She shook her head. "The cliff edge juts out. I can't believe they could've fallen from there. If they had, they'd be in the water. The glasses could belong to the killer who came down to check if the suitcase was submerged."

Colin said. "Maybe the killer didn't know they had to weigh down the suitcase to keep it submerged."

"Or they were in a hurry to dispose of the body," Katlyn added, glancing at the white egrets flying overhead, squawking.

Colin nodded. "I hope forensics find prints on the glasses."

"Let's head back." She started for the rocks separating the two beaches, with Colin in step.

When they set foot on the next beach, Colin glanced up and stopped. "There's a male up top staring at us."

She looked up. "I don't see him."

"He probably disappeared when he realized I noticed him. I'll race up and check if he's still there." Colin started up. "You take your time. I don't want you to have another accident."

"Thanks." She didn't want to admit the discomfort from her bruised ribs. Going up the steps was a little exhausting till her ribs healed. She saved further conversation until they reached the top of the cliff.

"He's gone," Colin said breathlessly.

As expected, the mysterious guy who had been watching them was nowhere to be seen.

Her phone rang, interrupting her focus.

"What the hell were you thinking?" White said. "Not having an adult present in the classroom during the interview with sixteen-year-old Poppy Connolly? I expect better from you."

"Poppy came to us willing to talk. I asked her if she wanted an adult present and she declined. If I insisted she wait until I organized an adult chaperone, she would have bolted."

"Don't justify your actions with me."

"Background info on Poppy's father. He's doing ten years for aggravated assault with a deadly weapon and robbery," Kat said.

"I see," White said. "I'll have to write a report about the complaint. You're very lucky that the girl's mother isn't making a fuss about this. But the school certainly is."

Katlyn sighed. "I understand, Chief. It won't happen again."

"You better make sure it doesn't. We need faster results on the Emily Green case ASAP."

"I'm doing my best, Chief. We found a pair of glasses on the beach that could belong to the killer."

"Well, that's something. Keep me updated."

Having finished the call, Katlyn returned her attention to the investigation. Colin called out to her, "I've found something!"

Katlyn hurried over to Colin. "What did you find?"

"Look at the bent grass here," Colin pointed to a depression in the bed of thrift grass near the edge. "This is where the guy must have been standing."

Something in the grass caught her eye. She pulled out an evidence bag and carefully picked up a piece of torn white cloth. "Let's see if forensics can get DNA from this."

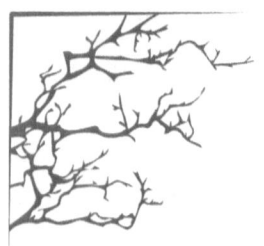

Chapter 33

"Here's what we know so far about Emily Green." She pointed to the pictures. "Her parents, Pam and Alexander Green, were on holiday when she was murdered. Seems they often left Emily on her own. The father, Alexander, is a salesperson. It wasn't unusual for him to be away a lot. The mother, Pam, a cleaner at the local pub, liked to visit her sister up north often. Then we have Emily's friend, Poppy, who told us Emily was seeing an older man with the initials HB. The two were seen arguing," Kat said. "Another friend of Emily's, Sophia, also said Emily was seeing an older man. To a teenager, an older man might be someone in their early twenties."

"That presents more questions than answers," Brady said.

Katlyn tapped the image of the suitcase. "The vinyl suitcase—no wheels, so possibly an older model—held Emily Green. A female, unless she was a bodybuilder, wouldn't have the strength to throw a suitcase with a body over the cliff without leaving significant drag marks. Therefore, probably a male threw the suitcase containing Emily's body from the cliff. This male, possibly HB, went down to the beach to check if the case was submerged. The designer glasses we found at the bottom of the cliff were prescription glasses. They could belong to the suspect." Katlyn turned from the big board. Okay team, does anyone have anything to add that we haven't covered?"

"When I showed the photo of the suitcase to the two luggage stores in town, both owners said the model was vintage one and hadn't been sold for many years," Amanda said. "I finally tried the local charity store." She smiled. "The woman at the store recognized it. She said a male in his late teens, possibly early twenties, came in a week ago looking for a large suitcase and when she showed him that one, he bought it. She only remembered because the lad seemed a bit agitated."

"Did you get a description?"

"Young, tall, and dark-haired was all she could remember," Amanda said. "Oh, and scruffy jeans."

"Bugger. That's not much to go on." Katlyn wrote on the board and drew a circle around the details and an arrow pointing to Emily. She turned to face the team. "Emily was pregnant and had a boyfriend. What we don't know is if she told him she was pregnant. If so, did he want her to have an abortion?"

"The money found on Emily complicates the issue," Brady said.

"Agreed. Anyone else have anything to add?" She turned to Derrick. "How's your investigation going on the initials HB?"

"I asked all the publicans in every local pub. No luck on either. That's if we can trust the teenager who told you that Emily called the boyfriend H.B."

"What makes you doubt her?"

Derrick grimaced. "She's just a teenager. They make things up."

"Did you do that as a teenager?"

He reddened. "That's different."

"No, it's not. I'll thank you not to malign any age group or sex from now on."

Sylvester jumped in before she could unleash her frustration. "If the guy had to buy the suitcase at a charity store, it may indicate he doesn't have a lot of money."

"That's possible." Katlyn nodded. "For the lad to have stuffed her in the suitcase and dumped her into the water means he was desperate. Maybe, a baby would ruin his university plans."

"Selfish bastard," Amanda said.

Katlyn continued. "Okay, so we're at a dead end on the boyfriend front. What about the parents? Colin, did you follow up on their alibis?"

Colin nodded. "I spoke with Pam Green's sister, and she confirmed that Pam and Alexander were staying with her for nearly a week. They stayed until the day you rang them to tell them the bad news about Emily."

"Okay, so far, the parents are in the clear. Amanda, did you have any luck with the CCTV footage?"

"No, unfortunately. The council car park cameras are broken. I checked with the council, and they're fixing them soon."

"That doesn't help us," Katlyn muttered. "Team, we've hit a dead end on several fronts. But we can't give up. Keep following up on any leads, no matter how small. We'll catch this bastard." The team nodded in agreement.

White had come out of his office to listen. His forehead creased into a frown and his eyes narrowed. Was he thinking of a way to unsettle her? Just let him try.

"We were told that Emily was a sweet girl, and everyone liked her," Kat said. "Though her friends could be air brushing the truth. It's also possible he's not as old as the girls have said. Anyone who's just in their twenties is old to a teenager," Kat said. Brady piped up. "Then the description about the lad being older doesn't stack up." "I'm wondering if the woman at the charity store made a mistake about the suspect's age," Kat said.

"The lab sent over the report on the glasses," Syl leaned forward from his seat. "They're designed for a male face and they didn't have any useful prints. The brand is available from that top online prescription glasses outlet. I contacted them. Seems they send out hundreds of glasses daily. They've sold 200 of these frames in the last two months. I asked if they had sold any in Casterton, Gyvennerville, or Winterton. Unfortunately, they only hold customer data for twelve months. She checked while I waited on the line and said no. I'm working on getting a court order so we can access the data and go through it ourselves."

"Thanks." Katlyn sighed. Time was passing, and they were no closer to finding the killer. "Derrick, can you find out how many unemployed males living in the area registered with the local job center office who wear glasses? Let's start with males from eighteen to twenty-eight years old."

He looked up from his phone. "What if there's a lot?"

"Let's see first," Kat said. "Amanda, go back to the charity store and ask the assistant if the male purchased anything besides the suitcase and if he was wearing glasses? And try to get a better description of the male."

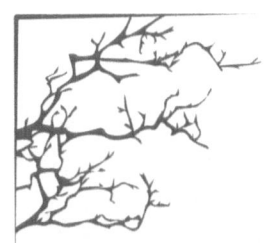

Chapter 34

"Kat, are you sitting down?" Dean Snowden, her ex, said on the phone. As it happened, she was at her desk filling out forms to keep the higher-ups happy. She usually said this to an unsuspecting family member when she had bad news to impart about their loved one. "What's the bad news?"

"Briony's been involved in an accident. She's in hospital."

"Oh, bloody hell. Is she seriously injured?"

"That, I don't know," he said.

"How can you not know?" Her stomach tightened with anxiety. "When did this happen?" She glanced at her watch and noted it was half-past eight in the morning. "Why didn't you tell me this sooner?"

"Now, just a minute, her boyfriend just called me. He was driving her to school. I'm on my way to see her."

Dean occasionally worked from home, but she suspected he had spent the night elsewhere. "Where are you now?"

"Are you going to interrogate me? I was at a friend's place."

She'd lost track of how many girlfriends he'd had before and after they split. "What? You're leaving Briony home alone while you go off to have a bit of skirt?"

"Briony's sixteen, in case you've forgotten. My bit of skirt, as you call it, is none of your business."

A wave of emotions welled up in her throat. "I'm leaving now." She hung up and turned to Colin. "My daughter has been in an accident. I'm heading to the hospital."

He stood. "Is it bad?"

"I don't know." Tears welled in her eyes.

"I'll come with you."

"You don't need to."

He grabbed his jacket. "You need some support."

She called White and told him. "I'll be back as soon as I can."

"Take your time. Family is important."

She couldn't help but wonder about White's changed demeanor. His response to her personal situation had been unexpected, and one she hadn't encountered before. She hung up and hurried downstairs with Colin.

He had his car keys in his hand. "You'll be in no fit state to drive."

"I can manage." But she was glad he'd offered.

She was in no mood for conversation, and Colin seemed to understand as he drove to Tellford Hospital. Just trying to hold herself together was challenging enough.

OVER AN HOUR LATER, Colin parked and locked the Jeep. They hurried up the steps to the entrance of St. Bernadette's Public Hospital. The brick building was undergoing renovations, with scaffolding forming a maze around the west wing.

The hallway was filled with people strolling, babies crying as mothers tried to soothe them, patients with crutches limping by, and others being wheeled down the seemingly endless corridors.

Reaching the emergency desk, the scent of disinfectant and the bustling medical staff greeted them. Katlyn rushed over. "I'm Kat Snowden, Briony Snowden's mother. I believe my daughter was involved in an accident and was brought here over an hour ago. Can you please tell me where I can find her?"

"Let me check." The duty clerk glanced at her screen. "Yes, I have her here. She's in Ward Two. Just go straight down to the end," she pointed, "and turn left. You'll find the ward halfway along. Ask at the desk for the room."

"Thank you," Katlyn whispered, her voice trembling with emotion.

She hurried through the doors, with Colin closely following.

Dean, her ex-husband, stood alone in the hallway, appearing refined in his custom-made shirt and trousers. He had an angular face, a slightly prominent nose, and short wavy hair. His appearance was not the reason she had once fallen blindly in love with him. What she had seen in this deceitful man completely escaped her now.

"Where is she?" she asked.

"In the room opposite. The doctor is with her now. I'm waiting for him to finish. Who's this?"

She introduced Colin to Dean.

Dean gave her partner a brief nod.

"What happened?"

"I still don't know."

A couple sat silently, holding hands. Another woman sobbed into her palms. The scene tugged at her heart. Briony had to be okay, she just had to be.

"Should we wait here?" Colin gestured towards a few vacant chairs.

She didn't respond. There was no way she could sit patiently and wait.

"There's a coffee machine in the hallway. Would you like one?" Dean offered.

She ignored Dean's question and approached the doctor as he emerged from the room. "How is Briony Snowden? I'm her mother."

"I'm Doctor Lindsay. Only immediate family members can see her now."

"Is she okay?" Kat asked. "What are her injuries?"

The doctor glanced at his phone. "I'm wanted elsewhere. I'll be back in shortly to have a chat with you."

"I'll wait here," Colin said to Katlyn.

Katlyn and Dean entered the room with four beds, two beds were curtained off. Her breath caught when saw Briony with cuts and bruises on her face. "Oh my god," she gasped. She gave her daughter a hug. "Are you okay?"

"I'm sorry, mum. I'm going to live. Promise."

Katlyn swallowed down a sob. Her daughter's pleading eyes squeezed at her heart. "Okay, love."

Dean gave Briony a kiss on her forehead, which was the only part of her face free of bruises. "We were so worried about you."

"I was in a car accident," Briony said, wincing as she spoke. "Jeff was driving. I don't remember much."

"I plan to have words with Jeff about his reckless driving," Dean said.

The doctor returned and glanced at his notes. "She'll be taken to X-ray as soon as we receive notification. We suspect Briony has fractured her left arm radius. She also has a significant bump on the side of her head. I'll need you to sign consent forms in case she requires surgery."

Katlyn wiped away the tears streaming down her face.

"Is she in pain?"

"There's considerable swelling around the suspected fracture. We've administered painkillers to make her more comfortable for now. We're also treating her abrasions. You can talk to your daughter for a moment. Then I'll need you to wait outside while we run some tests to ensure there are no other injuries. I'll have a nurse notify you when we're done." His phone beeped again. He glanced at it. "I have to go. The nurse will be here shortly." He hurried away.

A nurse entered the room with a wheelchair. "I need to take this patient to X-ray. "I'm taking Miss Snowden to X-ray. She'll be a while. You can go home or wait outside for her to return."

"See you soon, love."

"Are you leaving, Mum?"

Her daughter's request for her support tugged at her heartstrings again. "I'll wait until they bring you back."

"Thanks, Mum. You're always there for me."

It took a situation like this to bring them closer, and she didn't want it to be this way.

Katlyn joined Colin in the waiting area, her mind filled with worry for her daughter. She glanced at her watch. It had been over an hour since they'd taken Briony for X-rays.

Colin sat next to her, a cup of coffee in his hand. He had tried to reassure her, but she couldn't shake off the fear that Briony's injuries were more serious than they expected.

Dean continued pacing. "She should be out by now."

She glared at him. "You're not helping."

"It's a wonder you even came. You're too absorbed in your work to make time for your daughter."

"You're the father who's been lying to Briony about why we split."

"How dare you accuse me of anything!" He put his hands on his hips.

Colin stood and faced Dean. "Too right she is. If it weren't for diligent detectives like Katlyn, the country would be overrun with criminals doing as they pleased."

A doctor approached, holding some X-rays. "I'm Dr. Eunice Lee. I'll be looking after your daughter. The X-ray shows she has sustained a break to the ulna and radius, which are the bones between the elbow and the wrist. We may need to put in pins if the bones don't align the way we want them to. We need you to sign a consent form so we can administer general anesthesia to align the bones."

Dean nodded.

"Oh, hell." Katlyn put her hand to her face. "Do what you have to. Just make her better. Where do I sign?"

"I'll grab a release form for you. We'll schedule the surgery as soon as an operating theater is available."

They both signed the form.

Katlyn glanced up as a young man walked in. He had some cuts on his forehead.

Dean nodded to the young man. "Jeff, meet Briony's part-time mother."

Just breathe. Don't let him get to you.

She faced Briony's boyfriend and ignored Dean. He meant nothing to her anymore. "Are you alright? What happened?"

"Yes," Dean interjected gruffly, "Were you driving recklessly? If you were, you won't be seeing my daughter again."

Jeff appeared visibly uncomfortable. "I'm sorry about the accident. I was driving Briony to school."

She crossed her arms and waited for Jeff to continue. "It happened so fast. The car in front of us collided with the car in front of it. I tried to brake, but I couldn't avoid the other car. I'm so sorry."

Dean sighed. "Accidents happen all the time. You should drive more carefully."

Katlyn couldn't find the right words, so she stayed silent and nodded.

After a long wait, Dr. Eunice Lee walked toward them. Katlyn stood up, her heart pounding. "How is she?"

The doctor gave her a small smile. "Your daughter's very fortunate. The arm fracture was uncomplicated. She'll need to keep it immobilized in a cast for six weeks, but it should heal well."

Katlyn let out a sigh of relief. "Thank you. Can I see her now?"

"Of course. She's in recovery. She's awake but still drowsy. You can sit with her for a short while."

Katlyn followed the doctor to the ward, her heart in her throat. As soon as she saw her daughter connected to a monitor, tears welled up in her eyes. Briony appeared pale, but managed a weak smile when she spotted her mother.

"Mum," she whispered.

Katlyn took her hand. "I'm here, love. How are you feeling?"

"I'm okay."

Katlyn stroked her hair. "You scared me, you know that?"

Briony cried. "Oh, mum, I'm sorry."

Katlyn wiped tears from her eyes. "There's nothing to be sorry about. How are you feeling?"

Briony shifted awkwardly. "I'm fine."

"Are you in pain?" Dean said.

"A little uncomfortable but okay, dad."

She wanted to envelop her daughter in hugs and kisses, but she dared not because of her injuries. She took Briony's hand and forced a smile, though she was crying inside.

Her daughter had closed her eyes.

The nurse came in and noted her vital signs. "You can come back later. Your daughter has been through a lot. Best let her get some rest."

"Goodbye, sweetheart. I'll be back soon."

She joined Colin and Jeff in the waiting room.

"You fared better than my daughter. I hope this was an isolated incident, and you'll be more cautious while driving in the future," she said to Jeff.

Colin touched her arm, silently signaling her to take it easy on him, but she ignored the gesture.

"I'm sorry, Ms. Snowden, but it wasn't my fault."

Katlyn grimaced. "I apologize. I was completely out of line."

She nodded. They strode down the endless hallway, through more swinging doors, and exited the hospital.

Colin started the Jeep, but he didn't drive out. "Do you want to ask White to reassign the case to someone else so you can be with your daughter?"

She shook her head. "Briony's a broken arm, and as much as that worries me, it doesn't mean I can't concentrate on this case. I intend to return to the hospital. If it's late, I'll stay at Dean's. The house is still half mine, and I have a key."

He drove onto the road. "Are you going to hang around here tomorrow as well?"

"I don't know. I'm taking one step at a time. I'm on the phone, so if anything comes up, I can get one of the team to look into it."

THEY ARRIVED BACK AT Casterton station. Katlyn hurried up the stairs and made a beeline for White's office. She knocked on his door.

"Come in."

"I may need tomorrow off. My daughter is in the hospital. She has a broken arm, and the doctors are still running tests. I'm going back there as soon as I finish my report."

White wore his usual scowl. "I don't need to remind you of the importance of this case. Just tomorrow, then. Make sure you assign one of your team members to take over for you. Oh, and keep me informed."

Katlyn left his office feeling empty. White hadn't offered any kind words about her daughter. What had happened to his speech about family coming first? It seemed conveniently forgotten and discarded to suit his narrative.

She entered the squad room and assigned Colin to follow up on Emily's missing phone and Brady to investigate the neighbors where Emily had lived.

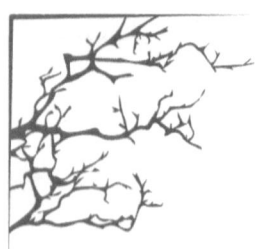

Chapter 35

"Good afternoon. Can you tell me how Briony Snowden is doing? I'm her mother," Katlyn asked anxiously over the phone.

"She's in a satisfactory condition. The doctor will decide whether to keep your daughter overnight for observation when he visits," the receptionist informed her.

Consumed with worry, her stomach in a tight knot, she said, "Thank you." Katlyn was about to dash out and head to the hospital. White waddled over with a sour look on his face. "Why haven't I received those reports from you yet?"

Just great. "I'm just finishing them now," she replied, her voice strained as she tried to contain her frustration.

She placed her handbag under her desk and spent the next hour completing the reports, her mind constantly drifting back to Briony. The weight of the situation bore heavily on her, intensifying her anxiety.

After she'd completed the reports and emailed them to White, she stood and spoke to the team. "I'm heading to the hospital to be with my daughter." After some brief well-wishes from the team, she rushed out, consumed with her daughter's well-being.

She turned onto the main road and increased her speed, eager to see Briony.

But fate had other plans. She was stuck in a traffic jam caused by a multi-car collision. Horns blared, and angry drivers were shouting and gesturing. Katlyn gritted her teeth, her frustration mounting with each passing second. She leaned back in her seat; her knuckles white as she tightly gripped the steering wheel, desperately wishing she could teleport herself to the hospital.

Two long hours later, she finally found a parking spot and raced into the hospital, her mind racing faster than her feet. Thoughts of Briony's condition and the minutes she had lost during the traffic jam weighed heavily on her.

She strode into the room where Briony had been when she'd visited earlier today. But Briony wasn't there. Heart drumming in fear, Katlyn headed for the nurses' desk.

"Can you please tell me where they have taken my daughter, Briony Snowden?"

"Just give me a moment." The nurse looked at the computer screen. "She just left with her father."

"Thank you." Katlyn dialed Dean. "Is Briony with you?"

"Yes. We're in the car and I'm taking her home. At least she can rely on one parent to be there for her," he said.

Katlyn gritted her teeth, fighting to keep her composure despite the anger welling up inside her. "I got held up at work." She didn't want Briony to worry, so she chose her words carefully, masking her true emotions.

"Are you okay, love? I'm driving to the house now," her voice filled with a combination of motherly concern and a desire to make up for her absence.

"I'm fine, Mum. I have a cast on my arm, and I'm feeling groggy." Briony sounded subdued. "Dad's going to look after me."

At least her ex-husband could cook, unlike herself. "I still want to see you. I'll be there soon," Katlyn said, determined to show her daughter that she was there for her, no matter the circumstances.

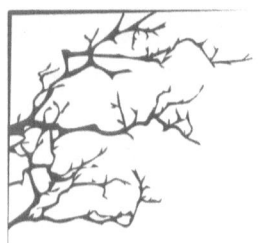

Chapter 36

Katlyn's eyes were dry from staring at the computer files for hours. Files she'd copied before leaving Tellford Police Station. These files contained evidence about the warehouse fire that caused Brian's death and left her with third-degree burns on her legs. Despite her efforts, she was no closer to finding the suspect who had deliberately started the fire.

Letting go of the past was something she'd have to work on. Her psychologist suggested she verbally acknowledge that Brian's death wasn't her fault. But this was easier said than done. If only she had tried harder to reach him, perhaps he would still be alive.

As she turned off the computer, tears welled up in her eyes. It was well after eleven. Time to get some rest. After a long, hot shower, she changed into her pajamas and joined Lucy, asleep at the foot of the bed.

Suddenly, a male laughed. "You're a funny girl. Why did you do that?"

Katlyn's heart skipped a beat as she sat up. A scream swelling in her throat.

Lucy hissed and sprung from under the quilt.

Her father's voice echoed in her ears, unmistakable and haunting. But he couldn't be here. He had been gone for over six months. Was it his ghost? Or was it her imagination playing cruel tricks on her?

Shivering with uncertainty, she was at a loss. All her defensive training seemed useless in this moment. She longed to turn on the lights and dispel her fear, but something held her back. Was she certain that the voice belonged to her father?

"You are a funny girl, kitten," her father continued, sending chills down her spine.

That's what he called her when she was little. Trembling with trepidation, she rushed blindly to the wardrobe, stepped inside, and crouched behind her dresses. After a moment, she regained her senses. What on earth was she doing? Her father was dead. She had to confront her fear, and face the truth.

Come on, buck up. Don't let this fear rule you. Move past it.

Taking a deep breath, she emerged from the wardrobe, her hands trembling but determined. She made her way through the darkened room, her mind filled with conflicting emotions. Memories of her father flooded her thoughts—his laughter, his comforting presence, and the pain of his loss. The possibility of his return, even in a spectral form, stirred a mixture of hope and fear within her.

Lucy hissed again. Katlyn's skin prickled with dread.

As she stepped into the hallway, flickering shadows in the second bedroom caught her attention, casting eerie shapes on the walls. She hesitated for a moment, torn between curiosity and fear. But she couldn't let her emotions paralyze her.

Keeping close to the wall, her hands outstretched, she cautiously went into the hallway, her heart pounding in her chest. A scraping sound on the window made her jump, and she instinctively retreated to her bedroom.

Gathering her resolve, she'd face whatever awaited her. Grabbing one of her hand weights, she crept into the second bedroom and crossed to the window. The noise resumed, echoing in the darkness.

Katlyn pushed aside the curtain, ready to confront whoever was outside. All she saw were the branches being blown about by the wind. A sense of relief washed over her, momentarily easing the tension in her body.

Lucy brushed against her legs. Katlyn screamed. Shaking, she hurried to the kitchen, turning on lights as she went. Checking every room, she couldn't see an intruder. Trying both the back and front doors she found them still locked. All this must have been a nightmare.

Filling a glass of water, she placed it on the bedside table, and left the lamp on to banish the darkness. Exhaustion weighed heavily on her, both physically and emotionally. The events of the day and the unsettling experiences tonight had taken its toll on her.

As she settled into bed, the scraping sound that had persisted suddenly ceased. Instantly alert, she sprang up once again. She peered out through each window, but all she could see was the darkness and the wind casting dancing shadows everywhere.

From the shadows, a silhouette suddenly emerged in the form of a man running away. Her heart leaped into her throat. Like a woman possessed, she rushed to turn on all the lights, then checked every window again to reassure herself that no one remained outside. She immediately called the police station to report the incident, her voice trembling with a mixture of fear and determination.

Soon after, two uniformed officers were knocking on her front door. She hastily tied her dressing gown and greeted them.

"Hello." She recognized the lads and asked them in. "I hope I haven't called you out on a wild goose chase, but I saw a male running away. I'm sure he was a peeping tom."

"We'll search the grounds and keep you informed, Ma'am. Please ensure your doors are locked," the constable replied. Their reassuring presence providing a sliver of comfort.

"I will," Katlyn assured them. She made herself a cup of tea with a dash of something stronger, to calm her nerves and sat, watching as they wandered around, illuminating the property with their flashlights. Her heart pounded, unable to shake the lingering sense that someone was still out there, observing her every move.

The tea did little to calm her restless thoughts.

The uniforms knocked on her front door. "We found some footprints at your bedroom window. But the peeping tom is probably long gone."

Katlyn hesitated to tell them about the man's voice because they'd think she had mental problems. As soon as White learned this, he'd take her off the case. "Thank you."

When they left, she turned off the lights and fell into bed, exhausted from lack of sleep. But when she closed her eyes, her mind raced with thoughts and fears.

Suddenly, she heard a noise, like someone tapping on the window. She froze, her heart racing. Slowly, she crept towards the window, half expecting to see a face peering in. However, all she saw was darkness. She tried to convince herself this was just that same branch brushing against the glass. But the eerie feeling persisted—a sense that someone was lurking outside.

Then she noticed a male figure moving in the shadows, the night obscured any distinguishing features. As fear and adrenaline coursed through her veins, Katlyn's conflicting emotions battled within her—fear, suspicion, but also determination and resilience.

Her heart pounding, she dialed the emergency number again. Within minutes, two police cars arrived, and the same officers diligently combed through the entire property, searching for any trace of the intruder. Yet, they couldn't find any evidence of an him. She apologized for calling them again.

Relief mingled with frustration in Katlyn's heart. She was relieved to know that she was safe, but the unsettling feeling of being watched refused to dissipate. And the emotional struggle she experienced regarding her father's voice grew.

Determined to remain vigilant, she resolved to stay awake for the rest of the night, and not to let her guard down. She lay in bed with her mind in turmoil.

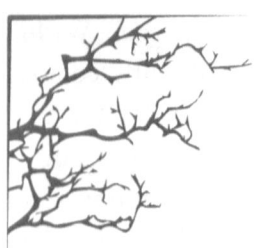

Chapter 37

In the morning, Katlyn opened her sleepy eyes with a sense of relief. She made it through the night unscathed. But she knew she couldn't let her guard down. She needed to find out who they were and why they were targeting her.

Yearning for some respite and clarity, she needed a walk to clear her head. She changed out of her pajamas and into a pair of leggings, a comfortable t-shirt. But before embarking on her morning stroll, she check in on her daughter. A phone call to Dean established Briony seemed well but for the purple and yellow bruising surrounding the cast.

Preferring to avoid the beach where she had discovered the body, Katlyn exited through the back gate, making her way to the common ground instead. She ran past the blackberry brambles and, as she reached the rocky outcrops, she stopped to look at the view of the imposing cliffs. Venturing into the laneway that snaked between homes, she eventually emerged onto the footpath. She continued her walk, passing by neighbors' houses until she found herself approximately three miles from her own residence.

Circling back, Katlyn picked up her pace until her skin grafts twinged uncomfortably. She wiped the sweat from her brow, determined to gather her thoughts and find solace in the familiar path. As she navigated the common ground again, a stumble sent her crashing down, coinciding with a sharp whooshing noise. An arrow grazed her shoulder, narrowly missing a fatal strike.

Stunned by the sudden attack, Katlyn lay motionless, her heart pounding in her ears. She strained to listen, but the overwhelming sound of her own heartbeat made it challenging to detect any other presence. The wind rustled the nearby nettles, heightening her anxiety. Slowly raising her head, she scanned her surroundings, yet no one came into view.

Cautiously, Katlyn surveyed the windswept shrubbery around her. The sparse gorse offered little cover, making it unlikely for someone to hide nearby.

However, she was unwilling to take any chances. A glimpse of a male figure wearing a beanie cap caught her eye in the distance, sending shivers down her spine. Holy Moses.

Pulling out her phone, she composed a text to Colin conveying her situation.

Katlyn: Someone fired an arrow at me. I'm in the common land behind my house. Send a patrol car, but no siren. I don't want to warn the suspect.

Colin: Are you alright?

Katlyn: Yes. A near miss with an arrow.

Colin: Will get there ASAP.

As she awaited Colin's arrival, a sharp pang of pain jolted through Katlyn's shoulder, accompanied by the sight of blood staining her fingers. A wave of concern washed over her—the arrow had caused more damage than she initially realized. Shit, shit, shit.

Katlyn refused to remain immobilized and wait for someone to rescue her. She couldn't afford to leave behind crucial evidence—the arrow. Despite the discomfort in her shoulder, she crawled toward the discarded weapon. Her knees took a battering on the rugged terrain as she moved. Carefully holding the arrow, she tried to remain calm, aware that help was on its way with Colin and the team.

A rustle in the nearby bushes startled her, putting her on edge. Was it another assailant attempting to approach, or perhaps the same one from before? Lowering herself back down, Katlyn forced herself to ignore the pain in her shoulder and maintained a watchful vigil for the patrol cars. Occasionally, she lifted her head, keenly aware that her attacker might still be lurking nearby.

As the distant sound of sirens grew louder, Katlyn's fear turned to frustration. She had asked Colin to ensure that the patrol cars approached discreetly, without activating their sirens. Yet, it seemed they had ignored her request. The element of surprise was lost, compromising their chances of apprehending the suspect.

Moments later, Colin made his way towards her. Katlyn mustered her strength, rising to her feet. However, a sudden bout of dizziness overcame her, causing her to falter. "I'm over here," she cried before collapsing into Colin's arms.

"Oh hell. You're bleeding." Colin caught her. "We need to get that looked at."

"I asked for no sirens."

"I told them. Seems my message didn't get through about that." He stared at her shoulder. "I'm taking you to the hospital."

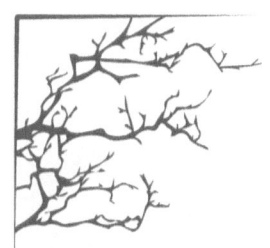

Chapter 38

K atlyn walked into the incident room. "Good morning, team."
She was late coming in to work after the accident and the hospital suggesting she go home and rest. But she couldn't do that. White told her to take the day off, which was surprising. That was so unlike him, even with health and safety obligations.

Katlyn had a premonition of an impending breakthrough on the case. She hoped this time her feeling was right.

"You look a little pale. Are you alright?" Amanda inquired with concern.

"Someone shot an arrow at me and it grazed my shoulder." Katlyn revealed, causing a murmur to ripple through the squad. She hadn't had the chance to inform anyone aside from White. "Colin came to my rescue. Thanks again, Colin," she expressed, acknowledging his help.

He gave her a nod.

"We should pull out all stops to catch this bastard," Amanda said.

Sylvester walked into the squad room, greeted by the team. "Hello, everyone. My flight was delayed because of a mechanical issue with the plane."

"How did the wedding go?" Katlyn said.

Sylvester shrugged. "It was over the top with the decorations fit for a king and desserts decorated with gold leaf for two hundred people, that were all dressed to the nines. I prefer simplicity."

Meanwhile, Derrick sat at his desk, pretending to pay attention while his focus remained on his computer screen.

"Are you with us, Derrick?" Katlyn addressed him, noting his lack of engagement.

He made a face and pursed his lips, clearly disinterested.

"I've the boys looking at the CCTV feed from my front and back doors," Katlyn said.

"Do you think they'll find something useful?" Amanda questioned.

"Let's hope they do," Katlyn responded.

Colin added, "This can't be an isolated attack."

"They've been cautious so far. My theory is that the suspect in Emily's case believes we're getting too close for comfort and is attempting to deter us," Katlyn explained.

"We need a breakthrough with this case," Colin said.

She sighed.

"Are you sure you're okay?" Amanda said.

"I took some painkillers earlier for my shoulder, but they haven't kicked in properly yet."

"You shouldn't be driving," Colin advised, his hands tucked into his pockets. "We can't predict if the suspect will strike again."

"Thank you for your concern. Even when I get my Corolla back, I'll be getting a ride until this case is resolved. And guess what? It was White who made the offer. With health and safety to consider, he had little choice." Katlyn was surprised, when White suggested she should use a taxi or an Uber until they caught this suspect. Especially, since his constant whinging about budget constraints. However, the recent incidents had raised concerns about her safety.

"Okay, let's summarize what we have so far," Katlyn began, as the team arranged their chairs in a semi-circle facing the board. She pinned up the image of the arrow for everyone to see. We found the glasses at Tide Cove and the suitcase with Emily Green's body, which was purchased from a charity store. Then there's the vague description of Emily's boyfriend, possibly in his early twenties, with the nickname or initials HB, whom no one seems to know. We have the incident with the white van that ran Brady and I off the road. The latest is a recent attack by an archer, which we can only assume is connected."

Sylvester stood up and expressed his doubts. "Are you certain the suspect is feeling threatened by our progress and is attempting to scare you off?"

"I can't say for certain, but it's the most logical explanation at this point. I'm open to other ideas. Anyone?" Katlyn invited the team to share their thoughts.

No one had any alternative theories to propose.

"Perhaps you shouldn't be living alone during this time," Syl suggested, taking a seat. "I have a spare room."

Derrick sniggered, but Colin intervened. "Keep your fly done up, Derrick." Colin glared at him. "She's not interested in what you have to offer."

"Thanks for the offer, Syl but, I've made other arrangements." She was grateful that her partner stood up for her. Syl was from old money and lived in one of the largest houses in the area. "Okay, enough distractions. Let's focus on the case."

Pointing to the image of Emily on the board, Katlyn continued, "The victim had been dead for twenty-four to forty-eight hours before I found her."

"I've read that smugglers used to land their contraband at Tide Cove and hide it in the nearby caves until they could sell it," Syl said.

"How interesting. Are you a history buff?" Katlyn inquired.

He nodded in affirmation.

"Will someone volunteer to check the caves? Emily might have been held captive there," Katlyn requested.

"I'll go since I know the location," Syl volunteered.

"Thanks. Now, has anyone any further questions?"

Derrick chimed in, "Did we find her phone?"

Katlyn turned to Colin for the answer. He appeared contrite as he responded, "I meant to inform you. The team conducted another search of Emily's room, but we couldn't locate her phone."

Another frustrating dead end. "Anything else?"

White stepped forward and delivered some news. "I've just received an update from forensics regarding your car. They retrieved a fingerprint. They're currently running a search on the database."

"Oh!" The news surprised Katlyn, raising her hopes for a breakthrough. "Let's hope we get some leads from this."

"Well, get back to it, everyone! We have two other cases waiting for our attention. If we don't make progress by the end of next week, I'll have to assign some of you to another case," White said before retreating to his office.

"Thanks, team. We all need to work harder," Katlyn acknowledged, said her gratitude.

Derrick complained, "I haven't clocked off on time for the past week. I have a life, you know."

"Doesn't everyone," Colin defended Katlyn. "Kat wouldn't expect you to put in the hours if she wasn't doing it herself."

"Still," Brady chimed in. "I've forgotten what my place looks like."

They were venting their frustrations, releasing some of the pressure that built up while working on such a challenging case.

Katlyn called her daughter. "How are you?"

"Oh, Mum, I'm fine."

"Did you get some sleep?"

"Well..."

"You poor love."

"Don't worry, I'm getting used to the cast, and it's not too bad."

That was a relief. "I'll come over to see you after I finish here."

"Dad's looking after me."

"Tomorrow then. I promise. Goodbye, love."

Next, she dialed forensics. "Hello, Noah. Brilliant work. I hear you've got a fingerprint from my Corolla."

Noah sounded sheepish. "Well, we've run the print through the database. And nothing. Zilch."

"Damn. I hoped." Just when it looked like they just might have a promising lead, her hopes were dashed again.

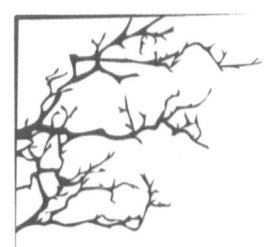

Chapter 39

C olin drove down the hedge-lined lane and turned into a gravel drive.
Katlyn slipped out of Colin's jeep.

Colin said as they walked down the gravel path. "There's someone in the chicken coop." "Calling it a chicken coop would be like calling a stately home a shack," Kat said.

The air was thick with the smell of chicken manure and dust. She made her way across the yard towards the coop, its double doors wide open. The clucking of the chickens created a cacophony. A spacious pen enclosed the area in front of the doors.

Inside, a burly man was scattering feed, attracting a frenzy of chickens. Despite the chill in the air, the man wore old jeans, a t-shirt, and boots.

"Mr. Streeton, I presume. His free-range eggs are sought after, I'm told," Colin said.

Metal Feeders and water dispensers hung in a circular array, with chains which secured them to the ceiling.

Streeton looked up, and noticed their presence. He let himself out of the chicken pen, and approached with a scowl on his face. "This is private property," he shouted over the noise. "What do you want?"

Katlyn stood tall, smiled, and presented her warrant card. "DS Kat Snowden, and this is DC Colin McKenzie. Mr. Logan Streeton. We need to ask you a few questions."

He stood with legs apart and hands on hips. "What's this about?"

"We're investigating an attack on my person earlier today."

"I don't know anything about that. You're lucky you caught me at home."

"I called your workshop and was told you had the day off."

"Yeah, and? Is that a crime?"

"Not at all. However, you may be able to assist us with our investigation."

"What's it got to do with me?"

"We are investigating an attempt on my life," she said again. "Someone shot an arrow at me this morning."

"You think I did this?"

"Everyone is a suspect at this stage. Can we move to somewhere quieter to talk?"

"I suppose you'd better come in"

He led them along the gravel path to the back door of the cottage. He took off his boots in the mudroom. "I keep a clean house, so I'd appreciate it if you remove your shoes here."

They both complied. As Katlyn removed her coat, she noticed Colin had a hole in his sock, but chose not to mention it. They followed Streeton into a tidy, albeit outdated, kitchen.

"My wife died a few years back. So, it's just me and my boy."

He let the statement linger, leaving Katlyn uncertain if she should respond or not.

"Would you like a cuppa?" Streeton said.

"We don't want to trouble you, Mr. Streeton. Thank you, nonetheless," Kat said.

Colin asked, "Do you mind if I record this interview?"

"I'd prefer it if you didn't."

"In that case, I'll just take notes." Colin pulled out a notepad and pen.

Streeton placed the kettle on the stove. "It's mid-afternoon, and it's time for my cuppa. Are you sure you don't want one?"

Katlyn glanced at Colin, who nodded. "Thank you. Two white teas, please."

He nodded to the wooden chairs around an eight-seater antique table. "Take a seat."

He picked up the box of tea bags and three mugs from the cupboard. "My wife used to keep the house spotless, and since she's gone, I've tried, but with work and the chickens. I get a woman to clean the house. We manage just fine."

"I'm sure you do." The kitchen was tidy, with only a few of items in the drying rack.

Streeton nodded. He tried to appear relaxed as he sat down at the table with his lips set in a thin line.

"I'm told you're the president of the local archery club. How many members of the archery club live in the area?" Katlyn asked.

He leaned back. "We're only a small club, with sixteen members, but only eight come regularly. The others join occasionally."

The kettle whistled, and Streeton poured the hot water into the mugs.

Katlyn took a sip of her tea. "Can I have a list of your members and their details?"

"I still don't understand why you want this," he replied.

Was he deliberately being thick-headed? "The person who shot the arrow at me may belong to your club."

Streeton set down his cup. "Well, you've come to the wrong conclusion. Our members do not loose arrows at the cops or the public. It's a dangerous sport, and we are very careful to vet each applicant before they can join."

"I'm glad to hear that. I still need to see the list."

"Why do you think the club has anything to do with what happened? It could have been a poacher or someone shooting at ducks. Or some kid just having fun."

"The list, please," she insisted for the third time. She was certain it would be difficult for a young kid to get their hands on the sort of arrow that was fired at her.

"I'll have to fetch it for you."

"We can wait," Colin interjected.

"The club records are in the shed. Not easy to access."

"As DC McKenzie said, we can wait." She tried to maintain a relaxed demeanor, but her nerves were on edge.

Streeton glared at her, put on his boots, and stepped through the back door.

Colin picked up his mug. "What do you make of him?"

"He's definitely hiding something," Katlyn replied.

Streeton returned with a black hardcover notebook in his hands. He tossed the book on the table, with a sour look on his face. "This is it."

"Thank you. Can you look at these?" She showed him the photos of the wound and the arrow

His face lost color as he stared at the arrow.

"I was fortunate that I stumbled, and the arrow only grazed me." She let the gravity of the situation sink in. "Who uses these types of arrows with such sharp tips and this type of fletching?"

He shrugged and looked away. "I don't know."

He's lying. His body language betrayed him. "Have another look." She pushed the photo closer to him.

He studied his mug.

"Mr. Streeton, we're not saying you're a suspect, but if you hinder our investigation by withholding vital information, you may face charges," she warned.

His eyes widened in alarm. "I recognize that fletching now. I suppose there are individuals who might use that type of arrow."

"Are any of them members of this club?" Colin inquired.

"I can't say."

"Can't say or won't say?" Katlyn pressed.

He furrowed his brows. "I resent the implication."

"I need a straightforward answer."

"I suppose some members have them in their collection."

Katlyn reached over and pushed the book to Mr. Streeton. "Please point out the members that use them."

He flipped open the book and sighed. "This is so childish. None of the members have any intention of harming a police officer."

Colin started tapping his foot impatiently. She, too, was irritated at his delaying tactics, but chose not to show it. "I'll ask you one more time. Tell us who uses this type of arrow."

"Just so you know, the members that I point out don't frequently use those arrows. They simply have them in their sets." He flipped to a listing of all the members, and pointed to three names.

Katlyn leaned over and studied the three names: Samuel Williams, the headmaster at the local school, Kasper Goch, and Doug Warley, a truck driver.

She took a photo of the page with her phone, and picked up the book. "Thank you for your assistance."

"I'll need that book back for the club records."

"Once again, thank you for your cooperation, and I'm advising you not to contact these men to warn them of our impending visit."

"I wouldn't do that," he said, glancing away.

Katlyn had her doubts.

"Why do you think one of them shot at you?" Streeton asked.

"We are attempting to eliminate suspects. They may be able to assist us in our investigation."

"You're completely mistaken about these men. They're upstanding citizens."

"We'll return the book to you once we've made the photocopies." Katlyn stood up. "Thank you for your help."

Streeton relaxed slightly.

But she wanted to ensure he understood the gravity of the situation. "We may need to speak with you again."

Streeton grimaced. "Please see yourselves out."

Colin drove as Katlyn called Amanda. "I'm sending you some names. Can you look them up and check if they have criminal records?"

"I'll get started right away."

"Doug Warley is a truck driver. Find out who he works for. Kasper Goch is a carpenter, and Samuel Williams is the headmaster at the local high school."

"That's interesting," Amanda said.

"We were interviewing his staff the other day, but we didn't interview him." She said goodbye and rang White. "Chief?"

"What is it?"

"I have some names for the individuals associated with that fletching. Samuel Williams, the headmaster at the local school. Kasper Goch, and Doug Warley, a truck driver. Kasper Goch has been doing renovations at my place." She crossed her fingers, hoping that her involvement with Kasper wouldn't lead to her being taken off the case, just as they were making progress.

"Did you give him a key?"

"No, Chief. My neighbor has a spare key. She lets him in."

"Very well. Keep me updated."

"Yes, Chief."

White hung up. He wasn't one to waste words and niceties.

She sent a text to Amanda, providing the details about the archery club members.

"We should interview Mr. Williams. Finally, we're getting somewhere," Katlyn said, a glimmer of hope in her voice.

"Don't count your chickens," Colin cautioned.

"Yeah, I know." She dialed the forensics department.

"Hello, Noel speaking."

"Hi, do you have any updates on the arrow we sent you?"

Noel sighed. "Sorry, no good news here. The arrow was clean. No fingerprints."

"Damn. I was hoping for at least a partial print."

Katlyn turned to Colin and relayed the findings.

Colin wore a disappointed expression.

"But just when I think we've hit another dead end, something else comes up."

"You mean the three archers?"

Katlyn nodded. "But Streeton claimed that only three members have those arrows. But we can't be sure he's telling the truth."

"Do you believe he's covering up for someone?"

She nodded.

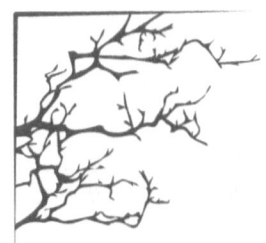

Chapter 40

Katlyn and Colin walked along the hallway of Casterton Community Secondary College to the headmaster's office. Analise, the office assistant, stopped typing and glanced at them with a startled expression.

"Good afternoon. Please inform Mr. Samuel Williams that we are here to speak with him," Kat said.

"You have an appointment?" Analise asked.

"Not exactly," Kat said.

The woman rang the headmaster.

"Excuse me," the woman said. "Mr. Williams is currently busy. Can you come back later?"

"We are not leaving until we speak with him," Kat said.

Analise raised an eyebrow and called the headmaster once again. Moments later, Mr. Williams emerged from his office and stopped in front of them. "I have a very hectic day."

"We need to speak with you," Katlyn stated.

Mr. Williams sighed. "I can't see what I have to add. You've already interviewed Emily's friends."

"We need to clarify a few things," Katlyn said.

His eyes widened with suspicion. "You'd better come into my office." He turned to Analise. "Hold my calls."

The woman nodded, and Mr. Williams opened the door to his office for Katlyn and Colin. "Please take a seat."

Katlyn glanced at the two metal and vinyl chairs and chose the one without a tear. The headmaster settled into his chair behind the desk. "I certainly can't be considered a suspect."

"I didn't said you were. Is there a reason you believe otherwise?" Katlyn asked.

He rolled his eyes. "Just get on with your questions."

"I must caution you that anything you say may be used as evidence in a court of law," Katlyn warned.

The headmaster folded his arms.

"You're a member of the archery club?" Katlyn inquired.

"Forgive me for failing to see the relevance, but what does this have to do with Emily's death?"

"Someone shot an arrow that could have caused me serious injury. I was fortunate that it only grazed my shoulder." Katlyn showed him a picture of the arrow's fletching on her phone. "I've been told that you own this type." Waiting to see his reaction when she revealed this information unexpectedly.

"I'm not sure if I do," he replied.

"I believe someone is trying to intimidate me and deter me from finding Emily's killer."

He sat up straighter in his chair. "How dare you insult me by coming in here and saying that I've got something to do with Emily's murder!"

"Mr. Williams, we are questioning everyone who possesses such arrowheads," Colin said.

Williams huffed. "You're damned impolite barging in here and... and accusing me without any evidence."

"Until we have apprehended the suspect, everyone who knew Emily and anyone who had access to these arrows is a potential suspect." Katlyn shifted in her chair. His exaggerated reaction and her intuition indicated that he was withholding something. "Are you certain you don't own an arrow like this?"

His chest seemed to deflate slightly. "Well... I suppose I might own a few arrowheads with fletching like the one in the photograph. However, it doesn't imply that I was the one who shot the arrow at you or killed Emily."

Finally, she was making progress. "What number of arrowheads do you own that match the one in the picture?" Kat said.

"Three and a fourth that needs work. Just so you know, I don't keep them at school. I store them securely in a locker in the shed at home."

"We need to see them. Can we call round later today?"

"I finish here at half-past four. I'll be home at five," he said.

Katlyn stood. "We'll sent an officer your home at five."

"I'll trust you won't alarm my wife. She has a heart condition."

"We'll do our best not to upset Mrs. Williams," Katlyn assured him.

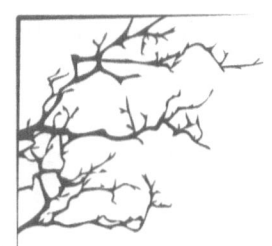

Chapter 41

After ringing the doorbell, Katlyn stood beside Colin at the blue front door of the gray-stone cottage.

A woman cracked the door open. "Good afternoon?"

They showed their warrant cards. "I'm DS Kat Snowden and this is DC Colin McKenzie. Is Mr. Warley home? We believe he may help us with a case we're investigating."

Mrs. Warley nodded. "I don't know how Doug can help you. He's driving a truck to the south of France. Left over a week ago."

"Is he a member of the archery club?" Kat said.

The woman nodded.

"Someone shot an arrow at me early this morning."

"Well, if you wanted to pin this on him, you're out of luck."

"We need to check his arrows."

"Can't you wait until he comes home tomorrow?"

"We would like to see them today."

She sighed. "Come in, then. He keeps them locked up in the garage."

They followed her through the house, which was cluttered with a full laundry basket and piles of newspapers in the kitchen. The rest of the house was in a similar state of disarray. Dirty dishes filled the sink, and open packets of biscuits sat on the countertop. Mrs. Warley led them to a side door and into a messy garage. She navigated between discarded furniture and car parts to a workbench with some tools hanging on the back wall. She ran her fingers underneath the side of the wooden bench for a key. "It's not here. Let me get the torch."

After Mrs. Warley went, Colin said, "Do you think her husband's genuinely away?"

Katlyn noticed some keys hanging on a hook on the side wall. "Let's see if she returns without keys."

Mrs. Warley returned with a downcast face and shone the torch under the bench. "They're not here. Sorry. You'll have to wait until Doug returns tomorrow."

"What about those keys on that hook? Why don't you try them?" Colin said.

The woman blushed and nodded. "I forgot about those."

She inserted each key with a shaking hand, but none of them fit the lock. "Doug's back tomorrow."

"What time is he expected?" Colin said.

Around 3 o'clock, barring any delays."

"Can you try ringing him?"

"I did while I was looking for a torch."

"Did he tell you where they are?" Katlyn asked.

"I couldn't reach him. In some parts of France, the signal is patchy."

"We'll return at three."

Mrs. Warley looked worried. "But he might be late."

"We can wait." Katlyn smiled. "What's the name of the trucking company he works for?"

"Winterton Transport."

"Their phone number, please?"

"I have a card in the kitchen. I can fetch it for you."

They followed her back inside. Katlyn noted three pairs of men's shoes near the back door. "Anyone else live with here you?"

"My two sons."

Colin took out his notebook. "Can I get their names, please?"

"Reece and Martin. Why?"

"Are they still in school?" Kate said.

"Reece works at the local butcher. Martin helps at the local petrol station."

"Were either of your sons dating Emily Green?"

"That's the girl they found murdered." She put her hand to her mouth. "Not my boys. They're good boys. Martin hasn't had a girlfriend. He's... mentally... handicapped. Reece has one shorter leg. Girls don't go for that." She said this as if it were an enormous burden for her.

Colin jotted down the information in his notepad.

"Thank you," Katlyn said.

As they walked to the car, Colin said, "That was a waste of time."

"Maybe, maybe not." Although Reece and Martin weren't among the three names mentioned by Mr. Williams. However, both Mrs. Warley's sons had access to the arrows with that specific fletching owned by their father.

Katlyn still needed to interview Mrs. Warley's sons. She called Brady. "Can you contact the local petrol station and find out what days Martin Warley works there? Also, ask if he wears prescription glasses."

"Do you think he's the one who attacked you?" Brady asked.

"Anything's possible."

Colin turned to her. "You're convinced the attack is connected to Emily's murder?"

"I can't believe you're not."

"I'm just not as certain as you are."

Katlyn shook her head. "You weren't the one who could have been seriously injured, but for a lucky break." She rang Amanda. "Can you check with Winterton Transport the times and routes assigned to Doug Warley over the past week?"

"You think his wife is lying?" Colin interrupted.

"Thanks," Katlyn said to Amanda. "I don't know if his wife is lying, but I like to double check everything."

"White has been bellyaching about the money being spent when we still don't have a solid suspect on the Emily Green case so far," Amanda said.

Katlyn sighed. "Everyone's doing their best. We can't do more than that." Katlyn ended the call.

"Let's have a chat with Reece Warley." Colin parked their car near the local butcher shop. They crossed the road and peered through the glass window. Rows of meat were displayed with plastic dividers separating the cuts. Katlyn opened the door and stepped inside. A young man with a scar on his face wearing a blue apron served an older woman. He limped to the back of the shop and returned with a tray of sausages. He weighed half a dozen and packaged them for the woman. Then he turned to Katlyn and Colin. "Can I help you?"

"Is Mr. Reece Warley here today?"

The muscular male nodded. "I'm Reece. Can I help you?" He put the tray in the display case.

They showed their warrant cards to him.

He raised an eyebrow. "Cops? What's going on?"

"Is there somewhere we can talk?"

"What have I done?"

"We believe you may be able to help us with a case we're investigating," she explained, not wanting to scare him off.

"The café across the road," Reece said.

That was a little too public. "Is there a back room?"

"No. The restaurant a few doors away has a private room."

Another man closed the cash register drawer. "We're not busy today, anyway. I'll tell the boss that you're at lunch if he calls."

"I owe you one, Sebastian," Reece said.

Sebastian nodded while observing Katlyn and Colin.

Reece washed his hands at the corner sink and removed his apron, and rang the restaurant owner. When he finished the call, he turned to them. "The owner agreed to let us use the room."

Once they were seated at one of the round tables in a small room with an oak ceiling and walls adorned with framed photos of local vessels at the nearby dock, Reece asked. "What's going on?"

Katlyn scrolled to the image she wanted to show Reece and handed her phone to him. "Have you seen this arrow before?"

Reece barely glanced at the image and shrugged.

A wait person entered, and took their orders.

"Someone shot this arrow at me this morning," Kat said.

Reece's eyes widened. "You think I did this?"

"We're exploring all possibilities at the moment," Katlyn replied.

"Do you have any arrows with this fletching?" Colin asked.

Reece shook his head as the wait person brought over their drinks and Colin's Devonshire tea, which included two scones.

"How long have you been a member of the archery club?" Katlyn asked.

He shrugged again. "About two years."

"Take another look at the photo," she insisted.

"I don't know," Reece replied hesitantly.

"Surely you would remember if you owned any arrows like this one," Kat said. Reece was proving harder to crack than she had expected.

Colin interjected, "Do you know anyone who may have access to this type of arrow?"

Reece thought for a moment before replying, "There's a guy at the club who makes his own arrows. He's a bit of a loner and keeps to himself."

"What's his name?" Katlyn asked.

"Peter. Peter Johnson," Reece said.

"Do you have his contact information?" Colin asked.

Reece shook his head. "No, he only comes to the club occasionally and leaves as soon as he's finished."

She glanced at Colin. Reece's nervousness didn't escape her notice. However, she chose not to reveal her awareness and instead said, "So, where were we... I believe you have arrowheads similar to the one in the image."

"What about it?"

"What are you hiding, Reece?" Katlyn pressed.

Reece stared at the tabletop. "Nothing. Nothing at all."

"Where were you this morning between six and seven-thirty?"

"Getting ready for work. I start at eight."

"Can anyone verify your whereabouts during this time?"

He sat back and folded his arms. "You're joking, aren't you?"

"We're very serious."

"My mum was still home. She can tell you," Reece said.

"I'll check," Kat said.

"Where were you last Friday night?" Colin asked.

"I can't remember. Probably out with the lads."

"I assume you've heard about the murder of the local teenager, Emily Green?" Colin inquired.

A visible pulse in Reece's neck betrayed his unease. "Oh, that's the girl everyone's talking about."

"Did you know Emily Green?" Katlyn asked.

"This is a small town. I've seen her around. Was Emily shot with that arrow?" Reece said, either genuinely unaware or choosing not to reveal his knowledge.

"I have to get back to work"

"One last thing. I need your employer's phone number," Kat said.

Reece provided the number and left the room, leaving Katlyn and Colin to discuss their observations.

"He was sweating," Katlyn remarked.

"I noticed that too," Colin agreed.

Katlyn called Arthur Nowak, the owner of the butcher shop, identified herself, and asked about Reece's work schedule for today.

"Why do you want to know?" Nowak questioned, surprised.

Katlyn explained they were following a lead regarding the attack on her life.

"What? You can't believe Reece had something to do with this? That's impossible. He's a bright, dependable lad and a good worker. He wouldn't harm a fly," Nowak defended Reece.

"Please check."

"I own two shops, and I'm currently busy at the one in Winterton-on-Sea. I'll have to look at the shift allocation when I find the time," Nowak replied, sounding evasive.

Katlyn sensed his hesitation. "I can wait on the line," she offered.

"I'll call you back," Nowak said before hanging up.

"Let's step outside," Katlyn suggested. "I think Mr. Nowak is going to call Reece. Let's see if he does."

They crossed the road and stood near a barbershop pole, watching as Reece conversed with a customer inside the butcher's shop. As soon as the customer left, the phone in the shop rang. Reece wiped his hands on his apron and answered.

Katlyn tried to call Nowak but received an engaged signal.

"Nowak's phone is engaged. He could be protecting the person who tried to kill me this morning," Katlyn remarked, a hint of suspicion in her voice."

"Reece was so nervous. He has guilt written all over his face," Colin said.

"We'll see." Ten minutes later, Katlyn's phone rang. "Mr. Nowak?"

"Yes, is that Kat Snowden?" Nowak said.

"Did you confirm the time Reece started work today?" Katlyn asked.

"Eight o'clock," Nowak said confidently.

"You're certain?" Katlyn probed further.

"Reece is always to work on time. I won't tolerate lateness," Nowak said.

"But you weren't at the Casterton shop today," Katlyn pointed out.

Nowak's breathing on the other end seemed laden with unease. "I can rely on Reece."

"Can you tell me the name of the other male staff member?" Katlyn inquired.

"That would be Sebastian Summers. You can't think he's the one who tried to harm you?" Nowak said.

"Everyone is a suspect until we find the perpetrator. If you think of anything that may help us with our investigation, please contact me."

"Thank you. Though I'm not sure I can help."

Katlyn hung up.

These men were protecting each other. "I'd been thinking that one person was the suspect in Emily Green's murder, but now... I'm not sure. It may have been a team effort. What made them kill that poor girl?"

"You think Reece is guilty?" Colin asked.

She sighed. "What I think is of no consequence without any concrete evidence to back it up. We'll need to dig deeper. Let's walk past the butcher shop and see what time it closes today."

"What are you thinking?"

"We need to have a chat with Sebastian." She called Amanda. "Can you see if Reece Warley has any priors? And there's a lad working with Reece by the name of Sebastian Summers. Can you check on him, too?"

"I'm on to it," Amanda said.

"Thank you."

Colin noted the shop hours with his phone. "Let's see if there's a rear entrance."

They walked up and down the service lane, trying to determine which back door belonged to the butcher shop. One had the aroma of bread wafting, another had two buckets of fragrant flowers, and a third cardboard box stacked on top of one another. They stopped at the fourth door. The meaty smell and the smears around the door handle were a telling sign. "This one for sure." Colin said. "We can't stand around here for two hours before the shop closes."

She arched an eyebrow. "A sob story now. Sure, you're in the right job?"

"Get off with ya," Colin said.

"Not likely," she said. "Kasper Goch isn't too far away. Let's have a chat with him, then return before the butcher shop closes."

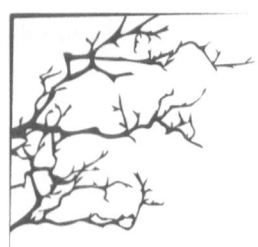

Chapter 42

Katlyn crossed the road and stopped when she noticed the side of Colin's Jeep. Her eyes widened, and a sharp breath escaped her lips. "Will you look at that! We've only been here for forty minutes, and..."

Colin ran his hand over the scratch. "Some damned kid with nothing better to do. Bastards. At least it's not too deep." His voice carried a tinge of annoyance, but beneath it, a hint of concern for his cherished car.

"Are you going to get the door resprayed?" Kat asked.

"Nope. It's too expensive. I'll try to touch it up myself."

"You good with a touch-up brush?"

"Now that could have other meanings." He laughed.

Katlyn grinned, but decided the safest way was to avoid taking it further. "I heard from the mechanic. I should have my car back tomorrow."

"That's good news."

"I hate depending on using a station car or getting a lift."

"I don't mind picking you up," Colin offered.

"Thanks."

They parked outside Kasper's house, the threat of rain looming in the air.

She opened the vehicle door. "Doug Warley was driving a lorry when Emily was murdered and when I was attacked. So long as his alibi checks out, it can't be him."

"Tick," Colin said.

"Reece Warley's alibi holds up so far, but I'm not convinced his mother is telling the truth," she reminded Colin. "Martin Warley has an intellectual disability, which makes it less likely for him to be the suspect," she said.

"We still need to verify if Sebastian confirms what Mr. Nowak told us," Colin said.

Katlyn nodded. "Let's have a chat with Kasper."

They walked up the path to a small semi-detached home. Kasper's semi looked freshly painted and his small front garden well-tendered, while the one next door seemed neglected. A faint scent of blooming flowers wafted through the air, mingling with the earthy aroma of damp soil.

Colin knocked on the front door, the sound echoing in the afternoon stillness. The door opened promptly, revealing Kasper dressed in form-fitting jeans and a jumper. His warm smile greeted them. "Good afternoon, Kat. I assume you're Colin?"

Colin displayed his warrant card briefly before tucking it back into his pocket. "No need for that. I know Kat. As I mentioned before, I don't know how I can assist you."

"Thank you for seeing us. We have a few questions to ask," Katlyn said, her voice calm but purposeful.

Kasper nodded, inviting them in.

They entered a tidy, albeit small, living room. The soft hum of a ticking clock filled the air, punctuating the silence.

"Tea or coffee? It's only instant coffee, I'm afraid," Kasper said.

"No thanks." Katlyn stared at the framed photograph of an elderly couple on the mantlepiece. They must be Kasper's parents, she guessed.

Colin took a seat, his eyes scanning the room, absorbing the details. He retrieved a notebook and pen from his pocket. "Mind if I take notes?"

"Go ahead. I have nothing to hide," Kasper replied, settling into a comfortable leather armchair.

Katlyn's gaze lingered on the photograph for a moment longer before she joined them, sinking into the worn fabric of a nearby armchair. "Where were you between 6 am and 8 am today?"

"That's easy. I was unpacking all the timber I needed for a wardrobe I'm constructing for a client. The pieces are pre-cut to size, so it's just a matter of putting them together on-site and installing it," Kasper replied, his voice filled with confidence.

Colin looked up from his notes, his gaze fixed on Kasper. "Can I have the client's details to verify your story?"

Kasper provided him with the information, his eyes meeting Colin's in an unspoken assurance.

Katlyn retrieved her phone and showed Kasper an image of the fletching on the arrow that grazed her earlier that morning. "We believe you own one or more of these arrows."

"I do. But I keep them locked away in the garage. Would you like to see them?"

Katlyn nodded.

They followed him to the garage with the scent of freshly cut wood wafting through the air. It awakened a sense of tranquility within her, a connection to a simpler, more tactile world. The garage was a surprised with its spaciousness, an unexpected contrast to the typical constraints of a semi-detached house. Woodworking machines occupied most of the area, with boards leaning against the walls, waiting to be transformed.

Kasper unlocked a tall metal locker, its hinges creaking softly as he opened the doors. The collection of bows and arrows showcased Kasper's skill and passion for craftsmanship. He bent down, his fingers tracing the fletching of the arrows. "All the arrows I own are here, including the ones with that particular fletching."

"May I look?" Katlyn asked.

Kasper stepped aside. "Sure."

She carefully studied each arrow. "Do you have receipts for these?"

"Somewhere. I'd have to search for them."

"Take a photo on your phone and send it to me when you find the receipts, please," Kat said.

"Right. Is there anything else?" He clicked the automatic button on the garage door.

"Can you tell us your schedule for the last seven days?"

He scratched at his stubble. "I'll have to check my phone diary. Give me a minute." He got up and went out.

"We need to return to the butcher shop to interview Sebastian?" Kat said.

Colin glanced at his watch. "We've time. Don't worry."

Kasper returned with his mobile phone and showed her his timetable. "It's how I stay organized with my work. I was at Victor's doing some work for him seven days ago. The next day, too. Then I dropped in to see you about what you were needing done. Then I worked at another other client's home."

The timetable had scheduled times and places on the calendar. "I'll need to verify this with Victor and your other client."

"Victor was at work."

"You were alone at Victor's place," Kat said.

"I had help with installing the new windows and with removing a kitchen."

Colin glanced at Katlyn. Her thoughts were in line with his on this. Their time was better spent interviewing Sebastian. But they had to follow every lead.

"Who helped you?" Colin said.

"Martin Warley. I only ask him on the two-man jobs. He works part-time at the petrol station."

Katlyn looked at Colin. "Does he work for you often?"

"It's not regularly, if that's what you mean."

This seemed to be a dead end.

"Did you know Emily Green?" Colin said.

"Right. Look... am I a suspect in this girl's murder?"

"Everyone is a suspect until we find the killer. Someone cut this young girl's life short, and I intend to find them," Kat said.

"Teresa is a wonderful partner. I don't need to look at silly schoolgirls? We're planning a wedding next year."

"That's great news." For some reason, she had a feeling that things would sour between the couple before then. How? She didn't know.

Colin tapped his watch.

"Thank you for your time," Katlyn said. "Mind if I drive?" She wanted to get a feel of how his vehicle handled. She was thinking of selling her Corolla and buying something different.

"Be my guest. Just be cautious when turning corners or parking. It's not as easy to maneuver as your car."

They returned to the Jeep and drove back to the butcher shop.

"He seems genuine, but we can't rule him out completely," Colin said.

She nodded. Katlyn pulled away from the curb. Driving the Jeep felt like operating a tank compared to her Corolla.

Kasper stood in front of his garage watching them leave.

"Reece is Martin's brother and Doug is their dad. Hmm, interesting." She wasn't sure why this disturbed her.

"Do you think the boys were in it together?" Colin asked.

"It's possible. Martin has an intellectual disability, but that doesn't rule out the potential for criminal or violent behavior. He also wears prescription glasses," she said. "Maybe, his brother coerced him into committing the murder."

"Then we need to check out Martin?"

She nodded. "Call Amanda and ask her and Brady to interview Martin."

"I'm on to it." He rang Amanda and conveyed the instructions.

Katlyn took her time finding a suitable parking space.

"Doubly careful, now are we?" Colin said.

"I don't want any more scrapes or dents on your car," Kat said. "Let's have a chat with Sebastian."

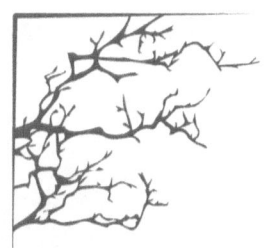

Chapter 43

K atlyn was about to open the Jeep door when her phone rang.

"Brady and I interviewed the other archery members who don't attend the club regularly," Amanda said. "A couple of members live two hours away. Brady rang one, and I rang the other. Then we focused on visiting the others."

"Where was Derrick?"

"He wasn't available. Apparently, he was running some messages for White."

That wasn't good. If she had known, she would have asked to have a floater, an officer from the team downstairs, assigned to assist them. "Any luck with the interviews?"

Katlyn put the phone on speaker for Colin's benefit.

"The short answer is no. But Heath Streeton, his father's the president of the club, mentioned Warley, Goch, Williams, Summers, and Nowak have those arrows. Only one of the other members remembered Warley and Williams had those arrows."

"The president, Logan Streeton, didn't mention Summers or Nowak," Amanda said.

Colin raised his eyebrows at the mention of Summers and Nowak.

"Anything else?" Katlyn asked.

"I get the idea that Heath Streeton hates archery, but his father was pushing him to participate," Amanda said. "Summers was in juvenile for assault three times when he was sixteen. He's got a temper. Maybe, now that he's twenty-four, he's settled down or keeping a low profile. Nothing on Reece Warley."

"Thanks. Criminal convictions for any of the others?" Kat said.

"Yes, Nowak has a conviction for assault with a deadly weapon—a knife. He spent a year in the nick. No records for the others."

"Nowak owns the local butcher shop and another in Winterton. Gets plenty of practice carving up meat," Kat said.

"Thanks for the info. I'll steer clear of him," Amanda said.

Colin said, "Good idea."

"Interesting that Heath's father didn't mention Summers nor Nowak," Kat said.

"You think they were working together and may be our potential suspects?" Amanda said.

"I'm not sure yet. Good work."

"One other thing. Brady and I called in to the headmaster's home. All his arrows are locked away. None missing."

She sighed. That was a dead end. "Thanks." She brightened up as an idea occurred to her. She rang Streeton. "Good afternoon, DS Kat Snowden here."

"I'm a busy man. What do you want this time?" Streeton replied.

"I believe there are two more archery club members that have those fletches. Slipped your mind, did it?"

"I ... um, I forgot."

"But, you know the Summers family well?"

"Sebastian's a good lad."

"So, you say. And you forgot to tell us about Mr. Nowak, too."

"I don't keep track."

A likely story. He was clearly hiding something. "How convenient." Katlyn intended to find out what. "Is this fletching easy to get, or is it exclusive to your club?"

"Look. What are you implying?"

"I don't need to spell it out, do I?"

"I think Doug had his made somewhere in France. Some of the members ordered some too."

"So, it was exclusive to one supplier?"

"Hmm, yes," Streeton said.

"I'll need the supplier's details."

"I'll have to look it up."

"Call me back ASAP when you have the information." Katlyn turned to Colin. "Let's get this done."

They entered the butcher shop.

Sebastian was loading pieces of meat into a mincing machine. When he saw who had entered, a shadow of worry crept over his features, his brows furrowing and his eyes betraying a hint of unease.

Meanwhile, Reece handed a package to a customer.

"Good afternoon." She was a little apprehensive in these situations. You didn't know how a suspect would react.

Sebastian Summers stopped loading meat onto a tray, washed his hands in the basin, and turned to them.

"Mr. Summers, I need to ask a few questions about the recent murder of Emily Green," Kat said.

A wary look passed between Reece and Sebastian.

"I know nothing about that," Summers said.

"We just need to take your statement," Colin said.

"Shit. You lot have it in for me."

"If you've done nothing wrong as you claim, then there's nothing for you to worry about."

"I'll have to close the shop. The boss won't like that."

"We can wait here for the fifteen minutes until you close."

Reece started loading trays of meat on a trolley and wheeled them to the cool room. He returned moments later. "Do you want me to finish up?"

"No, I'll do it," Summers said.

"See you tomorrow." Reece pulled off his apron. "I'll lock the back door."

Summers nodded to Reece, who disappeared through the doorway.

Summers pulled off his apron, hung it up and flipped the sign on the door to closed. While he was doing this, a woman knocked on the window.

He opened the door. "Sorry Miss."

"I hope you're not closed yet."

He forced a smile for her. "Not for you. Can I help you?"

He indicated for the two of them to go outside, but Katlyn ignored this. She watched as he made up her order. She sent a message to Brady for backup, just in case.

Once she was gone, he turned to them, fists clenched. "I swear you lot have it in for me."

"We'd like you to accompany us to the station where we can take your statement," Katlyn said.

"Why the station?"

"Six days ago, Emily was murdered. If you've nothing to hide, then it's in your best interests to cooperate with us," Kat said.

"I was here with Reece, working late that night. We cater for the Casterton Manor Weddings. They had put in a big order for a wedding happening the next day." His face had beads of sweat.

"Come on, mate. Let's go." Colin tensed. "We can do this the easy way or the hard way. Up to you."

Summers made his way to the door, as if he were coming quietly. He swung a left at Colin, knocking him to the ground.

The suspect shot through the door and sprinted up the road with Katlyn on his heels. He turned left and stumbled on the uneven pavement.

Katlyn grabbed her taser. "Stop right there!"

Summers dashed away before she used it. She raced after him.

A dumpster stood at the dead end of an access way. Summers jumped on the dumpster and vaulted over the wooden fence.

Katlyn clambered onto the dumpster. The smell of rotting food hung in the air, sour and overpowering.

Ignoring the smell, she scrambled across the discarded boxes and food, trying not to gag, she grabbed hold of the fence and made it over. Falling on a discarded pile of slate roof tiles, she slid and tumbled onto more building materials amongst the weeds. Getting up, she saw Summers barrel through thistle and long grass to the far side of the site.

Colin landed nearby. "Leave him to me."

Summers was halfway up a high brick fence as Colin neared.

Colin lunged and grabbed Summers' foot.

Summers kicked out. "Get off me, you shithead."

Colin fell backwards. "Bastard."

Summers scrambled up and over the brick wall.

Colin gave chase, clambering up. He extended a hand and helped Katlyn to gain a foothold. "I'll manage. Go," she urged her partner.

But Summers had disappeared. A row of cottages stood silent and dark, except where the streetlights threw shadows.

"Did you see where he went?" Colin asked.

She scanned the cottages and saw a faint moving shadow as it rounded the corner and vanished. "There." She pointed.

She dialed the station as she ran and gave a breathless precis of the situation, and was reassured reinforcements were nearby.

Rounding the corner, she darted along, hoping to see them. Moments later, she heard a shout.

"Get off me, ya shithead!" Summer cried.

Katlyn burst down a laneway between the cottages. Colin held Summers' wrists behind his back, with his knee pinning the man down.

"Ya got nuthin' on me. Cor, get off, ya piece of dirt," Summers said.

"Get the knife," Colin cried.

She kicked the penknife out of reach, grabbed a pair of cuffs, and secured them around the man's wrists. Summers was bigger than Colin, but her partner was super fit and worked out in the local boxing ring for fun.

"Are you okay?" she asked her partner.

"I'm fine," Colin said, pinning Summers as he struggled.

"Why'd you run?" Katlyn said.

"I thought you were goin' to pin som'n on me," Summers said breathlessly.

"A likely story." Katlyn pointed her tasker at him. "You can get up now." She nodded to Colin, who released Summers.

"Now, Colin is going to empty your pockets. Any problem from you and I won't hesitate."

Summers shrugged.

Colin searched Summers and found a small amount of cocaine in his pocket. He placed it in a bag and made a note of it on his phone.

"Mr. Summers, you're under arrest for possession of a controlled substance," Katlyn said. "Also, for possession of a dangerous weapon."

"What? That's not mine!" Summers protested.

"The knife?"

"Okay. That's mine. But, I work in a butcher shop."

"That may be so, but I don't see butchers carrying a penknife on their person." Katlyn read him his rights. "I can charge you for possession of an illegal substance or you can co-operate with us. Which will it be?" She knew she was crossing the line, but under the circumstances, she needed information.

If he didn't provide something they could use, then she'd charge him with possession.

Summers shrugged.

A police van pulled up. Two uniforms jumped out.

Katlyn said, "Mr. Summers has agreed to come to the station for an interview." She glanced at the suspect. He stood with his head down, but not cowered. "Can you bring him to the station, and take him to Interview Room 2, please?" Katlyn turned to Summers. "Any problems from you, and we'll slap that charge on you so fast your head will spin."

The uniforms led Sebastian Summers to the van, securing him in the back.

Colin climbed into the Jeep. "He's as guilty as hell."

Katlyn did up her seatbelt. "The man's got a temper. He was in juvenile court twice. I'm guessing he threatened the complainants he'd assaulted, and that's why they withdrew the charges."

Katlyn and Colin followed behind in their own vehicle. As they drove, Katlyn couldn't shake the feeling that there was much more Summers hadn't revealed. If he refused to provide any information, she would charge him with possession of an illegal substance. However, she didn't plan to charge him with possessing the penknife, as that article was a stretch. But, it wouldn't hurt to have Summers thinking they could charge him with that too.

Colin nodded. "Emily Green probably told him she was pregnant. He probably told her to get an abortion, and she didn't want to."

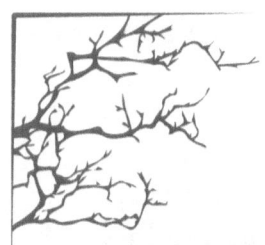

Chapter 44

Amanda hurried over to Katlyn, eager to share some updates. "Two things. First, I've got a copy of Doug Warley's time schedule. He's just returned from his trip to France, where he picked up some freight in Bordeaux. I emailed it to you."

"His wife told us he was delayed," Kat said. "And the second thing?"

"Just received a call from a contact at my previous posting. This is word of mouth, not officially documented. It came from a reliable source and it concerns Sebastian Summers. He'd was active in an archery club during his teenage years. His late father was a champion archer," Amanda said.

"That's interesting," Kat said. "Can you do a bit of digging as to where, when, and which archery club he frequented, please?"

"I'm on to it already. I'm just waiting for a callback from Winterton-on-Sea Archery Club. Our Mr. Summers grew up there. I'll send you the information as soon as I get it."

"Good work."

Amanda grabbed her handbag. "I'm going to get some dinner. Do you want anything, Kat?"

"Thanks for the offer, but I won't have time to eat it." Katlyn signaled for Brady to come over.

"What is it, boss?"

"Don't call me that."

He smiled. "Sorry."

"I need both you and Derrick to have a chat with Doug Warley," she said.

Derrick's head lifted and scowled when she mentioned his name. But, she ignored it for now, but if this kept on, she'd have words with him. "His wife rang and said he's back from France. I need you to ask him how many arrows he keeps with the specific fletching shown in this image." She sent the image to Brady's phone. "Ask him to open the locker in his garage. Check if all the arrows are there. If any are missing, let me know ASAP."

"Will do," Bradly said.

She gave a nod to Colin.

He acknowledged her and ended his phone call. "Right. I'm ready."

"Let's see what Summers has to say." Katlyn picked up a buff folder. She strode towards Interview Room 2, acknowledging the uniformed officer standing by the door, and took a seat beside Colin at the table. Sebastian Summers sat across from them.

Colin stated the time and date for the recording.

"Please state your full name, address, and date of birth for the recording."

After Summers had provided the information, Kat continued. "I need to caution you that anything you say may be later used in evidence in a court of law."

Summers nodded.

"For the microphone, please speak your answers," Kat said.

"Okay," he said.

"Tell me again, why did you run?"

"I thought you'd try to frame me. That's what cops do." Summers leaned back in his chair with a relaxed posture.

"Only if you're guilty." Katlyn slid a photo of the arrow that had grazed her early this morning toward him. "Do you recognize the fletching on this arrow?"

Summers glanced at the photo and shrugged. "Never seen it before."

"Have you ever tried your hand at archery before?"

"Nope."

"You don't belong to the local archery club?"

"Look what's this about? I done nothin' wrong," Summers said defensively.

She slid a printout across the table, showing Summers receiving an award for archery. "What's this, then? This picture tells me you were the best in the junior from 80 yards in the Outdoor Championship."

Summers pushed it away. "Okay, fine. I did some archery when I was younger. I haven't touched a bow and arrow in years."

"Where did you practice? Any specific club you attended?" Colin inquired.

"I don't remember the name of the club. It was ages ago. I used to go with my dad," Summers replied.

Katlyn exchanged glances with Colin. Seemed he was doubting Summers' story too. "We'll look into it," she said. "But let me be clear, Sebastian, if we find out you're lying, things will go much worse for you. We're trying to find the truth here."

"I'm telling you the truth!" Summers exclaimed, leaning forward, his voice laced with frustration.

"Why did you stop participating?" Kat probed.

"My dad was a champion archer. After he passed away, I left. I guess it held too many memories of my dad."

"Someone shot an arrow at me this morning. Where were you between 6:30 am and 8 am today?

Summers sat back and folded his muscular arms. "Getting ready for work. My misses cooked me a nice breakfast."

"What did she cook?" Kat said.

"We had a fry-up. Eggs, bacon, and mashed potatoes."

"Can your partner confirm you were together during that time?" Katlyn asked.

"Yep. Look, when can I go? I gotta get home. I usually go to the fitness center on my way home for dinner. It's past seven now. You lot with your useless questions. My misses be worried sick about me."

"Can we have her contact details, please?" Colin asked.

He told them.

Katlyn got up. "I'm going to pause the interview until we can verify your alibi. Do you want a coffee?"

"That's all I get when my stomach is talking to me?" Summers said.

"I'm afraid so," Kat said.

"What about a smoke?"

She pointed to the no-smoking signs. "Not allowed."

She walked out of the room with Colin and messaged Amanda, instructing her to ring Summers' wife and verify his alibi. It was going to be a long night.

Katlyn suppressed a yawn while waiting for the coffee machine to finish brewing.

She spoke with Amanda on the way back to the interview room. "How did you go?"

"Summer's partner confirmed he was home. She also mentioned they eat cereal for breakfast on weekdays," Amanda said.

"Thanks. You'd better get home yourself."

"I left a half a pizza on your desk for later," Amanda said.

Colin overheard the conversation and crossed the almost empty room. "I'm starving." He brought the pizza box over. "My favorite." He took a slice and began eating.

"Thanks. You shouldn't have. What do I owe you?" Kat asked.

"Nothing." Amanda turned to Colin. "Leave some for Kat."

He nodded and took another bite of pizza. "Next time, it's my shout," he said.

"I'll take you up on that," Amanda said.

"And I'll buy you a drink at the pub." Katlyn took a bite of pizza and realized how hungry she was.

"Did you pick up your wheels?" Colin said between mouthfuls.

She put her hand to her forehead. "I completely forgot. I'll do it first thing in the morning."

Colin scoffed down another slice of pizza.

They returned to the Interview Room.

Katlyn pushed the coffee toward Summers.

Summers scowled and took a gulp of coffee. He grimaced. "This tastes like dishwater."

Colin sat down next to Katlyn. "You get what you get."

Katlyn leaned forward. "Your wife told us you don't have a fry-ups on weekdays. Did this slip your mind, or were you lying?"

"I forgot. It still proves I was home," Summers said.

However, Katlyn couldn't dismiss the possibility that Summers and his wife were collaborating. "Did you know Emily Green?" She stared at him, trying to unsettle him.

"Why should I?"

"Just answer the question," Colin said.

"I watch the news. She was killed or somefin'," Summers replied.

"Were you in a relationship with her?" Katlyn probed further.

He thumped his palms on the table. "You lot try'n to pin this on me?"

"Answer the question. Were you in a relationship with her?" Katlyn persisted.

"I'm married."

"That doesn't stop some men." She knew only too well.

"Never even knew her," Summers said.

"Really."

He started jiggling his leg nervously.

"We have eyewitnesses who saw Emily Green with an older man."

His face reddened. "Alright. I had an affair last year with a girl, but she wasn't underage. She looked much older, and when I found out she was just eighteen, I broke up with her." He let out a yawn, displaying a lack of remorse.

The heartless bastard. Cheating on his wife and treating a young woman with such disregard. She couldn't help feeling disgusted. Katlyn leaned forward. "Mr. Summers, where you six nights ago?"

"I was home with my wife."

"Are you sure? Your wife told us you were at the pub," Katlyn said.

He rolled his eyes. "I forgot. I had a drink with some mates."

"We'll need their names to verify your story."

Summers slammed his hand on the table again. "Alright. The affair ended the other night. But it wasn't Emily Green."

"Are you saying you were seeing an eighteen-year-old girl, and recently broke up with her?" Katlyn pushed.

"Yes."

"Can you tell us where you were six nights ago?"

"I was with a girl."

"The girl you mentioned earlier, or some other girl?" His attitude irritated Katlyn, but she kept a calm exterior.

"Same one. I just broke up with her," Summers said.

"I'll need her details to verify your story."

He told them it was Lola Belcher.

This was the girl they'd interviewed yesterday. Was this a coincidence, or something more sinister? Katlyn paused the interview and stepped outside. She asked Amanda to ring Lola and confirm his story.

Returning to the interview room with Colin, Katlyn sat down opposite Summers. She pressed the record button and again stated the people present. She stared at Summers. "You know Lola Belcher isn't eighteen."

Summers seemed taken aback. "She told me she was."

"She's sixteen," Kat said.

"I swear I didn't know."

"Do you prefer having affairs with underage girls?" Katlyn asked.

He shrugged, displaying a complete lack of remorse or concern.

"Can you tell us about your relationship with Emily Green?" Katlyn pressed on.

"I told you I don't know the girl."

"You told us previously that you told your wife you were at the pub. But when pressed, you admitted you had lied and were seeing a female. And now you've just admitted to seeing Lola Belcher."

Colin said. "Mr. Summers, we know you're not telling us the whole truth."

Katlyn said, "We need you to come clean and tell us everything you know about Emily's murder."

Summers didn't answer.

"Mr. Summers, we have reason to believe that you're involved in Emily Green's murder. You're staying put until we get to the bottom of this."

Summers shifted in his seat nervously. "I want my solicitor."

"Of course, we can call your solicitor." She cautioned him again. "Before we do, I need to inform you anything you say can and will be used against you in a court of law."

Summers nodded and remained silent.

Katlyn knew they were getting closer to solving the case. Noting it was past ten o'clock, she knew it was unlikely they could arrange for a solicitor at this late hour. "I'm terminating this interview. We'll continue tomorrow with your solicitor present."

"Am I allowed to go home?"

"Not likely," Colin said.

They could only detain Summers for twenty-four hours without a charging him. "I can't guarantee that you won't scamper," Kat said.

She turned to the constable at the door. "Lock him up."

Summers stood to his full height of over six feet. "You can't hold me. Unless I'm going to be charged."

"Correct. You're being charged with possession of a Class B drug for personal use. You will be advised to attend a local drug agency for rehabilitation and you will be fined £2,500," Kat declared.

"But... but-" Summers stammered.

"You will be accommodated in one of the holding cells," Kat said. "Good night."

As Summers was escorted out of the room, Katlyn and Colin remained seated.

"What do you think?" Colin asked.

"We'll begin a thorough the background check on Summers."

"The way he reacted to the question about Emily Green was suspicious," Colin said.

"I agree. And his affair with a teen doesn't exactly paint him in a good light," Kat said. "If he's willing to cheat on his wife, who knows what else he's capable of?"

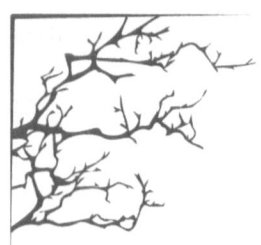

Chapter 45

"**M**orning, Chief." Katlyn entered White's office.

White kept typing on his keyboard and didn't bother to look up.

"Chief, you wanted to see me?"

"Sit down," he said, glancing up briefly.

She took a seat, but had her misgivings as his face bore a scowl.

"What's this about letting Summers go?"

"He's still in the holding cell. We haven't anything concrete on him. We charged him with possession of a Class B drug for personal use. I've set up the drug agency appointment, and I thought—"

"You thought, did you? Since when do you release a suspect before running it past me?"

She blinked in disbelief. She was definitely in White's office. "There's no evidence that would hold up in court that he's our suspect."

He pressed his lips together.

"I should have mentioned this with your earlier. For that, I apologize." Though he'd instructed her not to bother him with details when she had taken on this case.

He nodded, but remained silent.

"If you can allocate some funds to track his phone and a few lads to follow him when we release him, then we might get something on him that'll stick."

"We're under budget constraints, Katlyn, to reduce it, not increase it. I can't allocate additional resources for surveillance. You can track his phone messages. That's all I can offer. And you'd better be sure he's the suspect."

Katlyn sighed. "Summers has admitted to having affairs with two teenagers. One of them is Lola Belcher, who was Emily Green's friend."

He harrumphed. "Have you conducted a background check on Summers and Lola Belcher?"

"We haven't had enough time to sift through everything thoroughly. Chief, if he's not the suspect, he may be assisting the suspect."

"Get your team to do their jobs in a timely manner. If you can't do that, I'll have to take steps—"

While he was still talking, she marched out and went to the big board.

She stared at Emily Green's image. A sense of unease washed over her. Was this a forewarning? Would they finally get a break in the case? Last time, it had led to disappointment.

"Right, our daily prayers."

Katlyn pointed to the black marker with *'boyfriend?'* written below Emily's name. "She's been seen with a male. Possibly, a boyfriend, but she kept this a secret from her friends and parents. We can assume that the male was older. We know it wasn't someone her parents wanted her to associate with."

"What about Summers?" Brady said.

"We're releasing Summers," Kat said.

His jaw dropped.

"I need you...." She paused for a moment. Derrick was missing. "Anyway, I need you to go through the phone transcripts of Summer's phone to see if we've missed anything."

Brady nodded. "Will do."

She pointed to the picture of Summers on the board. "We'll put a trace on all Summers' calls and messages. Does anyone have anything to add?"

Derrick returned from the men's room. "He's the culprit. We should've charged him instead of letting him go."

Derrick seemed to have forgotten that they were having their regular meeting this morning. Something was off with Derrick.

She looked at her watch pointedly. "Nice of you to join us. We can't charge a suspect on a feeling. Where's the solid evidence?"

Colin nodded.

"Someone who lives across from that abandoned house where you and Colin were trapped in a few days ago rang," Derrick said.

"Did this person witness anything?" Katlyn asked.

The elderly woman witnessed two youths fleeing the cottage. She found that strange since the cottage had been abandoned for years. She assumed they were squatters. It didn't immediately click when she gave me the address."

"Well, it should have clicked," Kat said.

"And this woman saw them three days ago," White said as he approached.

Katlyn turned, startled by White's sudden presence. "Did she describe the lads?" she asked.

He shrugged. "I didn't think to ask. Her name's Pam Smith."

"You'd better get around there and take Mrs. Smith's statement."

He wasn't paying attention when he spoke to the woman. She made a mental note to have a talk with him about that later. He needed to pull his weight. "Get a description of the two guys. Also, check why she didn't report it to us on the same day."

"Okay," Derrick said.

"Anyone else have anything to add?"

"I don't know if they planned to come back and... or to let us go. But being locked up like that... well, it was scary," Colin said.

"Whatever their plans were, they certainly weren't good," Katlyn responded.

Brady stepped forward, holding a piece of paper in his hand.

"What do have you there?" Kat said.

"I've checked out the local optometrists who sell the type of frames you found on the cliff. One of them remembers selling similar frames. He sold a few pairs in the last six months, including one to a woman on your street, a Mrs. Babcock."

"The elderly widow who lives in that rundown house a few doors away from me," Katlyn recalled. She scratched her head in puzzlement. "I can't imagine her being involved in Emily's murder. Go and have a chat with her? First, ask if she has lost her glasses? If so, find out where she may have lost them?"

"When we canvassed the area and asked Mrs. Babcock if she'd seen anything. She said she hadn't," Brady said.

"Perhaps, she was too frightened to tell us. Take Amanda with you. A woman's presence might help her relax. See if she can recall anyone or anything acting strangely on that cliff?"

"Consider it done," Brady said.

As she walked past Derrick, she noticed him scrolling through dating sites on his computer. "Haven't you something to do?"

"Hey, I was just thinking," he said.

That didn't sound good. She gained the impression this job was beneath him. "Your wife would be none too pleased to know what you're doing. You can check out at dating sites in your own time."

Derrick flushed, quickly closed the website, and pretended to focus on a page on his screen as if he had missed something critical. Katlyn let out a deep sigh. She couldn't afford to have a lazy member, especially at this stage of the investigation. The killer was still at large, and time was running out. She decided to speak to Derrick after the meeting and give him a stern warning.

She'd recently overheard him complain to Brady about how his wife lacked fashion sense. "If you don't have more pressing matters, may I remind you about interviewing Mrs. Smith?" she reminded him.

He flushed again. "Right. You don't have to be like that." He logged off and stood.

Katlyn made her way to Amanda. "I need you to have a chat with Lola Belcher. Discover any details concerning her relationship with Summers."

"You think he's the archer?"

"Anything's possible."

Amanda grabbed her keys and purse. "When's Syl coming back from Paris?"

Did Amanda have a thing for him? "Tomorrow. He went to a wedding."

Katlyn returned to her desk. As she typed, she couldn't shake off the feeling something was distracting Derrick. She suspected he wasn't taking the case seriously, and his behavior was becoming increasingly erratic. She made a mental note to keep a closer eye on him and his actions.

Derrick walked in, looking flustered.

Katlyn asked, sensing something was wrong. "What's going on?"

"I've received a call from my wife's solicitor," Derrick said. "She's filing for divorce."

Katlyn could see he was upset, but she couldn't allow that to distract them from the case. "I'm sorry to hear that, Derrick, but we have a job to do. We need to stay focused and catch Emily's killer," she said firmly. "Everyone on the team needs to pull their weight."

Derrick nodded. "You're right."

"Interview Pam Smith and send me the report. As much as we need you on the case, take some time if you need to sort this out. Just keep me in the loop, please."

"Thanks." He walked to the exit without the usual spring in his step.

Katlyn turned her attention back to her work, typing up another report. It was certainly not her favorite part of the job, but a necessary evil. She was determined to catch the killer, no matter what.

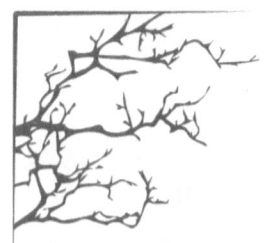

Chapter 46

"I've been thinking," Colin said. "We need to re-interview the three archers."

Katlyn yawned and sat back in her chair. Too many late nights were taking their toll on her. "Yep. It's been on my mind, too."

Her phone rang.

"Hello, Katlyn. We've just finished with Doug Warley," Brady said. "When we asked him about his arrows, he was sure they were all there and didn't want show us the storage locker. I pushed for him to open the locker. He kept stalling. He said he had other things to attend to. Said he knew what he owned."

"Was he nervous?" Katlyn asked.

"He had beads of sweat on his forehead. When he finally opened the locker, the arrows were all neatly arranged in rows. But there were three empty spaces. When I asked him about it, he said he had recently thrown some away. And when I showed him the image of the fletching, he denied ever owning arrows of that type."

"Now. That's interesting," she said. "Yet Logan Streeton was sure Doug had some of those arrows."

She heard Derrick speaking in the background. He said he'd done enough for the morning and was going to grab some lunch. She would speak to him later to see if his personal life was affecting his focus on the job. The team members needed to work together if they wanted to solve cases successfully.

"You think he removed them because he knew we were coming? Or was it because the one fired at me was missing, and he removed the others to make it look as if he didn't own any similar ones?" Katlyn speculated.

"There's definitely something suspicious going on," Brady said.

"Hmm. I'll have a chat with him later. Thanks."

No sooner had she hung up and her phone rang again. "DS Kat Snowden."

"I work at the local petrol station and your detectives came to talk to Martin, Martin Warley," a woman said.

"That's right. Can I get your name, please?"

"Carol Belcher. I manage the station where Martin works."

Could this be Lola's mother? "How can I help you?" Kat said.

"I'm sure Martin didn't work that day in question. Why would someone write on the timesheet that he was at work?"

That was indeed suspicious. "Do you know where he was?"

"No. Just saying, he wasn't scheduled on for that day."

"Is he on today?"

"No."

"Can you check his timesheet on the dates he worked and email me a copy?"

"I'm supposed to be placing an order, and I'm alone here now. Give me a couple of hours and I'll get it to you. What's he supposed to have done?"

"I'm sorry. We can't comment on an ongoing investigation," Kat said.

"Oh. What investigation is that?"

The press didn't know she had an arrow shot at her. They didn't know the two of them were trapped in a farmhouse. And she wanted to keep it that way. "I'm not at liberty to say. Have you noticed any changes in his behavior lately?"

There was a pause on the line. "I can't say I have."

"Please, this is important."

"I don't like to tattle on anyone. He appeared distracted and nervous at work a few days ago. Kept putting stock away in the wrong places and that's not like him. And he usually can't wait to play the old video game machine we have in the shop, but he didn't touch it that day on his break, which was unusual."

Katlyn needed Carol's cooperation. She saved asking her about Lola's relationship with Summers for another time. "Thank you. I appreciate your help. Call me if you think of anything else and email me that timesheet, please."

As soon as she ended the call, she remembered she hadn't followed up with Amanda yet. She dialed her number.

"Amanda, any news on the arrows?"

"No luck. The manufacturer wouldn't give me any information. They cited confidentiality and didn't want to breach any data protection regulations," Amanda responded. "I tried my best, Katlyn. But they were adamant. However,

I mentioned the attempted murder to them, hoping it would sway their decision, but it didn't work."

"Alright, thanks for trying." Kat said.

"Oh, and I think we're finally getting somewhere. I spoke with the president of the archery club in Winterton-on-Sea."

Colin listened in.

"He told me that Mr. Summers senior was an active member until he died of a heart attack a few years ago. Sebastian did very well and won some championships, but once his father died, he stopped going."

"That backs up what we were told. Good work."

Katlyn ended the call and glanced at the clock. She had a few hours before Carol would email Martin's work schedule. She needed to gather more information about Martin and Doug. As she contemplated her next move, her phone rang again. This time it was Doug Warley.

"Is that DS Kat Snowden?"

"Speaking. I was about to ring you."

"The cops had been round asking about my arrows. I don't want anyone coming here bothering me or my family. I've had enough of all this."

"Mr. Warley, we're investigating an attack on my person. We need to have a chat with you."

"I showed the cops that my stock of arrows is all there."

"You say none are missing?"

"I didn't say that. Three of them were too old, and I threw them out. I keep all the archery equipment stored in a locker in the garage. Only my family knows where they are kept."

"I'd like to check this locker. I'll send forensics over shortly."

"Shit. No!"

"I'm afraid that I must insist. I'll obtain a search warrant if necessary? Then I can get them to search your home as well."

"You think I've time to wait around for you lot! I told you I don't want any cops coming around." He sighed and spoke again. "I have to check the truck and wash it before I do the next trip, anyway."

Katlyn said goodbye and hung up.

Amanda rushed over. "I've just spoken with a company that makes fletching for arrows again. Seems they've reconsidered. Must have scared them when I mentioned I planned to get in touch with the French authorities to gain the information."

"You said that when we haven't run it past White?"

Amanda put her finger to her lips. "I was stretching the truth a little. They mentioned they sent a batch to the UK two months ago."

"Did you get addresses?"

"The owner said he'd get that to us tomorrow because the accounts department was short-staffed."

"Keep on top of it."

"I'll speak to the owner again if he isn't forthcoming with the information."

"Good."

Colin sat on the edge of her desk. "What was that about?"

"Let me deal with this first. Then I'll tell you."

She went to Brady's desk, and he looked up mid-typing.

"Something wrong, boss?"

She shook her head. "White is the boss. Anyway, I need you to pay Martin Warley another visit. His boss, Carol Belcher, just told me that the day Colin and I were locked up in that abandoned cottage, Martin wasn't working. Though he told us he was."

"So, he's lying?" Brady said as Colin joined them.

"Yes," Kat said.

She recounted the information about the missing arrows, she'd shared with Brady, about Martin Warley and his father, Doug. "Amanda's waiting on the manufacturer of the arrows with that specific fletching to supply the details of the buyers. Hopefully, she'll get that tomorrow."

"You're thinking the person who shot at you is the same one who locked the two of you in that house?" Brady asked.

"It's possible Summers and Reece are working together," Colin said for Brady's benefit.

"Martin is Reece's brother. Could it be the three of them are in on this?" she said.

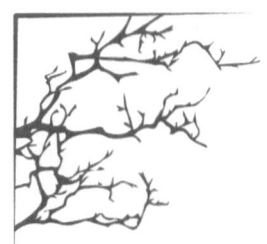

Chapter 47

Katlyn exited Colin's Jeep, bracing herself against the chilly wind. She zipped up her puffer jacket. Doug Warley was washing down his truck, which was parked on the street.

"Martin's mentally disabled, right?" Colin said.

Katlyn nodded, her breath forming a mist in the crisp air. "D.S. Kat Snowden, and this is D.C. Colin McKenzie."

Doug Warley, unshaven and unkempt, looked at them with a scowl. "What do you lot want? I told the coppers that just left. None of the arrows I own are missing. But they dusted for prints. Made a terrible mess, which I'll have to clean up." He scowled. "They took photos, as well."

"We need to have a chat with your son, Martin," Kat said. She'd told Brady to speak with Martin, but considering his handicap, thought it may be wiser if she met the lad herself.

He put his hands on his hips. "What's he supposed to have done?"

Colin stood to his full height of 5'10' with legs spread. "If he's not here, then tell us where he is?"

Doug glared at them. "You'd better come inside."

They followed him through the front door, past a cluttered lounge, and into a messy, dated kitchen.

"You be careful with my boy. He's not right in the head. Take a seat and I'll get him." Doug disappeared through the doorway.

A lanky, tall young man wearing black-rimmed glasses strolled into the kitchen. He pulled out a chair and sat at the far end of the table. "Dad said you want to talk to me."

Katlyn introduced Colin and herself. "We need to ask you a few questions."

"Okay," Martin said.

"Where were you three days ago?"

"Gosh. I don't remember." He scratched his head. "I was probably at work. Yeah. That's where I were." He blushed.

"We've checked. You weren't at work that day."

Martin's brow furrowed as he struggled to recall. "I have trouble remembering sometimes. Maybe I got confused with the dates."

Colin folded his arms. "Well, you'd better think hard."

"I can ask my dad, 'cause he'll remember."

"We're asking you," she said.

He scratched his head again. "I remember now. I was helping my friend. He installs kitchens and does stuff."

"Can we get his contact information?"

"You mean name?"

Katlyn nodded.

"Kasper Goch."

Katlyn maintained a poker face, but inside her stomach was in knots. Goch had been working unsupervised inside her home. Could he be the one behind the attempts to run her off the road, trying to scare her or worse? This revelation could jeopardize her position in the case? "We'll need to verify this with Kasper."

Martin nodded. "I need a cup of tea. Would you like one?"

"No thank you," they both said.

"We'll take our leave now," Kat said. "Thank you for your cooperation."

As they walked to the Jeep, Colin said, "That was a waste of time."

"No. It raised questions that need answers." Katlyn's thoughts raced with the implications of Kasper's involvement. She vowed to dig deeper into Kasper's background and any potential connections to the ongoing investigation.

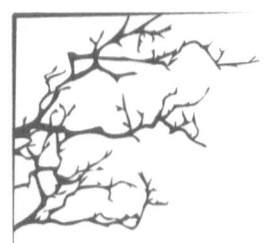

Chapter 48

Katlyn's phone rang. "DS Kat Snowden."

"Good afternoon. I'm... Emily's mother." The woman's voice was flat. It was obvious she was grieving.

"If you're calling to ask how the investigation is going? All I can tell you is we're making progress."

"I wanted to know. Thank you. But the other reason for my call is Clare. She's the mother of Emily's friend. Clare came over last night. Her daughter told her Emily kept a diary. Emily used to talk about it to her daughter. I can't bring myself to go into Emmy's room. I'm asking if you could you look for her diary."

"Do you have any idea where she might have kept it?"

"That's just the thing. I don't."

"Can I get the girl's name and her mother's details, please?"

"Oh. I don't know if she'd want me to tell you."

What was wrong with some people? Was privacy more important than finding her daughter's killer? "It's vitally important we have a chat with the girl and her mother."

"It's Clare Connolly and her daughter Poppy."

Frustration welled inside Katlyn. When interviewed, Poppy withheld this information from both Colin and herself. It would have saved a lot of time, if they'd known this sooner. "Thank you. I'll come over with D.C. Colin McKenzie shortly."

Katlyn went to Amanda, who was at her desk talking on the phone. She pushed aside some papers at the far end of Amanda's desk so she could perch on it, but papers fluttered down. She picked up the mess.

Amanda indicated she'd be a moment. As soon as Amanda hung up, Katlyn said, "Will you contact Mrs. Connolly and her daughter, Poppy? See if you can find out where the diary was kept? I spoke with Poppy when we interviewed the schoolgirls at the local high school. She only mentioned that Emily was spending time with an older male."

"I'll get on to it," Amanda said.

"Call me if you find out anything of use."

Amanda nodded as she picked up the phone.

Katlyn joined Colin, making himself a cup of coffee.

"Want one?" he offered.

"That'll have to wait."

He pulled a face and put his cup down.

"Emily's mother, Pam, said Emily probably kept a diary."

"Why didn't she tell us this before?" Colin asked.

"Grief can play with your memory." She recalled when her mum died and how difficult it was to organize even simple tasks for the first month. How she had thought that the Easter eggs on the supermarket shelves were from the previous year, only to realize that they were not. "We need to search Emily's room."

He started for the stairs. "Looks like we'll be using my car again."

"Of course."

"Such confidence in my driving skills, though yours isn't so stellar."

Katlyn laughed as she went after him on the stairs. "That's a low blow." She slowed down as she reached the ground floor, feeling the slight tightness of her healing skin grafts. A small reminder the they were finally healing.

They drove to Mrs. Green's home.

A little while later, they stood outside a cottage with a front door painted bottle-green and a tiny front garden overgrown with weeds.

After a single knock, Mr. Green opened the door. "Thank you for coming. I'm afraid my wife's not so good today. Our poor Emily...." He couldn't bring himself to say the word. "I'm taking Pam to see a therapist tomorrow."

"We are sorry to disturb you at this difficult time. Can we come in?"

"Of course." He stepped aside to let them in and closed the door behind them. Mr. Green led them into the reception room.

"We'd like to search Emily's room for that diary."

"I'll take you up. Neither of us has been in their since ... since." He shrugged and his mouth turned down at the corners. He led them up the stairs and unlocked his daughter's room. "I've kept it locked so... well, it's been hard." Tears welled in his eyes.

Katlyn nodded. "We're terribly sorry for your loss." She stepped inside.

Mr. Green stood in the entrance. "I know it's messy. But, that's how she left it. I guess...."

"You can leave us to it, thanks." She snapped on some disposable gloves and handed a pair to Colin.

Mr. Green disappeared down the hallway as Katlyn and Colin began. Clothes were strewn all over the floor, and the wardrobe doors were open. A small desk had the usual textbooks, pens, folders, and a laptop.

Colin glanced at the laptop. "Did forensics discover anything helpful on the laptop?"

Katlyn shook her head as she glanced at her phone. "I was hoping Amanda would send a message after she spoke with Poppy."

"A watched kettle never boils."

Katlyn grinned. "That saying is older than me."

"Should we wait for Amanda?"

"Nope. Let's split up. You search that side and I'll search this side."

"Sure." Colin pushed aside the few hanging dresses. "Nothing at the back of her closet." He kneeled and pulled out boxes of shoes. "Did you find out what sort of diary we're looking for?"

"It could be any color and size." She opened the top drawer of the desk stuffed with makeup and hair accessories.

As they continued their search, her phone rang.

"I spoke with Poppy," Amanda said. "She's still saying she doesn't know where Emily kept her diary."

"That's not the news I wanted to hear. Colin and I are at the Green's home."

"The boys didn't find it in her room?"

"I know. But we're searching Emily's room again for the diary," Kat said.

"Good luck with that."

"Yep. Typical teenager's room. We'll probably be hours."

"No dinner, then?"

"It's too early for that yet. We might grab some fish and chips on the way home."

She hung up and dumped the contents of the drawer onto the floor and rummaged through them. "I can't remember keeping so many hair ties and hair bands when I was living at home."

Colin laughed. "That was surely only yesterday."

A smile crossed her face. "I wish. On second thought, I don't wish. First dates hold no good memories for me. I usually wore the wrong thing, said the wrong thing, or just messed up."

He paused in the act of opening another box. "I'm all ears. Tell me about them."

"My lips are sealed."

She threw the contents of the top drawer back in and started on the next one. That one had plenty of pens and papers. The next drawer would not budge. She pulled harder, but it was jammed. "Bugger." She jiggled it and tried again. It opened so fast she landed on her bottom.

"Nice," Colin said.

"It's bloody not."

The drawer, now on the carpet, was filled with cheap cosmetics, hairbrushes, and hair clips. She pulled each item out. Found nothing of significance.

Replacing the drawer, she moved to the next one, which opened easily. It contained packets of costume jewelry, nail files, and clippers.

Colin gave a whistle. "I think I've found something."

He pulled out a shoebox from on top of the wardrobe. She had her fingers crossed, hoping it contained the elusive diary they needed.

He placed the box on the floor. Inside were notes and trinkets. "No point in crossing your fingers. No luck here."

He must have noticed. She had to stop doing that. It was just superstitious nonsense. "Keep looking."

Colin continued searching, lifting each corner of the mattress, moving the bed back and forth, but they found nothing.

"Emily must have something she was hiding from prying eyes. I know Briony has hiding places. Hmm." Katlyn went to the desk and pulled out the bottom drawer and saw nothing of interest. She went to push it in, but it wouldn't go. She noticed something taped to the bottom of the shelf. "Let's see what this is." She flattened herself on the floor.

She removed a small pink hard-covered book. It had a little fancy catch and lock. Grabbing a hairpin from the next drawer, she fiddled with the lock until it sprung open. She flipped open the pages. "Bingo. It's Emily's diary."

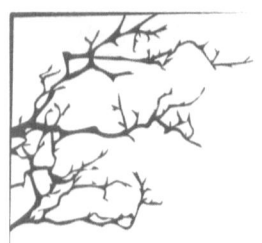

Chapter 49

Katlyn and Colin walked into the squad room.

With a sense of cautious optimism, Katlyn held up the diary in an evidence bag, her expression guarded. She didn't want to jinx their progress in case the diary provided no useful information. "We found it."

Amanda smiled. "Let's hope it sheds some light on this case."

Katlyn took a seat at her desk. "I've my fingers and toes crossed."

Derrick sauntered over before she could start reading. "I have a good description of the two lads who locked you and Colin in the basement on Bransgrove Road," he glanced at his notes. "Firstly, the elderly woman said they looked like brothers. One was tall and skinny, the other limped. She thought she'd seen the one with a limp at the butcher shop in the high street."

Colin chimed in. "The one with the limp could be Reece Warley."

"That's a possibility," Kat said.

"The woman was reluctant to come in to identify them," Derrick said. "But I persuaded her. Told her it was only a video ID. She wouldn't have to face the suspects in person."

"Well done," Kat said.

Derrick's chest seemed to swell at this praise. "I know."

Was she finally getting through to the lad to do the job he signed up for instead of thinking it was beneath him? She'd reserve further judgement until later.

Colin said, "Let's call the Warley brothers in."

"Not yet," she said. Katlyn nodded. "Before we proceed, we need to confirm that they are the same lads witnessed by Pam Smith. Let me know when she arrives."

Derrick pursed his lips. He didn't look too pleased. "But... alright, we'll wait for her to ID the lads."

"I want to interview her before you show her the photos. We have to ensure she's not seeking attention by fabricating something."

"Fine!" He tramped away.

Katlyn settled back in her chair, scanning through the thick folder in front of her. It contained statements, photographs, and witness accounts, all crucial pieces of the puzzle they were trying to solve. She flipped through the first few pages of the diary when her phone rang.

"In my office," White said.

Katlyn glanced again at the diary before she got up.

"Evening, Chief."

White looked up from a thick folder on his desk. "The mayor wants to speak with you personally. He wants an update on our progress on the Green case. I'll trust you'll not reveal any sensitive information."

"I haven't time to visit the mayor. We're just found Emily's diary and I need time to read it."

"You hoping it'll reveal who the boyfriend was?"

She nodded. "And possibly if he was the one who killed her and why."

"You're pinning your hopes on that." He shrugged. "I'll speak to the mayor and try to delay him."

"Appreciate that, Chief." She went back to her desk as Derrick approached, scowling. "She's here. Shall I bring her in?"

Katlyn nodded. "Yes, let's get this over with." She asked Colin to join them.

Shortly after, Derrick brought Pam Smith into a spare office. Pam was a thin, nervous-looking woman in her late sixties. She appeared to be afraid and kept glancing around the room.

Katlyn gestured for her to take a seat. Katlyn greeted her warmly, putting her at ease. "Thank you for coming, Mrs. Smith. We appreciate your help."

Pam nodded, her hands clasped tightly in her lap, and nodded.

Katlyn leaned forward. "Now, I understand you witnessed two lads a few nights ago. Can you tell us what you saw?"

Pam spoke nervously. "Will the two lads know who identified them?"

Katlyn assured her with a gentle smile. "Your identity will remain strictly confidential. We are here to ensure your safety."

Pam nodded again. "I glanced out of the window and saw two lads, young men I suppose, running away from a cottage. I thought it was odd because the cottage has been deserted for years. I thought they had stolen something or were squatters."

Colin took detailed notes while Katlyn probed further.

"Can you provide a more detailed description of the lads? Any distinctive clothing or features that you noticed?"

Pam hesitated. "Well, they were both quite tall, and they appeared to be in their late teens. One had brown hair, and the other had blond hair. Sorry, I didn't notice anything else."

Katlyn acknowledged her response with a nod. "Thank you for your help. We will arrange for you to view a digital line-up to see if you can identify them."

"I don't want them to see me."

"I can assure you, that won't happen." She explained to Mrs. Smith, she would only view the line-up on a computer.

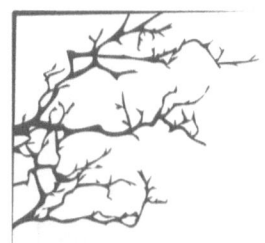

Chapter 50

Katlyn rang the officer's downstairs and instructed them to bring in Martin and Reece Warley. "Colin, can you arrange two separate interview rooms? We should question them individually."

"Good idea," he said.

She then turned to Derrick. "Will you oversee the officers escorting the two brothers? Ensure they don't cross paths. Also, take a photograph of Martin and Reece for the digital line-up for Pam Smith."

Derrick grinned. "Sure thing." He hurried off to carry out his tasks.

Time to explore the contents of Emily's diary. Katlyn expected it would reveal Reece as the father of Emily's unborn child. She put on a pair of disposable gloves and began reading. The earlier entries covered her parents' frequent arguments and Emily's school friends. Finally, she found what she had been searching for.

Saturday

I met the most delicious guy today at the High Street shops. I hope I see him again.

Monday

We had our math test today. I didn't study for it. Mum doesn't know. She's too busy planning her holiday with Dad to care about what I do.

Tuesday

The supermarket today. I didn't see him. So sad. My bad. I've such a crush on him.

Thursday

He spoke to me today. He remembered me. But he was with some woman. I shot her daggers.

He smiled at me when I was paying for my chewing gum. I think I'm in love with him. He's such a hunk.

Saturday

I saw him again today at the supermarket. He's got the most kissable, luscious lips. He wears those tight jeans that reveal he's all man. He didn't notice me, so I pretended to crash into him. Then he asked me if I was okay. My heart melted. I told him I was more than okay. He asked if I'd like to meet up with him. Stupid question. I'm melting here. Of course, I said yes.

We're going to meet next Saturday afternoon in the park. I'm so excited. I can't wait.

Saturday afternoon

OMG. He likes what I like. We talked for hours, and he held my hand. His touch felt like electricity running through my body. Melting here. And he's so sweet. He asked me to go for a drive next Friday night. Of course, I said yes. I'll sneak out when Mum and Dad are at the local pub for their usual Friday night booze up.

Friday night.

He picked me up in his work van at the High Street shops and drove to the common ground. We made out. I'm in heaven. He's my Honey Bear. HB is such a nice guy, and he was so gentle because he didn't want to hurt me. Woo hoo. I'm not a virgin anymore.

I'm dreaming about him a lot now.

Saturday

I stole some of Mum's pills, so I don't get pregnant. Should have thought about this before.

Seeing HB again next Friday night. I can't wait. I wish I was older, and we could move in together. But mum and dad wouldn't approve. They'd say he's too old for me. But I know what I want and I want him.

Thursday

Can't wait to see him again. I'm having sexy dreams about being with him and wake up in a sweat all the time.

Friday night.

We made out, which was amazing. HB is so beyond gorgeous, I melt when he touches me.

I asked him about the girl I saw him with weeks ago. He said she's a cousin. I was beyond relieved. I don't want him two-timing me.

He wants me to have a breast implants. Something I've wanted for ages. He's going to take me to the clinic and pay for it. I love him more. I want to look hot for him.

Wednesday

I blabbed to Poppy that I have a diary and she told me she had one, too. She asked me if I had a boyfriend. What? She thinks I'm going to tell her. Never.

Thursday

Mum ran out of her pill prescription. She still doesn't know that I've been secretly taking a sleeve from the packet. I don't want to go to the doctor because he'll tell her. But I think it'll be okay.

I skipped school two days to get the op. My boobs are so sore. But, they amazing. HB was there for me. Parents are clueless and think I'm staying with Poppy.

Friday night.

I snuck out as usual. Mum and dad were at the local pub.

HB told me he's Polish. He's soooo sweet. My very own Honey Bear and I told him this. He told me he'll call me his Sugar Baby. I told him he had a nice, earthy smell. He said that's from working with wood.

Thursday

I checked and rechecked the date, but I've just realized I missed my period this month. I'm hoping it'll start late. Though they never have before. I'm seriously sweating over getting them. Usually, I'm glad when they're over. I hate the first day when I feel like my body is so heavy and all achy and stuff.

Tuesday

Not a drop of blood. Shit. Shit. Shit.

Friday

I bought a pregnancy test at the pharmacy on the way home. But it's still in the packet. I'm too scared to use it.

HB splashed out and took me for a lovely meal in Winterton-on-Sea. He'd booked a table in the back corner 'cause he was nervous in case anybody recognized us. But no one did. He's calling me his Sugar Baby all the time. I love it.

After dinner, we went to the seaside. It was so windy. But we didn't get out 'cause we made love. I want to be with him forever. I told him I love him. He said, "Me too." I wish he'd said the words like I did.

Wednesday.

Finally, used the pregnancy test. Shock. I'm pregnant. Mum and Dad will have to let us move in together. I can see us raising kids together. It'll be so nice.

I rang HB, though he's told me never to ring, but to send a coded message we'd agreed on. Then he'd ring me when he could.

He was crazy mad when I told him. Told me I was stupid and should have been on the pill. I cried buckets. He wants to see me Friday night to sort this out.

He loves me, too, and I'm sure he'll want to keep the baby. But I can't sleep with all the worry. I'm crying buckets every night.

Friday

I vomited this morning when I got up.

My eyes are red, and I look awful. Mum didn't even notice. But she asked why I wasn't getting ready for school. Told her I'm sick and need to stay in bed. She believed me. It was sort of true, but I'd finished with the vomits for the day.

I saw HB tonight. He told me to have an abortion. That he'd pay for it. I said I want to think about it. But I want this baby. It's going to be a beautiful boy, I just know it. Just the image of HB. I love this baby already.

Saturday

I hardly sleep all night. Heaved again.

Mum asked why I looked so down, which was a first. She rarely notices. I told her I must have the flu.

I cried buckets again.

Monday

Before PE, Poppy asked what was wrong with me. I lied and said I thought it must be the flu.

I went home after trying to eat lunch. I knew it was going to come up again. The thought of food makes me want to heave. I finally kept down the pizza mum bought at Tesco's.

Wednesday

HB wants to meet up tonight. I'll have to sneak out. But I know mum will be glued to the TV watching a show about ABBA, anyway. She's been going on about it for days.

He kept offering me money to have the abortion. Gave me a card from a clinic in Winterton. I kept saying I'll think about it.

HB told me he's got a partner and I can't have the baby.

I was so mad. Screamed at him. He's been lying to me all this time. He said I was a stupid girl.

How could he say that? He loves me.

He's booked me into the clinic for next Friday. He'll drive me. After I went home, my knees started to shake.

I'm scared. But I'm going to keep the baby.

It might be the last time I see HB. I'm crying inside. I don't know what I'm going to do. Mum will be mad at me when I tell her. Dad, I can't think what he will say. I'm so scared.

They'll kick me out. I don't know where I'll go.

Thursday.

He rang me this morning when I was on the way to school. I told him I don't want to go to some clinic. I want to keep the baby.

We're going to meet and talk about it tomorrow night at our usual spot. He said that he understands and will look after me. It's such a relief. Mum and dad will be going on their holiday for a week. It'll be perfect. I'll ask him to sleep over.

Friday

I just found out some shit about HB. He's been lying to me. I don't know what to do.

Katlyn's hands trembled as she finished reading Emily's heartbreaking entries. Emily's diary exposed a difficult relationship with HB that included lies, manipulation, and the discovery HB had a partner. Emily was facing an incredibly tough decision regarding her pregnancy, with pressure from HB to have an abortion.

The last entry was dated the day Emily died.

Colin stood by her desk. "Is that Emily Green's diary you're reading?"

She nodded. "Revealing, too."

She flipped it to the page that revealed HB was Polish, and he worked with wood. She showed this entry to Colin. "Are you thinking what I'm thinking?"

"It must be that carpenter Kasper Goch. The only other carpenter nearby is gay, so he's not a candidate. Isn't Goch doing some work at your place?"

"Was. Not anymore after this." The kitchen Kasper planned to install next week was sitting in her garage. If Kasper was the primary suspect, which from

Emily's diary showed he was, then this kitchen would stay in her garage until she hired a different handyman to finish the job. If he was Emily's killer, she would ensure he was behind bars for a long time.

"Did you give him your key?"

Katlyn stood. She knew where he was going with this. "No, thank goodness. If I had, the entire case would have been compromised. We'll need to interview Teresa, Kasper's partner. Two constables from downstairs are bringing in the two Warley lads for an interview." She photocopied the most revealing entries, crossed to White's office with the copies in her hand. She was lucky to catch him, as he often left early.

She knocked and opened the door. White motioned for her to enter.

"Have you got a minute?"

"Stop wasting my time and get to the point." He stared at her. "What's that?"

He must have noticed her holding something in her hands. "Excerpts from Emily Green's diary."

"Well? Out with it."

She gave him the photocopies of the revealing pages in Emily's diary.

"Go on. You expect me to read all this?"

There wasn't that much to read, but she summarized what the pages contained. "Emily knew she was pregnant and wanted to keep the baby. However, the boyfriend wanted her to have an abortion. Nicknamed him Honey Bear once the relationship moved on from just kissing. She refers to him as HB from then on. Emily mentions this boyfriend works with wood. Colin and I suspect it can only be Kasper Goch. The other carpenter in the area is gay. But here's the interesting part: Kasper doesn't wear prescription glasses."

"Then that rules him out."

"He may have had one of the Warley brothers helping him. Martin wears glasses." She paused, letting this information sink in. "Also, we have an eyewitness when Colin and I were locked up in that derelict house on Bransgrove Road."

"Eyewitness?" White asked.

"Derrick spoke with a Mrs. Smith, who saw the two male suspects. She mentioned one of the men walked with a limp, and the other was tall and skinny. The woman identified Reece Warley from a digital line-up. However, she didn't get a good look at the other male."

"Good work. Finally, you're making progress instead of dawdling."

That was back-handed praise.

"The press has been criticizing us for not solving the case yet." White blew his nose into a crumpled, yellowed handkerchief.

She found him repulsive.

White stuffed the handkerchief back into his pocket.

She held her tongue, though she wanted to give him a piece of her mind.

Colin pushed open the door and entered. "Evening, Chief."

White ignored him. "So, talk, girl," White said.

"My mother always said it costs nothing to be polite," Colin quipped.

The support was welcome. Katlyn would remember that he had her back.

"The team downstairs is bringing in Reece and his brother Martin. We'll be questioning them first thing tomorrow morning."

"You should have had the suspects behind bars days ago."

"Kat's done an outstanding job on this, and you give her crap," Colin said.

White reddened, and Katlyn wasn't sure if it was with anger or embarrassment. Not that she cared either way.

"I believe the brothers assisted Goch with trying to scare Colin and myself. Locking us in that abandoned house, running me off the road, the arrows, and tampering with my brakes. But, killing and disposing of Emily Green's body... I believe that was Kasper Goch? We have yet to confirm this. Also, why did they assist Goch? What does he have over them?

"What do you think, Colin? Is Goch our main suspect?" White said.

"We both believe it's Goch, but until we are 100% certain, we can't arrest him," Colin said.

"Bring in this suspect and question him. Put pressure on him to confess. While you're at it, interview his partner, too. Do you think she's his accomplice?"

"Our plan was to interview her. And I don't think she's involved. But still need to establish this," Katlyn said.

She turned on her heels and marched out of White's office with Colin beside her.

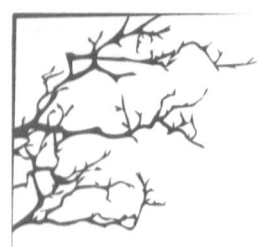

Chapter 51

Katlyn strode into Interview Room 1 with purpose, taking a seat next to the weary-looking Colin. On the other side of the table sat Teresa Holgate, the mortuary technician. "Hello. You know I'm D.S. Kat Snowden and this is D.C. Colin McKenzie."

Teresa nodded. "I know who you are."

"We appreciate you coming in," Kat said. "We have some questions regarding Emily Green's murder."

"I didn't know Emily personally. I only assisted with the autopsy." Teresa appeared puzzled.

"This is an informal interview, and we're not recording the interview, but I'll need you to provide a written statement later," Katlyn informed her.

"That's fine," Teresa replied.

"Where were you on Friday night?" Kat asked.

"I don't understand." Teresa brushed her shoulder-length hair from her face. "Why? Are you accusing me of having something to do with her murder?" she asked.

Katlyn reassured her, "No, we just need to eliminate you from our inquiries." She wanted the answers to be spontaneous and unhampered by any rehearsed responses. If Teresa had assisted Kasper, then she might reveal this either in her body language or in her reply. "These are routine questions."

Teresa paused. "I stopped at the shops and picked up some dinner on the way home. Kasper was meeting up with friends, so I didn't cook for him."

"You were home alone all night?"

Teresa's eyes widened. "You're surely not accusing me of having anything to do with... I can't believe this."

"No, we're just asking routine questions." She wanted to ensure that Teresa didn't feel accused of any wrongdoing and her responses were genuine.

"Kasper can tell you this is our usual routine every Friday night. He goes to the pub with his mates. Sometimes he comes home to change first, sometimes not."

"You don't accompany him?"

"No. I usually watch that quiz show on Friday nights," Teresa said. "I'm totally addicted to it. Kasper loves his football, so I get to watch what I want on the nights he's not home. I'd love to be on that show and win the money."

"Can you recall the amount of money that the contestant won on Friday night?"

"Yes. It was twenty thousand pounds. I was cheering for her. But I can't remember her name."

Teresa didn't show any signs of lying. "Thank you for coming in." She'd get Brady to check what time she left work on Friday night. "PC Cromwell will show you downstairs where you can fill out the statement about where you were last Friday night."

"Then I'm free to go?"

Katlyn nodded. "I may need to ask a few more questions, so don't leave town."

Teresa's thin brows furrowed. She followed the constable out.

Colin rose. "What do you think?"

"That she's telling the truth or very good at lying. But her responses seem genuine. Send a couple of lads to talk to Reece's neighbors. See what you can find out. And check what time he left for work yesterday."

Her stomach rumbled. Lunch wouldn't happen today. They still had three more interviews to conduct, and it was late morning already. "Let's grab a coffee, then see what the Warley brothers have to say. We'll interview Goch last."

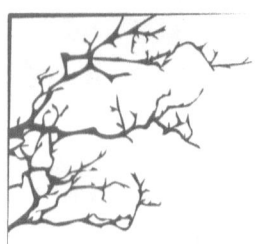

Chapter 52

Katlyn ended a call from Sergeant Hardy. He'd informed her one of the Warley's neighbors said Reece had left his house earlier than usual on the morning of the incident. That gave Reece enough time to get in some target practice using Katlyn as the target.

Gathering up her folder, she joined Colin, Brady, and Amanda in the hallway near the interview rooms. "Martin Warley has an intellectually disability. I've modified the questions accordingly." Slipping out some pages from the folder, she handed one set to Brady and another set to Amanda. "Familiarize yourself with them and ad-lib if you think it's necessary."

"I believe we can manage that," Amanda said.

"When are the guys bringing in Martin Warley from the holding cell?" Brady said.

"I've asked Constable Cromwell to bring him in ten. If Martin's uncooperative during the interview, then inform him—his brother claims he was the one who shot the arrow at me and locked us up in that abandoned house."

Brady nodded. "Are you doing the same with Reece?"

"Yes," Kat said. "Cromwell took him into the interview room about five minutes ago, so they won't see each other."

"Brady, let's review these questions," Amanda said.

Meanwhile, Colin positioned himself at the door of Reece's interview room. "Are you set to interview Reece?" he asked Katlyn.

"As ready as I'll ever be," she replied.

Katlyn strode into the interview room with Colin, and slammed the folder onto the table. "Good afternoon, Mr. Warley." She stated the date, time, and who was present for the voice recorder. "This interview is being recorded, and anything you say may be used as evidence against you in a court of law. Can you please state your full name and date of birth, please?"

In the observation room, White sat with a video screen and voice feed from the two interview rooms. He could alternate between them.

Reece Warley leaned back in his chair with his arms folded. "Tell me what this is about? What am I accused of?"

Ignoring his question, Kat said, "I need your full name and date of birth, please?"

He told them.

"You may request to have your solicitor present."

"What for?" Reece demanded. "What are you accusing me of?"

"We are interviewing you concerning the murder of Emily Green, as well as several attempts to cause me bodily harm." Katlyn repeated, "You can request to have your solicitor present at any time while we're conducting the interview. Is that understood?"

"Yes!"

"Tell us where you were yesterday morning?"

Reece pursed his lips. "You've already asked me this."

"We've received some new information regarding the attack on my person."

"I don't own a gun or any other weapons."

"But, you're familiar with using a bow and arrow."

"I haven't been loosing any arrows at anyone. Archery is a dangerous sport, and I'm not stupid enough to use a moving human target."

"How do you know I was moving?"

"An assumption, I guess," Reece said.

Katlyn persisted. "I'll ask you again... what time did you leave home yesterday morning?"

"This is getting tiresome. The usual. About 7:30 a.m."

"We have an eyewitness who saw you leave home far earlier than this yesterday morning."

Reece looked up at the ceiling. "You're wasting my time. I had to take care of some personal business."

"Can you elaborate on what that personal business was?"

"It's private."

She asked, "Can you provide any witnesses or evidence to corroborate your statement?"

"No, I can't," Reece replied, a touch of nervousness creeping into his voice.

Colin lent forward. "I'm afraid we need to know the details."

Reece's eyes darted around the room, his nervousness evident.

"We also have an eyewitness who saw two young men running away from an abandoned house five days ago. She provided a detailed description of both individuals."

Reece stared at the worn Formica-topped table, suddenly finding it the most interesting thing in the room.

"I'm not saying nothing."

"Your brother informed us that both of you were involved in locking Colin and I in that abandoned house."

Reece's nostrils flared, and a flush of red appeared on his neck. "Stupid idiot." He stared at the floor.

Katlyn smiled. "You've practically admitted that you and Martin locked both of us in that farmhouse."

"No. I never said anything like that."

Colin leaned forward. "Your brother stated it was your idea. He claimed you wanted to scare us off from investigating the Green case. He told us he assisted you in locking us up in that farmhouse."

"He's too stupid to do much of anything."

"That's precisely why we believe him when he suggested you were the mastermind," Kat said.

Reece jerked up at the sound of a knock on the door.

Constable Cromwell opened the door. "A word, please?"

Katlyn went into the hallway and closed the door behind her.

"You know Mrs. Smith picked out Reece Warley from the digital line-up, but she's now retracted this statement. She rang and said she couldn't be certain it was Reece Warley."

Katlyn sighed. "She was initially scared, but Derrick convinced her to come in. I'll have to speak with her again and see if she'll change her mind. Thanks. I'll wait a moment and go back inside."

She walked confidently back into the room, ready to deceive. "Okay, Reece. We've an eyewitness who saw two lads running away from the house on Bransgrove Road. She has identified you from the digital line-up."

"Bullshit. I wasn't there."

"Either you cooperate, or I'll ensure the judge isn't lenient with you or your brother. He'll be fresh meat for the criminals inside."

Reece closed his eyes and leaned back in his chair, sighing. "Alright. We locked you up in that stupid house. It was meant to be a lark. We planned to let you go. But when we returned, you had both scampered We only meant to scare you a little. You were so full of yourself on TV and we just wanted to rattle your big head."

Well, that was news to her. She sure didn't feel confident during the TV interview. In fact, she'd been incredibly nervous and had made a total fool of herself. "You're too old for that. Pranks like that are only for teenagers. And causing damage to DC McKenzie's vehicle, is also an actionable crime. Next one on the list... is stalking me in the common area near my house, and causing me bodily harm? Was that to bring me down a peg or two as well?"

"I don't know what you're talking about."

"Your father is missing some arrows. Indications are that the arrow shot at me is your father's?"

Reece looked at the ceiling. "I do not know what you're talking about," he repeated.

"We have some clear prints on the tip of the arrow shaft fired at me, and they match yours. Care to explain how they happen to be there?"

Reece frowned and tapped his foot. Finally, he was edgy.

"If you want to take the blame. So be it." She wanted him to be anxious and confess he was working with Kasper. "Don't think your supposed friend will save you from the lockup. Book him, Sergeant."

"Who do you mean?"

Katlyn rose and picked up the file. "Come clean and we can negotiate."

"I want a solicitor. I'm entitled to one."

"I'll arrange it. But a solicitor won't save you with all the evidence stacking up against you. Whoever you're protecting will walk free. I wouldn't like to be in your shoes. He'll let you rot in jail. You know that, don't you?"

Reece closed his eyes for a moment. "Okay. Okay! I get it. Will you make sure I don't get charged and my brother doesn't either if I cooperate?"

"I can't make any promises."

He put his head in his hands. She glanced at Colin and shrugged. They'll have to wait and see how this goes.

Finally, he looked up. "I guess I'm in a mess."

Katlyn let the silence stretch while she waited for him to continue. His nerves would get the better of him if she played it right. He tapped the table. "My brother did loose the arrow. But we were only following Kasper's orders. He helped me when I was in a tight spot. I owed him some favors."

Now they were getting somewhere. "What favors?"

"That's between him and me. He organized for us to lock you two up and told Martin to scare you with loosing the arrow. He didn't mean to hurt you."

"What about... causing me crash into that tree?"

"That was Kasper's doing."

She shivered, knowing Kasper had spent time in her home. Was it sheer luck that he hadn't tried to attack her there? "Did you help Kasper kill Emily Green?"

Reece shook his head.

"For the record, Reece Warley is shaking his head in the negative. Did you help him dispose of the body?"

"No. I had nothing to do with that."

"So, it was Martin who aided Kasper?"

Reece's eyes widened, and he jerked in his seat. "No, it was me. Leave Martin out of this."

Reece was covering for Martin. She stood up. "Right. Book Reece Warley for holding Colin and me captive in that farmhouse on Bransgrove Road," she instructed the constable at the door.

"Aren't you going to book me for disposing of the body?"

"Tell me how you did it?"

"I put her in a plastic bag and threw her into the water." He grimaced.

At least he did find the act repulsive. He was protecting for his brother. She grabbed the folder. "You were following Kasper's instructions?"

"That's right."

"Wrong. Miss Green wasn't in a plastic bag when we discovered her."

Reece put his head in his hands and swore. "Please leave my brother out of this. He can't survive in jail."

"I can't make any promises, but I'll try to have him put in a secure facility." She walked out with Colin by her side.

Brady frowned as he leaned against the wall in the hallway.

He put on a sour face for her, but it wasn't genuine.

"How did you go?" Kat asked.

"He wouldn't talk. I said his brother told us all the information we needed. Then he said he couldn't cope and started crying," Brady said.

"Not a peep?"

"Not initially."

She tilted her head. "Ah. You're trying to get me going."

He grinned. "But after he finished crying, he told us that Kasper needed help and he couldn't let him down. He helped Kasper get rid of the body. He broke down and cried again. Then he confessed to shooting an arrow at you. Claimed he didn't mean to harm you."

"Geez. A lethal weapon, and he didn't mean to hurt me." She ran her fingers through her hair. "Reece confessed to locking us up in that farmhouse on Bransgrove Road."

"You're kidding?"

"These brothers are something else. We need to identify which brother is guilty of what crime. They're covering for each other."

"Should I re-interview Martin again?" Brady asked.

"Let's leave them to stew awhile before we revisit who shot the arrow. I'll study the transcript of the interview with Martin before I interview Kasper Goch."

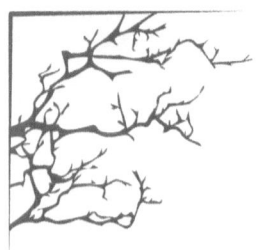

Chapter 53

Goch sat across the table in the Interview Room. His bored gaze flicked over Katlyn. "Good afternoon Mr. Goch."

Katlyn nodded for the operator to start the video. She stated the usual details for the voice recorder. "This interview is being recorded, and I need to caution you that anything you may say may be used as evidence against you in a court of law. Can I get your full name and date of birth, please?"

He told them.

"You may request to have your solicitor present at any time during this interview. Is that understood?"

"Yes."

In the next room, White watched the live feed on the video and voice recorder.

He adjusted his prescription glasses.

"Are those glasses new?" Kat asked.

"That's not a crime," he said. "I mostly wear contact lenses, but my eyes are irritated today."

"I see," Katlyn said, making a mental note of his response. She observed a nervous twitch near his eye, potentially caused by the irritation from his lenses.

"You're wasting my time and yours," Kasper's voice tinged with annoyance. "I don't know what you think I've done. I can assure you I drive within the prescribed limits and don't steal, drink to excess, beat my partner, or start fights at the pub. Nor did I harm that girl you found."

Katlyn maintained her composure. Can you tell us again your schedule for Friday, twenty-third, including the evening?"

"I told you I was at Victor Sabrige's all day installing a new kitchen." Kasper leaned back and crossed his arms.

Katlyn glanced at her notes. "Martin Warley has now withdrawn his statement about working with you at Victor Sabrige's place. It seems you were there alone, coming and going as you pleased."

"I'm telling you, I was there," Kasper insisted. "That new kitchen didn't levitate into place."

A smart-arsed answer. He was proving to be a tough nut to crack.

Colin interjected, attempting to establish rapport, playing the good cop and she, the bad one. "Would you like some tea or coffee?"

Kasper glanced at Colin, slightly taken aback by the unexpected offer. "No thanks. I want to leave. You can't keep me here." He pushed his chair back and stood up.

The uniform standing at the door stepped forward. "Sir, will you please sit down!"

"You've nothing on me!" Kasper snapped out.

"Please, calm down." Colin said, playing up the good cop role. The sooner we finish the interview, the sooner you can leave."

Kasper reluctantly resumed his seat, crossing his arms once again. His guard was up, his expression defiant.

"Where were you Friday night, the evening of the twenty-third?" Kat said. This suspect was cool under pressure and would prove a hard one to crack.

"I was probably at the pub," Kasper said.

"We were informed you didn't always go to the pub on Friday nights. That particular Friday, you weren't there," Kat said.

"Who told you that? They must have forgotten about the darts competition. It's on once a month. I never miss it. My name is on the player's list." He seemed confident in his alibi.

She sent an SMS to Amanda, instructing her to verify the information. "I'll get someone to check."

She nodded to the officer standing at the door. "We're pausing the interview for fifteen minutes."

"When are you letting me go?" Kasper pressed, growing impatient.

"We won't keep you longer than necessary," Colin said.

Katlyn observed Kasper's body language. His eyes darted around the room, his fingers drumming lightly on the table. He was more complex than he appeared.

"I'll return shortly," she said.

She left Kasper and raced into the squad room.

"Did you get in touch with the pub manager?"

Amanda nodded. "I've confirmed with the pub they had a dart comp that night. I told him to check the list of competitors. Goch competed, but was eliminated early on."

"How long would it take to walk from the pub to the park where he and Emily met last Friday night?" Kat said.

"I'd estimate, only a few minutes. And that's not running."

That's what she thought. "So, he had enough time to meet Emily Green, kill her, stash the body nearby, return to the competition, and make it look like he hadn't left." She held up her hand to Amanda and they high-fived. "Can you walk the route just to be sure?" "Okay. I'll message you with the exact time."

Colin held two coffees and a packet of biscuits under his arm. "Here you go. Get this into you. We head back in."

"Thanks." She grabbed the digestives.

"Hey, I didn't say those were for you." But he smiled.

She offered his biscuits to Amanda and handed the rest back to Colin.

Katlyn set the half-finished coffee and biscuit on her desk. Her stomach was in knots.

Colin sipped his drink and munched on a digestive. "Lost your appetite?"

She nodded, returned to the interview room and sat opposite Kasper.

Colin set down a mug of coffee for Kasper. "Here you go. I grabbed some sugar in case you need it."

"Thank you." He took a sip of the coffee. He was cool as ice.

"Mr. Goch, it seems your alibi isn't as solid as you claimed," Katlyn stated, her voice filled with determination. We're told that you competed, but you left early. You weren't in top form that night. The pub is just minutes from where you met Emily in the park."

"I didn't meet this girl in a park or anywhere else. Friday nights, I go to the pub and have a beer with my friends."

"Do you know that Emily Green kept a diary?"

His eyes widened. "You're making that up."

Katlyn held up the diary in a plastic sleeve.

Goch started tapping his foot. "So what! Kids nowadays have nothing better to do than make stuff up." He pointed at the diary. "Whatever she wrote in that diary was a figment of her imagination."

"You speak as if you knew her," Kat said.

"Look, this is not a very large town. Everyone knows everyone. I don't think I've ever spoken to her."

She slid a photo of Emily Green lying on the mortuary table across to him.

Goch blinked, and his expression softened.

If Katlyn hadn't been watching him so closely, she'd have missed it. It seemed he wasn't a complete psychopath. "You won't be speaking to her anymore, will you?"

She pushed the photos of her smashed-up Corolla toward Kasper. "I believe it was you who forced my vehicle off the road and caused me to crash. I could have been killed."

Kasper shrugged.

"You tried to scare me. But no matter what you did, it didn't work, did it?"

Kasper's eyes narrowed, his fists clenched by his sides.

There was a knock on the door. The uniformed officer opened it. Brady poked his head in. "Got it." he smiled. "You can proceed."

Katlyn returned his smile. "Thanks." She turned to Goch. Now came the set up. "As I mentioned before, Martin is no longer supporting you. His statement indicated that he helped you dispose of the Emily's body." She kept her fingers crossed under the table.

Goch snarled. "That lying git."

Katlyn leaned forward. "Why don't you tell us what really happened?"

"I'm going to sue you if you keep this up. Once I've been a suspect, it doesn't matter if I committed the deed or not. These accusations will ruin my business."

"We haven't charged you with anything. Please answer the question."

"Like I said, I didn't know the girl. How should I know what happened?" The vein at his neck pulsed with tension. "Martin's pissed off because I told him I can't use him anymore. I couldn't even trust him to hammer a nail in straight. He was pretty useless."

Katlyn sat back. "I find that hard to believe since you only used him for brawn when you needed to install something heavy, like kitchen cabinets."

"You trust that half-wit."

"And he thought he was your friend and tried so hard not to betray you."

Kasper snorted.

"Do you have a thing for underage teenage girls?"

"I told you I have a partner."

"But she doesn't satisfy your hunger for young, untouched girls?"

"That's rubbish."

"Get your juices going, do they?" Colin said. "You like enticing underage girls to have sex with you."

"You're daft. I have a partner," Goch said.

"Was she upsetting your plans with Teresa?" she said.

His face betrayed him. He winced.

"Emily wouldn't give you up?"

"That's nonsense, since I didn't even know the girl."

"Why did you do it?" Colin asked.

"That's rubbish."

"You killed her and made Martin help you dispose of the body," Kat said.

He shook his head, refolded his arms, and tapped his foot.

"I had someone talk to the staff at the local thrift store. It appears they sold a suitcase identical to the one we Emily found in. The staff member gave us a description of the lad who purchased it."

"Nothing to do with me."

"You're a piece of work," Colin lent forward. "You don't care Martin will be in prison for years because of you."

"How many, Goch?" Katlyn pushed. "Two, three, or more girls? You use them and move on when you get tired of them."

"You're making this up."

Katlyn slid another photo of Emily's body in the open suitcase toward him. Kasper looked away.

"Emily found out about Teresa, and she was planning to tell your partner everything," Colin said.

"You didn't want to leave Teresa, and you couldn't let Emily ruin what you had, could you?" Katlyn said.

"She was just a bit of skirt on the side, was she?" Colin said.

Goch gripped the table. "Shut up. Shut the fuck up!"

"She was an inconvenience, wasn't she?" Kat said. "Discarded when she refused to cooperate and have the abortion."

Kasper's expression turned ashen, and beads of sweat formed on his forehead. The walls he had constructed were crumbling, leaving him exposed. He had reached a turning point, caught in the web of his own lies.

"I told her ... Shit! Shit! Shit!" He thumped the table. The constable stepped forward.

She nodded to the constable. "It's okay."

She ran with Goch's revealing answer. "What did you tell her?"

"Nothing. I don't know what you're talking about."

"Yes, you do. You said... I told her. Shall I replay what you just said?"

He looked down at the tabletop. "I don't know. I didn't mean to do it."

He put his head in his hands. "It was an accident."

As if the apology would solve everything. "My heart bleeds."

"Emily was a sixteen-year-old girl who you seduced. But she was an inconvenience to you," Colin said. "You tired of her. She had dreams of moving in with you. She didn't know you had a partner at the beginning of your relationship. That you had plans to get married."

He looked up. His hands were shaking. "She was arguing with me. Emily wouldn't stop. She fell and hit her head."

"What did you argue about?"

"Nothing."

"I don't believe you."

"I don't remember."

"She was pregnant, and you wanted her to get an abortion," Kat said.

"She wouldn't listen. I just wanted her to get rid of it. I gave her money to pay for it." He shook his head. "It was an accident."

He called the baby, an it. That spoke of how unfeeling he was. "Why didn't you report the accident?" she said.

"I didn't know what to do."

"But you knew how to dispose of her body easily enough," Kat said.

"You're twisting this to suit you. I was upset. I didn't know what to do. Martin said we should dispose of her."

"Are you telling us Martin would know what to do? That he knew to take her pulse to check if she was still alive?" Kat said. "He's mentally handicapped. But you're sure he's capable of figuring out what to do," Colin said.

"I don't know."

"How about you tell us what actually happened?" Kat asked.

"I told you."

"No, you didn't. Let's start again. You argued with Emily. She must have been pushed with some force to break her neck."

"I didn't mean to push her so hard. But she was arguing with me. I only wanted her to stop arguing."

"You were angry because she wouldn't listen to you. You took it out on her," Kat said.

"I'm sorry. It was an accident."

As if that would make it okay. "You persuaded Martin to shoot that arrow, didn't you?"

Kasper shrugged.

He was a skilled manipulator. "The list goes on. Forcing me off the road and causing my car to crash into that tree... was it you?" His eyes took on a sly look. "Will I get a lesser sentence if I cooperate?"

Please give me strength. "I don't know."

He smiled. "I don't know how to use a bow and arrow."

"How'd you convince Reece and Martin to do that?"

He shrugged.

"Trapping my partner and me in that abandoned house was just stupid."

He glared at her and rose from his seat. "You calling me stupid?"

The constable stepped closer.

"Sit down," Colin said. "You've just admitted to locking us in that farmhouse on Bransgrove Road."

"It wasn't me."

"One of your lackeys, then. Martin does your bidding," Katlyn said.

Kasper smiled.

"How many other young girls did you prey on?"

Kasper didn't answer.

"We have a statement from Martin that you asked him to fire that arrow." She collected the file and the photos. "Society will be all the better to see scum like you locked away for a very long time."

She turned to Colin. "Book him. Then take him down to the holding cell."

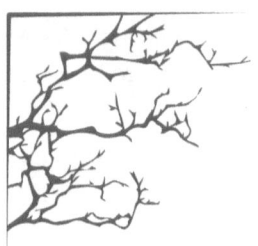

Chapter 54

Billy surveyed the empty, blustery street, the moon partially obscured by dark clouds. A malicious smile crept across his lips as he pulled a balaclava over his face, his gaze fixed on Katlyn's bedroom window. Tonight, he would finally rid himself of the thorn in his side: Kat Snowden.

Billy recalled his once thriving business as he walked along the laneway between Katlyn's and her neighbor's houses. Katlyn was the injustice he was forced to endure, and his desire for revenge consumed him.

Staying hidden in the shadows, he maneuvered through the common ground, deftly avoiding low shrubs and rocks. However, a misstep on uneven ground sent a searing pain through his leg, causing him to cry out in agony. Cursing softly, he attempted to soldier on, but the pain grew. Limping slowly, he opened Katlyn's back gate and slipped into her backyard, shrouded in darkness.

With each labored step, the more he dwelled on his motivations, and the more his actions became fueled by a sense of justice.

Billy unlocked Katlyn's back door. Thanks to his contact, a tech-savvy individual, the video feed remained on a loop, ensuring he was never here. He let himself in with an eerie sense of familiarity.

STARTLED AWAKE, LUCY jumped from the bed as if on-fire and jolted Katlyn from her sleep.

She rubbed her eyes, grogginess tugging at her thoughts. Perhaps her cat was too warm under the duvet. She pushed the covers down, glancing at Lucy's retreating figure.

Lately, Lucy had become more skittish. Seeking professional help from a behavioral animal specialist had crossed her mind, but the daunting cost of a consultation held her back. "Come on, Lucy. Come snuggle with me."

Lucy darted under her bed, clearly spooked by something unseen. Katlyn, exhausted from her interview with Kasper, struggled to summon the energy to investigate. Peaceful sleep was her only wish. She closed her eyes, her senses remaining on high alert.

She felt for the Glock 17 hidden under her pillow. She had taken the gun to bed since spotting the stalker outside her home. It was still there. The gun's presence brought a modicum of reassurance, attributing her cat's odd behavior to her own anxiety. With a yawn, she drifted back into slumber.

BILLY PULLED THE BACK door closed carefully, causing a clicking sound as the catch caught. The sound, loud in the still of the night. He tensed with the gun in his hand, and the safety released, his senses attuned to any sign of Katlyn stirring.

He navigated the mudroom, but an accidental stumble into the scattered cat litter increased the pain in his ankle.

Billy froze, waiting for any sign of disturbance. All was silent. He continued down the hallway, his injury causing discomfort with each step.

At the entrance to Katlyn's bedroom, he observed her iridescent form as the moonlight caressed her partly exposed curves. She was breathing softly, asleep.

She reminded him of an image of a goddess from a storybook his mother would read to him when he was a child. In those stories, the goddess took what she desired, but eventually, her comeuppance arrived. Katlyn too, would face a similar fate. A surge of excitement grew in his veins. This moment promised an intoxicating rush of power, which would be better than sex.

He took aim.

Katlyn Snowden would pay for the misery she'd caused him. Bye, Katlyn.

As he prepared to pull the trigger, something sank its teeth into his ankle, and he fired blindly, agony coursing through his body. Swatting away the ferocious creature, he saw it was a bloodied, crazed feline. He aimed the gun at the maddening creature, ready to silence it, but to his bewilderment, the cat vanished into the darkness.

Katlyn screamed.

Limping, Billy retreated through the back door and vanished into the night.

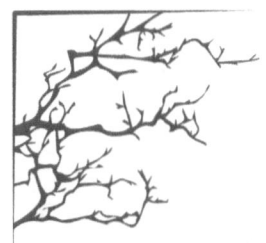

Chapter 55

Katlyn woke as something tore at her leg. A shot? Was she dreaming? No! The pain in her leg, very real. She screamed.

Lucy jumped, pounced, and hissed, like a cat possessed. Another shot rang out.

A shadowy figure stood at the bedroom door.

The ache in her leg asserted itself. She turned the bedside lamp on and blinked.

Lucy, hair on end, back hunched, hissed at something.

Her kitty was possessed and darted away.

"Shit!" Blood stained her sheets. Pain radiated through her thigh.

She felt under the pillow. Her Glock 17, still there. Closing her fingers around it, she slipped from the bed. Gritting her teeth with pain, she limped towards the doorway and peered into the darkness.

A scream ballooned in her throat when she heard the back door banging shut. She grabbed her phone from the bedside table and sent a message to Colin.

Katlyn: 'Help. Intruder. Wounded. No siren.'

She slid down the wall. Would she still be alive by the time Colin reached her?

Willing herself to move, she rose and limped to the kitchen. Moonlight slanted in the windows and threw shadows everywhere.

Unable to stand, Katlyn sank to the floor and slumped against the kitchen cupboards.

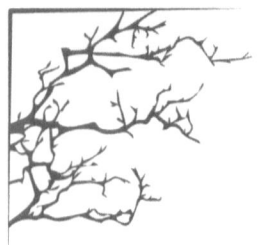

Chapter 56

Katlyn groaned. Her head feeling as though it was stuffed with cotton wool. Where was she? The smells of antiseptic and illness hung in the air, strong and pungent.

She tried to push herself up, but the effort was too much. Her left thigh hurt like hell.

A nurse hurried to her bedside, offering a reassuring smile. "Glad to see you're awake. You were unconscious. The doctor said you're very lucky the bullet only grazed your left thigh, causing minor skin damage. If you're in pain, I can give you some stronger painkillers."

The events of the previous night rushed back to her like an oncoming freight train. Lucy's odd behavior. An intruder had shot her... she shuddered at the realization of what might have been if his aim had been true.

She tried to lift herself up with the support of her right elbow against the bed, but the nurse intervened upon hearing her groan. "Thank you."

Taking Katlyn's pulse and jotting down some notes, the nurse replied, "There's nothing wrong with your heart. We removed the monitors a few hours ago, but I need to keep track of your vital signs regularly."

Katlyn sighed. Her thoughts were in turmoil as she tried to process last night's events with Lucy and the intruder.

"I'll fetch you some painkillers." The nurse hurried out and returned moments later with a cup of water and a container of pills.

"Take these for the pain."

Katlyn eyed the two capsules. "Thanks. But it's not that bad. I can manage."

"As you wish."

The nurse left the pills on the tray, and hurried away. She soon returned with a large bunch of white lilies. "You're a popular woman." She arranged them in a vase, unpinned the card, and handed it to Katlyn.

Opening the envelope, Katlyn read the message.

Dear Kat,

I'll be over to see you soon. I've been worried since I found out what happened to you.

Victor.

Katlyn smiled. He was a sweetie. She put the card back on the flowers as Victor walked in.

"Hello," he said. "You're one for drama to get attention."

"Yeah, I know. Thanks for the flowers. They're lovely."

"My pleasure." Victor leaned in and gave her a feathery-light kiss on her cheek, his hand brushing against hers. "How are you feeling?"

"I'm okay."

"Until you install an alarm, you shouldn't stay at your place."

"It may never happen again," she said.

"But it could. I've a spare room and I'd enjoy having some company."

"I appreciate the offer. Let me think about it."

"The doctor will call in to see you later." The nurse puffed up Katlyn's pillow. "He'll probably sign the release form tomorrow morning unless there's something else going on."

"Thanks," Kat said.

"You've a visitor waiting just outside," the nurse said.

"Who is it?"

"I'm told it's someone you know." The nurse headed out the door.

Colin walked in with a small bouquet of white and pink roses. He hesitated upon noticing the vase filled with lilies and placed the roses on the side table. "Hello there. Taking a well-deserved rest, are you? Going to great lengths to avoid work."

She stared at him and started laughing. "Not funny. Thanks for coming to see me."

"Hello, Victor," Colin said.

Victor returned his greeting. "Work awaits," he said softly. Leaning in, he blew a gentle kiss in the air, sending it floating toward her like a whispered promise. "See you later."

Kat blushed a little, at his affectionate gesture. "You know how to brighten my day, Victor."

After Victor left, Katlyn turned to Colin.

His brows furrow, and there was a faint tightening around his lips at her exchange with Victor. However, he quickly regain his composure, and his face bore a neutral expression.

Hmm. She wasn't sure if Colin disliked Victor. "Thanks for the roses and for rescuing me," Kat said.

"I didn't want to lose a partner."

"Is that all it was?"

Colin laughed. "You're trying to make a joke now. You can't be too bad."

"It's either laugh or cry. And I'm not into crying."

"Everyone was so worried about you. Some scumbag broke into your house and tried to kill you."

Katlyn nodded. "Lucy attacked him. OMG! What's happened to her?"

"Don't worry. Your neighbor's taking care of her for you."

"I hardly know the woman. Will you thank her for me?"

"Of course."

"Amanda offered for you to bunk at her place until you get yourself sorted."

"I might take her up on that offer." She was reluctant to accept Victor's offer, even as a temporary arrangement. It may lead to some complications she didn't want to consider at the moment.

"Forensics have dusted your place for prints. No luck there."

"That's disappointing."

He shook his head. "The scumbag must have worn gloves. Glad your cat disrupted his aim otherwise...." Colin's expression turned grim.

"Yeah. I know, I'd be dead." A sobering thought.

Colin seemed ill at ease. He glanced at the flowers. "I'll hunt down a vase for these."

Her partner looked troubled.

She found herself in a single room with a large picture window. The view of the sheep-dotted fields was soothing. However, she didn't want to be in the hospital while her attacker roamed free. She longed to be on the case, to track down this psychopath before they could harm someone else. What did they want? Were they planning to rob her home or simply kill her for the thrill of it? She shuddered.

Colin returned holding a vase and had shoved the flowers and paper wrap into it. "The nurse can sort this out. I'm hopeless with this sort of thing."

"Take a seat and update me on the Goch case?"

"Kasper Goch has been officially charged and remanded and will appear before the courts in a month's time."

"A good wrap-up to the case."

"Lucky you rang me."

Her head ached. "I don't remember."

"Well, you did. I came over and knocked on your front door. When you didn't answer, I went around the back and tried the door. It was unlocked. Do you usually leave it like that?"

"I always lock it. Someone must have tampered with the latch. I'll check my phone."

"The CCTV footage should have captured me entering through the back."

She clicked on the app. "What? No images of you at all, or even the forensics team when they arrived. I think your friend hasn't set it up correctly." She'd stay with Amanda until they changed her locks, the CCTV fixed and a new alarm system installed.

"I'll have him go right over and check the video feed."

"Thanks. Also, check with my neighbors to see if they saw anything?"

"Already done. One of your neighbors recalls a van parked on the street a few times over the past few weeks."

"Did she note down the number plate or provide a description of the vehicle?"

"I'm afraid not. She paid little attention to it because she assumed it was a repairman or someone getting some work done. No help there."

"Thanks."

"I've also checked the database for any break-and-enters and attempts to cause bodily harm. Such incidents aren't common in the area."

"Any signs of forced entry?"

"No. The intruder must've had a key or picked the lock."

"Hell. I had the locks changed."

"I know."

"Kasper didn't have a key, and he's in custody."

"We'll keep searching. Brady's got an ear on the street. He's been pushing for information from his sources."

"Good. There must be something somewhere. Maybe, you need to widen the scope of the investigation."

"Yes, boss."

"Can I ask you to arrange for my locks to be changed again?"

"Happy to do it. And hear this... White's urging the team to pull out all stops on finding the perp responsible for this."

"Is that what it takes for him to appreciate the hard work I do?"

"Sorry to bring you down, but after Chief Superintendent Higgins visited and commended your efforts, Derrick got loaded up with two more cases. He's been moaning about the extra workload."

"He might surprise us yet," Katlyn laughed.

Watch out for:
Book 3 "Softly He Sleeps" which will be out in a few months.

BOOKS WRITTEN BY O.N. STEFAN:

Amanda Blake Thriller Series

The Deadly Caress – Book 1

https://getbook.at/B00I0DI0MY

Deeds of Darkness – Book 2.

https://mybook.to/DeedsOfDarkness

Hidden – Book 3.

https://mybook.to/Hidden-thriller

Standalone thrillers: *Sleep then my Princess.*

https://getbook.at/B016G5T7AG

Katlyn Snowden Detective Mystery Series.

Softly, He Dies – Book 1

https://mybook.to/SoftlyHeDies

Acknowledgments

A big thank you to all my wonderful beta readers, my street team, the wonderful book groups, readers, book bloggers and reviewers.

I want to say that word of mouth is such a powerful thing and without all your hard work and passion, talking up and blogging about my books, I would have far fewer readers.

Please leave a review on your favorite book retailer and Goodreads.

Follow me on Bookbub: https://www.bookbub.com/authors/o-n-stefan

Thank you.

Want to join my subscriber group to get my latest news and offers?

Find out when my next book is launching.

https://landing.mailerlite.com/webforms/landing/l5u7p9

Want to join my Facebook fan page? https://www.facebook.com/groups/632508307256042

Find me on my website. Click on the link below and sign up on the pop up.

http://onstefan.weebly.com/

Natalie Stefan.

Please leave a review. It need not be more than a sentence but it helps other readers to try out my stories.